The Forsaken Dimension

Book 5 of Motionless

Daryl Walker

Contents

CHAPTER ONE

Letters

C hris turned the phone over and over in his hands, staring at it. It had been uncharged for the past year or so, as he hadn't had any need for it whatsoever within that timeframe.

He sighed and placed it face down on the hard wooden surface of the bar. He leaned his head on his hand before turning his attention back to the diary sitting next to the phone.

Picking up his pen, he wrote on the blank white sheet of paper.

> *Dear Ash,*
>
> *I know it's been a while since I've written anything. I don't know how long this one will take to get to you.*
>
> *Nothing new has really been happening here, which is the main reason I haven't sent anything your way recently. If there was anything new or important happening over here, I'd let you know straight away.*

Hope everything's going well for you and Alex. Let me know how everyone is and how everything's going there. If there're any developments on me returning home and to the correct dimension from this end, you'll be the first to know.

Miss you all,

Chris

He put the pen down and quickly read through what he'd written before tearing the page out of the diary and folding it in half. He put it in his back pocket, grabbed the now-closed diary, stood up, and headed for the door.

For the past year, every night had been the same. He'd sit at the bar, write something, and either send it off to Ash before the night really kicked in, or he'd just sit and contemplate what he had to do.

The usual few regulars occupied their usual seats at the bar or at tables but, tonight, Chris didn't acknowledge any of them as he headed out through the door and onto the sidewalk, the door staying open behind him as it always did.

He headed down the paved sidewalk, passing groups and individuals as he headed to his destination. It was a Friday night, so there were a lot more people walking around town than other nights. It would take him a bit to get where he was going, but he needed the time to think.

A few people greeted him as he passed by, getting a half-hearted greeting in return. The town was small enough that nearly everyone knew everyone. There were only a few people Chris didn't really know.

Finally reaching the town's border, Chris walked down the stone road in the dark, knowing the way to his destination without having to think about where he was going. He'd done this walk so many times now, he wasn't about to forget the way.

It was always best to walk through the night as long as he stayed on the road. This dimension luckily didn't have much in the way of danger like Oz and Wonderland did. It was something Chris appreciated, but he still missed his home, and he hoped he'd be able to get back soon.

If you didn't stay on the road, the worst thing that could happen is that you would get lost. Chris hadn't heard much in the way of anyone being eaten or attacked outside of town. That was partially why he'd ended up in this town, Treadway Valley. It was a nice place, out in the green fields and not far from the major city of the county. He was glad he'd managed to find such a nice place.

The only problem was Marion.

Chris shook his head, not wanting to dwell on that one fact right now. He had somewhere to be, and he wasn't about to let his mind wander to somewhere he didn't want to end up.

He continued to walk, trying not to think too much. It wasn't going to be an overly long walk, but it would take an hour, two at the most if he dawdled, to get to wher he was going. Once he was there, he'd go about his task and then return to what he'd come to call his home.

As nice as Treadway Valley was, hopefully it wasn't going to be his permanent residence. It wasn't somewhere he wanted to live out the remainder of his life.

The road surface eventually turned to dirt, and after a long and tiring walk, Chris saw his destination up ahead. You couldn't really miss the large rock formation of Grogan's Gap. It was massive, the light brown stone towering up into the sky on either side of the road.

Chris headed down the slight incline, the ground around the road having now turned to dirt as well, the road now nothing more than a worn track. A few lights on the rocks signaled Grogan's Gap, lighting up the entranceway into the area. The gap was rather narrow as it led travelers further inland.

Chris headed into the gap without any real thought, having done this many times before. There were enough lights set up along the rocks, so he was able to see where he was going. Not that there was really anywhere else to go within Grogan's Gap except forwards.

There were no twists, no turns, just a straightforward walk that led to the closed off end. It wouldn't take long, just a few more minutes at the most.

The only sound he heard was his own footsteps walking along the dirt track, going deeper into the Gap. The silence was something he'd gotten more used to every time he visited this area.

A bright light at the end lit up a large area of dirt and rocks, reaching past it and reflecting up into the sky.

He came to a halt in front of the Dimension Portal and looked at the stone border and the shimmering, bright light in the middle of it, something he'd missed seeing over the last couple of months. *How long had it been since he'd been down here?*

Not wanting to dwell on the topic, Chris switched his gaze to the medium-sized square stone feature on the right-hand side of the portal. Something motionless sat on top of it. He walked over and the creature sitting atop the stone slightly opened its eyes.

It had clearly been sleeping, and Chris had disturbed it.

The little creature was no bigger than a small dog. It was a dark gray color, made of some kind of stone and it looked a little bit like a gargoyle, just without the horns and other disturbing features.

Chris ignored it and grabbed something from the basket that was next to the creature, who had now lost interest in Chris and was now back to sleeping.

Chris took his pen and the folded piece of paper out of his pocket. He moved out of the way a bit, placing the paper inside the envelope that he'd taken from the basket and making sure the envelope was properly sealed before addressing it:

Ash; Dimension 1; Wonderland.

He'd done this many times before and, once he was done, he put his pen back in his pocket and placed the sealed envelope on the rock on the creature's right, getting another glance from it as it slightly opened its eyes again.

Chris knew the process. His letter wouldn't be delivered until the morning, but he was confident that the creature would make sure it got to Ash.

The creature shut its eyes again, having silently acknowledged Chris's request, not needing to say anything out loud. It knew its job and, when the sun came up, it would go about it.

Chris left, heading back the way he'd come, through Grogan's Gap, towards Treadway Valley. It would be late by the time he got back, but he knew there would still be a lot of people out and about since everything was open late on Friday nights.

He put his hands in his pockets as he strolled along the dirt road, gaze down on the ground as he made his way back.

Hopefully he'd hear back from Ash soon.

CHAPTER TWO

Contacts

A lex turned the corner at such a fast pace he slid and nearly lost his balance.

He rushed into the room and stopped in front of Ash. She was sitting on her throne as she usually did when she had nothing to do within the castle, and she looked up at the disturbance.

"Mail! Chris!" Alex managed to say, out of breath from his mail collection running.

He held the envelope out and Ash took it, much more alert now that Chris had been mentioned. Alex waited impatiently, watching her open the letter that was addressed to her. He never opened mail addressed to anyone that wasn't him. He knew it wasn't for him, so he left it alone.

Over the past twelve months, Ash had been receiving letters from Chris, and she made sure that whenever she got one, she sent one right back.

It had been an interesting and exciting discovery. None of them had been aware that they were able to send mail back and forth between dimensions.

Chris had been the one to somehow discover it was a thing. Ash had known they could send mail back and forth through counties, but not between dimensions. It had been quite the surprise when she'd received the first letter from Chris, but now it had become a normal thing, although it had been a little while since the last one.

"What does he have to say this time? Anything we need to know to get him back?" Alex asked hurriedly, not wanting to wait any longer as Ash read the brief letter over a few times.

Ash sighed. "Not yet, Alex, nothing." Disappointment appeared on Alex's face. "He's just checking in. He hasn't found anything that can get him back home yet."

Alex gave a disappointed nod, looking down at the floor as a castle guard appeared in the doorway.

Ash indicated for him to speak.

"They've pushed past the border," he informed her, the look on Ash's face changing as she glanced at Alex who now looked worried. He knew what they were talking about. "They're pushing inland."

Ash looked at him for a few seconds before giving a nod. "Alright, we'll handle it."

The guard seemed unconvinced but nodded nonetheless before leaving the room.

Alex looked at Ash, who was looking across the room, thinking.

"Maybe it's about time we asked for help," he suggested timidly, knowing this wasn't something Ash wanted to do. "I know you don't want to, but if they're now in Wonderland, we could all be in serious trouble, Ash. It's been twelve months with no trouble, but now? We need the help."

Ash sighed, knowing he was right. She reluctantly pushed herself up out of the throne.

If the Legion was now across the border and in Wonderland, there was a very high chance they'd take the Room of Doors and make it Upstairs. That wasn't something they could let happen.

It had taken the Legion this long to get past the border, thanks to help from the Banshee's End outposts, but having them actually making it past the outposts was very bad news. Something must have gone wrong.

Ash strode off through the castle, gripping Chris's note in her hand. Alex hurried along behind, not wanting to be left on his own.

Ash reached her bedroom, went in, and put Chris's note on the desk before sitting down and grabbing a blank piece of paper.

"I hope you know I'm only doing this because if I don't, they'll push further in and we'll be forced to leave," Ash said, grabbing a pen and beginning to write on the page. "This is the last thing I want to do, and you know it."

Alex was standing beside her, and he nodded, knowing exactly that.

Ash wasn't happy as she finished writing. She quickly read through what she'd written, then folded the paper, put it in an empty envelope, sealed it, and addressed it:

Craig Taylor; Banshee's End Outpost; Oz.

"Captain?"

Danny looked up from what he'd been half-heartedly looking at, feet up on the table and disinterest on his face. He wasn't ever going to get used to being addressed like that. It didn't matter how long he played this role, it wouldn't ever get any less weird.

"What?"

The recruit who'd addressed him shifted awkwardly, clearly intimidated by Danny. Danny didn't care, because it meant people wouldn't try to mess with him. The recruit glanced at the other three bandits. Ted, Jordan, and Shawn all waited to hear what this recruit had to say for himself.

The recruit looked back at Danny who was just watching him. That was the issue with a lot of these newer recruits. They never understood the concept of wasting someone else's time.

"What?" Danny asked again, a bit more forceful this time, making the recruit flinch at his tone. "Speak or fuck off. I don't like having my time wasted, we're busy."

The recruit nodded, realizing he needed to speak or else something unpleasant might happen.

"Remington's outside. He wants to speak to you since Commander Taylor's not here and neither is Jacob."

Damn vampires, thought Danny. It was always the same whenever Craig and Jacob weren't at Banshee's End and Remington showed up. Danny was always the next in line, and he didn't get why Cain couldn't take care of it. Why did it have to be him?

He'd made it very clear multiple times that he didn't like Remington, mainly because he was still a vampire.

Danny really didn't like vampires. His hatred had only gotten worse over the past twelve months, and it wasn't about to change.

"Can't he wait until Craig gets back?" Danny asked, turning his focus back to the map he'd been looking at before the interruption. "I'm busy."

"Doing what?" the recruit dared to say.

Ted and Jordan exchanged brief looks as Danny's focus remained on the map.

"Slackin' off, what do you think I'm doing?" Danny snapped. He looked away from the map, seeing the intimidation on the recruit's face. Danny looked him over judgmentally. "What's your name, kid? You're new around here, right?"

The recruit didn't look to be that old, eighteen at the most. Danny knew he was new and hadn't been at Banshee's End very long. He knew who was who under his command, and he knew who was new and who wasn't.

One thing Danny prided himself on was knowing everyone who reported to him. It annoyed him that he didn't know who this kid was, and he wanted to find out. He was sure this kid had been picked up from somewhere in Oz, he just didn't know where.

The recruit shifted awkwardly again, clearing his throat before answering, knowing that since Danny was a captain, he had to answer.

"Daniel Mitchells, sir," he said, trying to keep his tone steady.

Danny looked him over, a bit of interest on his face now.

"Daniel, hey?" Daniel gave a nod. Danny looked back at his face. "Where are you from, Dan?"

The intimidation was still very clear on Daniel's face as he answered. "Waterwall Incline, sir."

"Hm, the coastline, hey?" Daniel nodded again, Danny back to looking him up and down. "What are you doing here then, if that's the case?"

Daniel frowned. "I'm sorry?"

"You're like, what, eighteen?" Danny mused, resting the map in his lap and crossing his arms. "What's a kid like you doing here at Banshee's End if you're from the coastline? Nice area down there, wouldn't wanna trade that view in for this place. Nothing but dirt and sand here, kid."

Daniel tried to keep his expression as neutral as possible, but Danny saw the slight shift in it as Daniel avoided his gaze.

"Wanted to help out with the issues going on around the county, sir," he said. Danny wished he'd quit calling him 'sir', but he knew it wouldn't happen. They were taught to respect their officers at Banshee's End. "Signed up when they came around to sign people up that were interested."

Danny still wasn't convinced. There had to be more to this kid's story.

"Is that so?" he asked. Daniel nodded and Danny narrowed his eyes at him. "So, you signed up for this crusade willingly, and now you're here. I know you haven't been here for long, and they did the recruiting at Waterwall Incline months ago, so you've only been here for a few weeks at the most."

Daniel didn't say anything, and Danny shifted how he was sitting, resting his hands in his lap on the map as he linked his fingers together.

"You ever stood across from a real vampire, kid?" Danny asked. Daniel shook his head, looking uncomfortable again. "And you said this can't wait for Craig?"

"Remington said he wants to talk to you. He knows Commander Taylor won't be back for a while." Daniel shifted again. "Someone asked me to come and tell you this because apparently Remington won't wait around for long."

"Well, he's got a fuckin' eternity, not like the rest of us," Danny commented. He sighed, taking his feet off the table and placing the map back on the table. "Alright, we'll go see what the vampire wants." He looked at Daniel. "You're coming with us. See how you go in a situation with the undead."

Worry crossed Daniel's face, but he tried to get rid of it quickly, knowing he would have to deal with vampires later down the line if he lasted long enough to go out with a field team.

Danny stood up, indicating for the other three and Daniel to follow him as he headed out of the room, leaving the door wide open as he went outside. It was dark out, but Danny wasn't surprised. Remington only ever showed up at Banshee's End under the cover of darkness.

"He say where he'd be?" Danny asked as he came to a stop a few paces outside the lodgings.

Daniel wasn't far behind him and Ted carelessly pushed past him to join Danny.

"Around near the church."

Of course, that's where Remington was going to hang out. It was where he was every time he came around to Banshee's End. Why would Danny have thought that he'd show up somewhere different?

Danny didn't quite understand why Remington always hung around the church. He couldn't get very close to it and it's not like he was able to get inside it. It didn't make any sense to him.

Danny headed off without another word, Ted walking beside him and the other three not far behind. It was late, so there weren't many people around and Danny was glad about that. He didn't like interacting with too many people and, whenever Craig wasn't around, everyone came to him.

Sure enough, as the church came into view, so did the figure of a person just near the borderline.

"What do you want and why can't you just find which outpost Craig's at and go there?" Danny called. Remington looked over, but Danny knew he'd heard them way before he'd spoken. "This'd better be worth it."

As always, Remington stood with his arms crossed across his chest, the usual look on his face. He didn't much like Danny and he knew Danny didn't much like him. Their relationship hadn't changed or improved over the past year, and Remington knew nothing would change between them as long as he was the living dead.

"No, I walk across the barren, open landscape of a desert, just so I can come and tell you irrelevant bullshit," Remington said as the group halted near him. He narrowed his eyes, seeing Daniel trying to keep out of the way. "Who's the kid? He's nervous, that's for sure, heartbeats don't lie."

Danny looked at Daniel briefly before grabbing his arm and moving him up to stand next to him, the worry clear on Daniel's face.

"This is Daniel. He's never come into contact with a real vampire before."

A sly smile lit up Remington's face as he looked Daniel over. He flashed his teeth, the light from the church making it that much eerier.

"Is that right?" Remington looked Daniel over again before moving forward a bit, closing the distance between himself and the others. "I'll take it you haven't been here long, then, I mean, if you haven't come across the real living dead before. Correct me if I'm wrong."

Daniel shook his head as Remington stopped just in front of him. Danny still had hold of Daniel's arm, making sure he couldn't go anywhere. Remington pretended to think as he looked Daniel over a third time, summing him up.

Remington turned his attention to Danny, temporarily ignoring Daniel who was only a step in front of him.

"I don't know which outpost Craig's at," he said. "I was hoping you'd be able to tell me. If you know, I can leave you and your little clique alone and I'll go talk to the big boss myself. Commander is higher than captain, after all."

Danny glared at him, and Remington switched his gaze back to Daniel. He leaned in closer, as if he was about to whisper something to him.

"You know where Craig's posted?" he asked, very aware that he was intimidating the young man. "Because if you happen to know, then I don't need to worry about harassing Danny here and he can go back to being the vampire hater that he is. The less time I'm here, the happier your captain will be."

Daniel looked at Danny, then back at Remington who was watching him with interest. Daniel shifted uncomfortably and got an amused smile from Remington.

"Can't remember the number of the outpost but it's not in Oz or Wonderland," Danny said. "C'mon and I'll show you on the map."

He let Daniel go and headed back the way they'd come, the others following with Remington trailing behind.

Once they reached the lodgings, Danny went in and straight over to the table where he'd left the map. He gestured for everyone, including Daniel, to take a seat at the table with him.

Remington sat on the seat closest to Danny on his right, wanting to see the map and be on his way.

"Last time I heard, Craig was over here at Outpost Fourteen, over near Dreamer's Ledge in Marshore County," Danny began, wanting the vampire out and gone as soon as possible. If he cooperated, it would be easy to get him out. "If he's not there, then I dunno where the hell he's gotten to. They'd be able to tell you when you get there, though, if you don't happen to find him."

"How long's he stationed there?" Remington asked, studying the map on the table.

Danny had hoped he'd be able to get him out with just the one answer but now, here he was, asking more questions.

"Don't know, don't care. I don't get told everything. You wanna know, ask him when you see him. It's not my business and not my place to ask."

Remington gave a nod of understanding, pushing his chair back and getting to his feet.

"Alright, I'll be on my way, then. Outpost Fourteen in Marshore County, right?" Danny nodded and Remington looked at Daniel, who'd taken the seat furthest away from him. "No need to be intimidated, kid, I don't bite. Much."

He gave him an amused smile, seeing the uncomfortable look on Daniel's face was still there.

Danny grabbed something off the table and held it out to Remington who took the sealed envelope curiously.

"Can you give this to Craig when you see him?" he asked. "Came in the mail yesterday, but he's not here and, by the looks of it, it's important."

Remington looked the envelope over, turning it over and reading the name on the back.

"Ooh, it's from Ash," he mused, the amusement clear. He indicated to the letter as he looked at Danny. "Those two still messing around?"

"Don't know, don't care."

Remington grinned. "I'll make sure Mister Taylor receives this letter." He saluted. "You can count on me, Captain!"

CHAPTER THREE

A Call for Help

Craig sighed, leaning his head on his hand. He'd had enough of Dreamer's Ledge and just wanted to go home. Banshee's End was ten times more exciting and at least there were more interesting people to talk to back there, even if it was in the middle of the desert.

The only people here were recruits and none of them were overly interesting to talk to. Most of them didn't wish to engage in conversation with their commander about things that didn't involve their job.

Outpost Fourteen was going to be the death of Craig if he didn't get out of here soon.

"Commander Taylor?"

Craig reluctantly looked up. Arley Beckett, one of his top recruits, was standing in the doorway. She'd been with Banshee's End since before Craig had arrived and she was very dedicated. Craig had considered promoting her many times, but he hadn't had the opportunity yet.

She was definitely next in line to be a captain. If he'd had it his way, she would have been the one in Danny's position, but he hadn't had the final say. Jacob was the one in charge of the entire Banshee's End operation, not Craig, so the decision was his.

Craig indicated for Arley to speak.

"Outpost Six has gone down," she said. Craig sighed. This wasn't good. "Banshee's End received the distress call about a day and a half ago."

"Jesus Christ," Craig said, putting his head in his hands. He looked up at Arley. "That's the third one this month." He pulled the large map on the table closer and grabbed the pen. He crossed out Outpost Six and wrote something next to it. "The Legion have control of it?"

"From what we've been told, they've left it unoccupied," Arley informed him, Craig writing something else as he listened.

Craig looked up and met her gaze. "They turn anyone?"

Arley shrugged. "They haven't said. Banshee's End were going to send a scout team to see what's happened and what's going on, and whether they've left anyone alive."

Craig gave a reluctant nod, not liking the way this was going. He indicated for Arley to take a seat at the table with him.

"Did they say anything about which of the Legion's team pushed through Outpost Six?"

She sat on the seat closest to him, on his right, and looked at what he'd written on the map. "They haven't said yet, but there's been some speculation that it was Graith's."

"Wrong."

They both looked at the doorway to see Remington leaning against the doorframe, hands in pockets.

He indicated between them. "You two discussing important things?"

Craig rolled his eyes as Remington came into the room, leaving the door wide open. He took a seat on Craig's left and placed his arms on the table, resting his chin on them as he looked at Craig, not saying anything as Craig just returned the look.

"Something wrong, Remington?" Craig asked, seeing that Remington wasn't about to say anything.

Remington gave a shrug, shifting and grabbing something from his back pocket, chin back on arms on the table as he held it out to Craig, getting a frown from him.

"Your GF wants to talk," Remington said as Craig took the envelope, turning it over to see who'd sent it. "Didn't realize you guys were still a thing, what with you being in a separate county and all."

Craig shot him an annoyed look. "We were never a 'thing' and we never will be."

Remington gave another shrug, still in the same position. "Everyone has a type, not judging."

Craig shook his head, opening the letter to see what Ash wanted. It had been a long time since Craig had heard anything from her. She tried to avoid contacting him in any way possible, so the fact that she'd written a letter and addressed it to him directly made him think it was important.

Craig,

Sorry to bother you and, believe me, if I didn't have to write this, then I certainly wouldn't, but Alex made a good point earlier on and pretty well forced me to write this and get into contact with you.

The Legion has pushed past the border. They're in Wonderland and are most likely going to be pushing further inland, which means that they could easily stumble across the Room of Doors that leads back Upstairs.

As mentioned by Abel last year before everything went so wrong, this could end very badly if they push through the Room and make it Upstairs. There are a lot of people up there (including Abel and the others, at the moment) that would be seriously affected if this were to happen.

I know you wouldn't want something like this to happen since you most likely have some form of family existing up there (even if you aren't there and they don't even know where you've been for the past however long). With Alex mentioning this kind of thing, it's unfortunately made me come to the decision that this isn't something that I want to happen.

With that said, I reluctantly ask for your help. If you need to, I give you one-hundred-percent confirmation and permission to put up outposts within Wonderland's borders, AS LONG AS they manage to keep the Legion's threat down and control their influx of vampires within Wonderland.

Ash. ♡

Craig stared at the letter for a minute or so as he thought over what Ash had written. Remington leaned in a bit, pretending not to read the letter as he, very obviously, read the letter.

"I love the little heart she put next to her name at the end," he noted, getting another annoyed look from Craig. Remington looked at him blankly. "What? I think it's cute."

"You're full of it, Remington. If you weren't already dead, I'd kill you myself." Craig turned his focus back to the letter, looking at the date at the top of the page. "Sent a couple of days ago." He looked at Arley. "What day did Outpost Six go down?"

"Roughly three days ago," she said, Craig looking back to the paper. "The distress call only came through a day and a half ago, though."

Craig sighed. "If it was only a couple of days ago, then they've most likely just pushed forwards. I doubt they'd have turned anyone if they're already pushing inland through Wonderland."

"It was Cole's unit, so I wouldn't bet on it," Remington said. Craig and Arley looked at him. "By the way, Taylor, I was listening to that rock band of yours earlier this week, and you guys were good. Hadn't ever really listened to you guys much before I came down here."

"Oh, shut it," Craig snapped, not in the mood for Remington's antics right now. He indicated to Ash's letter. "This is some serious shit, Bell, stop trying to change the subject."

Remington shifted, sitting up and holding his hands up in his defense. "I was just trying to praise my wonderful commander." He lowered his hands, going back to resting his arms on the table, chin back on his arms as he looked at Craig. "Just thought you might want a bit of a break from this shit for a bit and reminisce on old times, that's all."

"I appreciate the concern, but the last thing I'd want to do is talk about my life before I came down here."

Remington gave him a bit of a sad look. "You miss it?"

"Everyone misses it," Craig snapped again, the sad look staying on Remington's face. "Right now, though, I have more important things to worry about. If we don't move against the Legion, they're going to make it to the Room of Doors in Wonderland and then they're going to make it Upstairs. That means they'll take as much of that area as they can. They won't stop with just the Underground Worlds,

Remington. If they push through the Room, they're going to take the entire world."

Remington shifted, resting his head on his hand as he spoke.

"That's part of the reason I came over here. I wanted to talk to you about this situation," he said, not playing around anymore, seeing that this was serious. "There's been a lot of talk recently about what's gonna go down if they pushed into Wonderland. They've known for a while that you guys aren't patrolling or set up in the area. They're convinced they can take on Ash and, if she's not careful, they'll do just that."

Craig indicated to the letter. "That's why she's asked for help."

Remington gave a bit of a nod. "Right. But remember, we've already seen what happened with Danny and his crew because of the Legion."

"That's a different situation. Their home was already gone by the time they went to leave."

"Yes, but Ash has an entire county depending on her," Remington said. "If you're setting up outposts in Wonderland, then you're gonna need more people. Recruiting isn't easy lately, so I've heard."

"I'm sure you have," Craig said reluctantly. He sighed. "Either way, we have to set up a couple of outposts and push the Legion back into Oz. If we can contain it mainly in these two counties, and they steer clear of Pandelon and Haymarc, we should be able to get this threat more or less under control."

"You said it was Cole's unit?" Arley asked, getting a nod from Remington.

"It sure was, sweetheart," he said. "So, you'd best get someone out there to check to make sure that the amount of dead bodies matches the right amount of people you had there."

"I thought Cole wasn't able to turn people," Craig stated.

Remington sat up, arms still resting against the table.

"That was before Old Man Wickor got staked last week," he said, staring at the table and making a violent stabbing gesture.

Arley glanced at Craig, but he didn't look away from Remington.

Remington settled down, arm back on the table and gaze back on Craig. "Cole's moved up the food chain."

Craig sighed, leaning back in his chair and crossing his arms. "Terrific." He looked at Arley. "Go mark Wickor off the board and put down Cole."

Arley nodded and pushed her chair back, getting to her feet. Remington got to his feet as well, getting a curious look from Craig.

"Gonna come help revise your board of the high ranks!" Remington said cheerfully. He looked at Craig, who was still watching him. "If that's OK with you, Commander Taylor."

"Take a day walk for all I care."

Remington smiled at him as Craig waved him and Arley away.

CHAPTER FOUR

Revising the Board

Remington caught up to Arley, hearing Craig shut the door even from this far down the hallway.

"You totally have a thing for your commander," Remington said as he walked alongside her.

They passed a few people who glanced warily at him, knowing the deal by now, but some still not too relaxed about the situation.

Arley glanced at him as they turned a corner.

"What? You're joking," she scoffed. "Craig was right, you're full of it, Rem."

"Am I, though?" Remington said, making Arley shake her head.

Remington watched her as they stopped at a closed door and Arley scanned herself in. He followed her through, shutting the door behind him and hearing it automatically lock.

"You forget how well I can hear things, Arls. Human heartbeats are quite easy to identify and yours increased a bit when he spoke to you."

"You don't know anything."

Remington scoffed as he looked around, casually leaning against the closest table.

"You also just referred to him as Craig, not Commander Taylor," he noted, arms crossed as he studied the photos of all the recruits on the wall. Everyone at Outpost Fourteen and involved in this operation was there, their individual information underneath their picture.

He looked back at Arley, who was crossing a name off a rather long list on a board hanging on the wall. "I heard that he was going to get you promoted to captain before Danny and his gang of misfits found themselves homeless."

Arley glanced over her shoulder at him before turning her focus back to the board, writing another name on it.

"What's that got to do with anything?" she asked.

Remington noticed that his name wasn't on the board. It looked like Craig hadn't told anyone about Remington's rank and that he could turn people into vampires.

Remington gave a shrug, going back to looking at the photos on the wall.

"It means you're clearly working hard, and Craig has faith in you," he said, continuing to look at the photos. "Either that, or you've been sleeping with your boss to get that promotion."

Arley stopped what she was doing, turned, and stared at him. "Excuse me?"

Remington looked at her face for a few seconds before looking her up and down, then studying one of the silver rings on his finger. "Well, I guess it's the hard work that's gotten you in line for a promotion, then."

Arley wasn't in the least bit happy. "Sometimes, you're seriously unbelievable."

Remington held his hands up in his defense as Arley crossed her arms and continued to glare at him, the board forgotten.

"Didn't meant to offend. Men sleep their way to the top, too," he said. "Luckily in the vampire hierarchy, that's not something that's possible, but that's a story for another time. The point I'm trying to make is that you're a hard worker and Craig's noticed."

Arley shook her head, understanding more now why Craig didn't want to put up with Remington for long periods of time. Although she was used to Remington, his undercover work of infiltrating the Legion meant she hadn't spent too much time around him.

She indicated to the board, getting Remington's attention to it and away from whatever he'd been staring at previously. "You said you were here to revise."

Remington nodded, pushing off the table and going over to stand next to her in front of the board, though he didn't need to be this close to read it. His eyesight was ten times better than a normal human, but he wanted to be close to the board to make it look like he was important, and so it wouldn't look as awkward with him staring at it and having Arley standing near it.

Remington scanned the list of names, seeing Graith's name at the top. A few names had question marks next to them, and he indicated to a couple of them.

"Why the question marks?" he asked.

Arley switched her gaze to the specific names he'd pointed out.

"They're the ones that we aren't sure about," she said. Remington frowned. "Craig ... Commander Taylor ... wasn't sure if they were still around or not since we haven't heard anything about any of them in a while. He was thinking that maybe they'd been killed and someone else had taken their ranks."

Remington looked back at the board. "As far as I know, Wickor is the only one that's been recently redeceased. Everyone else on the board, as far as I know, is still out there and moving around. I think a couple might have gone back underground, but I don't know for sure. I only know of the most recent rank turnovers. Cole's the only one and that was last week."

"So, everyone else is still relevant?"

Remington gave a slow nod as he looked the list over again. "For now." He pointed one name out. "Casper's moved up in the ranks. He's directly under Graith now. Apart from that, the rest of the list seems to be correct."

Arley nodded and wrote on the board, while Remington went back to where he'd previously been leaning against the table.

"What was the deal with Craig and Ash?" Arley asked.

Remington looked at her and gave a bit of a shrug, not wanting to tread on her hopes of possibly hooking up with Craig at some point.

"Don't know, never really known," he said, trying to sound convincing but not doing a great job. "But Ash isn't even in this county, so it doesn't really matter either way, right?"

"Right."

Remington moved over to the wall with all the profiles and pictures on it.

"You mentioned something about Craig earlier on," Arley said. "About him being in a 'band' or something? What did you mean by that?"

"You're not from Upstairs, are you?" Remington asked.

Arley shrugged. "Honestly, Rem, I have no idea. I've only ever known the Underground Worlds. For all I know, though, maybe I am actually from Upstairs. Maybe we all are but we just don't remember."

Remington gave her a slight nod before he spoke again.

"A band is a group of musicians," he explained. Arley looked interested. At least she knew what musicians were, as they had them down here in the Underground Worlds but, in Remington's opinion, they weren't anywhere near as good as the ones from Upstairs. "Craig used to front the band, meaning he was their singer. I was just listening to a bit of their stuff the other day, that's all."

Arley seemed rather interested in what she was hearing, but Remington spoke again before she could say anything.

"I know Craig misses home," he said sadly. "He misses Upstairs. I don't blame him, I miss home, too."

"You're from Upstairs?" Arley asked.

Remington gave a nod, turning his focus back to the wall of photos.

"I am, my family still lives up there," he said, unable to hide the sadness in his tone. "Which is why we need to stop the Legion from ever reaching the Upstairs exit. If they get up there, they're going to kill a lot of people and I don't want to see that happen to anyone, let alone the people I grew up with." He sighed. "They all probably think I'm dead by now. I've been missing for seven years. That's enough time for them to declare me legally dead. Technically, they're not wrong and I *am* dead, but that's not quite the way things work up there."

Arley wasn't too sure what to say in return, so she didn't say anything. She didn't know a whole lot about Remington. He never really spoke much about himself and Arley had always assumed there was a reason for it. She didn't even know how he'd ended up working for Banshee's End, or even how he'd become a vampire in the first place. Maybe one day he would tell her.

She wondered if Craig knew much about him or if he was also in the dark. She hadn't ever brought it up with him, as he was always busy with everything and didn't have a lot of time to just talk.

Remington indicated to the pictures on the wall.

"What's the deal with this?" he asked, looking over to her. "I see you're on the wall, but Mister Taylor is not."

"He doesn't just stay at this one outpost, so he doesn't need to be on the wall here. He moves around to the different ones, checks how things are going, and gets the new ones up and running," she explained, coming over to where he was standing. She indicated to the wall. "This shows who's here in case something happens. It has everyone's information and how long people are here for before they get moved to other outposts, if that's the case."

Remington nodded, understanding a bit more now, his gaze back on the wall. "Interesting."

"Every outpost has them," Arley continued, seeing the thought on Remington's face. "Which is how we're going to know if anyone's missing from Outpost Six when a team gets sent over there."

Remington nodded again before looking at her. "Believe me, Arley, if Cole was the one in charge, which he was, then you're most likely going to be missing a good few bodies."

Arley wasn't too happy to hear it, but she knew Remington was most likely right. Cole was someone Remington knew well. He knew what he would do if he was given the chance.

"How did you meet Cole?" Arley dared to ask.

Remington raised an eyebrow. "Why do you wanna know? Fishing for info, young lady?"

Arley gave an awkward shrug, Remington looking her over while he decided whether to answer her or not.

"You don't really talk about the vampires much unless it's to tell Craig or Jacob what they're up to and what their next move is going to be. I was just wondering, that's all," she said, defensively.

Remington hesitated before he sighed, knowing that she'd probably ask again one day if he didn't answer her now.

"Cole was my first friend when I got turned," he explained. "He helped me through a lot with the turn, taught me how to control myself and the hunger. If he hadn't been around, I don't know what would've happened. I know I would've killed a lot of people if Cole hadn't been there to help me through everything. He's always been there for me, not just at that one point in time, either."

Arley didn't say anything, and Remington looked at the ground as he spoke again.

"I know it's probably not something you want to hear me say," he said quietly. "But, if push comes to shove and Cole's in the same room as me with anyone from Banshee's End, it's not going to end well." He looked up, meeting Arley's gaze. "I owe Cole a hell of a lot and he's never once asked anything from me. He didn't have to help me like he did, but he went out of his way without asking for anything in return. That's why I wished he'd never be able to turn people, because now it puts him on your radar and means you guys are gonna be hunting him. As bad as it sounds, I can't let you take him out, I'm sorry."

Arley once again stayed quiet, Remington looking back at the wall before speaking again.

"I need to head out. If there's anything else I need to tell you, I'll make sure I come back and inform Taylor." He looked at Arley, giving her a slight smile. "You look after yourself, Arley. I'll see you around."

CHAPTER FIVE

Strangers at the Bar

Chris leant his head on his hand as he stared down at the wooden bar. He was starting to get sick of seeing the same dark wood every damn day and he was starting to wish that something exciting would happen in this town.

The most exciting thing that had happened over the course of the year that he'd spent here was when the circus had come into town and that wasn't even that exciting. The circus hadn't even been that great but at least they'd tried. This town needed something to happen, or Chris was going to go crazy.

Marion was enough to drive him insane, and he had to live with her. He made sure that most days he didn't have to see her, which was why he spent pretty well every day and night in this bar, even though he didn't even drink.

He was surprised she hadn't driven him to drink yet.

"You're looking miserable, what's gotten you so down?" a female voice asked.

Chris didn't recognize the voice, and he looked up to see who'd spoken.

The young woman behind the bar looked at him. She was leaning against the bar a few spaces down, on the opposite side to Chris. She wasn't very tall, her hair was dyed black, and she had tattoos down both of her arms.

He was positive he'd never seen her before and, around this town, that was very odd. He looked her over with a bit of a frown. Something about her wasn't quite right but he couldn't pick what it was, yet.

"Would've thought everyone here is miserable for some reason or another," Chris said as the woman moved down the bar and leaned against it again, right in front of him. "Only miserable people come out to bars, don't they?"

The woman gave him a bit of an amused smile, shifting and mirroring Chris's position, so her head was on her hand as Chris just looked at her.

"True," she said. "But you're here every night. I don't think I've been here when you haven't been. There's clearly a reason you're here at the bar. Never seen you order anything, either, might I add."

"I don't drink," Chris said, confirming her suspicions.

"Then why come to the bar?"

Chris gave a careless shrug. "Honestly, your guess is as good as mine."

He got another amused smile, the woman shifting her position again and holding her hand out in a friendly way.

"The name's Maddie," she introduced herself.

Chris shook her hand, noticing straight off how cold she was. That was his indicator.

He let her hand go suddenly and Maddie raised her eyebrows in surprise at him.

"You're a vampire," he stated, keeping his voice down. "No one's that cold unless they're dead."

Maddie didn't say anything for a few seconds, Chris being rather cautious now. You could never tell what type of person a vampire was by the first impression. For all he knew, Maddie was very dangerous. He wasn't about to take that risk.

"I'll take it you've run into vampires before, then."

"I guess you could say that."

Maddie looked him over, back to leaning against the bar.

"You never told me your name," she said, trying to steer the conversation away from the fact that she was part of the living dead. "You know mine, so fair's fair, tell me your name."

"Chris," he reluctantly introduced himself.

"It's nice to meet you, Chris!" she said cheerfully, Chris nowhere near as enthused as she was. "Tell me what brings you all the way to Treadway Valley, because something tells me you're not from here."

Chris watched her for a few seconds before responding. "Depends on why you want to know. I don't know if you've noticed yet, but there's not really a lot of trust with me and vampires."

"You don't have to be so negative about us, you know," she said. She leaned in more and lowered her voice. "I can help you get back home if you let me."

Her words made him frown. What was she talking about?

"I'm sorry?"

"You probably don't know that you've had someone on your trail for months," she stated, still keeping her voice down. "I don't personally know why they're following you, what their reasons are. But, put it this way, if you let me help you, I can get you back home before this dimension collapses."

"Wait, hang on a second," Chris said, trying to get his head around what she was saying. "Did you just say that this dimension is going to *collapse*?"

Maddie raised an eyebrow. "You didn't know that was happening?"

"No!" Chris exclaimed, a few people looking over at the minor disruption to the quiet bar. It was always too quiet in there. He lowered his voice. "How would I know that? If I knew, you think I'd still be here? Seriously?"

He figured that by now, Maddie knew he wasn't from this dimension. She'd already mentioned getting him back home and now he was even more determined to get the hell out of here and back to his correct home.

Maddie looked around the room before returning her gaze to Chris. She moved back from the bar and headed around to the same side as he was on, Chris watching her the whole time.

"Let's go talk," she said, indicating for him to follow her as she made her way to the open door.

Chris hesitated, then got up and followed her outside, into the cool night air. There weren't many people around tonight, but it was only Tuesday, and there were never many people around on a Tuesday night.

It had also been nearly four days since Chris had sent that last letter to Ash and she hadn't responded yet. He was worried because it never took her this long to answer. Maybe she was just too busy this time around?

He hoped that his letter had actually reached her and that nothing had happened to her over the time when he hadn't written. He was sure Alex or someone else would've informed him if something had happened to Ash.

He was just hoping that everything was OK back home with everyone.

He followed Maddie to the outskirts of town. Maddie walked a few paces in front of him, and he followed her a bit further, seeing that she was headed towards the small lake not far from the town.

Once the two of them reached the lake's edge, Maddie stopped. Chris caught up and stopped a few paces in front of her, crossing his arms as he regarded her.

"What did you want to talk about and how long is this going to take?" he asked, past the point of being tired.

He just wanted to call it quits for the night, even if that meant that he had to go back to the lodgings he unfortunately had to share with Marion.

"Won't take long, just wanted to explain a few things, seeing as you clearly don't trust me," Maddie said defensively.

"Well, I don't know how much you know about vampires, how long you've been one, but from my experiences with the living dead, they're not always the most trustworthy beings."

Maddie rolled her eyes. "We're not all like that you know."

Chris stayed silent, not wanting to continue talking about vampires.

"You're aware of abilities," she stated straight off, already knowing that Chris wasn't stupid and he had a pretty good idea of everything that was going on. "If you know a thing or two about vampires, it's that when people get turned, they lose their ability. Still with me?"

Chris nodded, once again not saying anything and letting her continue to explain.

"My ability was very rare," she continued, not missing a beat whatsoever. "I was able to travel through dimensions, hence why I'm unfortunately stuck in this one."

Chris frowned. "You could travel through dimensions?"

"Very few people have that ability," Maddie said with a bit of a nod. "I think there's about six in total over the entire dimension spectrum, five since I've been a vampire. Part of that ability, though, stuck with me when I got turned. I can't travel through dimensions anymore, but I can still tell who's from what dimension."

"How?"

"Everyone has an aura, different colors. Yours is the wrong colour for this dimension, yours is gold. It's a Dimension One aura."

"Meaning what exactly?"

Maddie shifted slightly. "Every dimension is very similar; some only have slight differences. Whether it's one person not existing in one, but existing in another, or someone in a different line of work, you get the idea of it. Each dimension is labelled depending on when it was created. You being from Dimension One means that you're the original Chris. Any other dimensions are copied from the original dimension: Dimension One. If that makes sense."

Chris gave a bit of a nod, understanding what she was saying. It was hard to believe, but he didn't really have much choice at the moment.

"Any idea how many dimensions are out there?" he asked curiously.

Maddie shrugged. "No idea. Could be millions. I know of over three hundred different dimensions."

Chris was surprised, but there was also a part of him that wasn't surprised about there being hundreds of different dimensions. He wondered what some of the other ones were like, how different they were.

"OK, so what's this got to do with getting me home?" he asked. "Because you said so yourself: you can't travel through dimensions anymore, so how does this help me in any way whatsoever? Also, what's the deal with this dimension collapsing?"

"If we can find someone who can travel through dimensions, they can get you home," Maddie emphasized.

Chris was unimpressed. "You said it's incredibly rare for anyone to be able to do that."

"But I can still sense people who are out of place. If we find someone who can travel like that, I'll know."

Chris sighed. He knew she was trying to help but, right now, he couldn't see this plan working in the slightest.

"OK, say we do find someone," he said. "They can get me back home. The only problem with that is that I'm currently spell-bound to someone, which is the reason I got dragged into this dimension in the first place. How do you suggest that we untie me from her because I'll be damned if she's coming back with me."

"We'll figure that out when we find someone who can move through dimensions," Maddie said. "Right now, that's our main focus."

"So, why is this dimension collapsing exactly?" Chris repeated.

"Some disturbance in between the dimensions," Maddie said with a bit of a shrug. "That's all I know. If we find someone who can move through the dimensions, we can get a clearer answer on it and how long we've got. I only tell what I hear from the carriers."

"The gargoyle things near the portal?"

Maddie nodded. "Mmhm. Not from them exactly but news that comes through from others in other dimensions. There's a group that keeps tabs on everything and everyone that can—or used to be able to—move through dimensions. We're kept up to date on what's happening in case anyone needs to be warned to stay out of certain dimensions."

"There are some dimensions you guys aren't allowed in?"

Maddie nodded again. "There are a couple of locked dimensions," she explained, the interest clear on Chris's face. "Only the Dimension Guardians are able to access those dimensions. They get locked for a reason."

A frown appeared on Chris's face. "Like what exactly?"

"We'll use Dimension Fifteen as an example. It's currently locked and won't ever be unlocked unless the threat of the zombie apocalypse there dies out. Rare, but it happens in some dimensions. Fifteen happened to be the first one plagued by the undead and so it got locked. That way the zombie virus can't spread to other dimensions if someone travels there and gets into trouble. Things like that are what causes dimensions to get locked."

Chris sighed. This was all so confusing.

"OK, well, I guess I'm going to have to take your word for it then," he said. Maddie smiled at him. "But now, it's getting late, so I'm going to head back into town and get some sleep. I'll come find you tomorrow night and we can figure something out to get out of this ... Godforsaken dimension. Goodnight."

"Night!" Maddie called with a wave as Chris headed back into town.

He walked back into town and through the quiet streets. Some of the streetlights were on, lighting his way as he made his way back to his lodgings. As usual, the front light had been left on and he went in through the front door, shutting it after himself and making sure it was locked.

It was quiet. That was the reason he came home late most nights, as it meant that he didn't have to put up with Marion and he could avoid the situation as best he could.

He frowned as something on the table caught his eye. It was a small white envelope addressed to him:

Chris; Dimension 4; Treadway Valley.

It was Ash's handwriting and Chris grabbed the envelope and sat down, tearing it open and unfolding the piece of paper he took out.

Chris,

I was starting to think that maybe something had happened since we hadn't heard from you in a few months. I hope everything is actually going OK for you over there and that you can make your way home soon.

We've had no new developments on this side in the way of getting you home yet and for that I'm really sorry. The moment we know something, we'll let you know.

The Legion have forced their way past the Banshee's End outpost on the border. They've managed to make their way into Wonderland and we're now trying to stop them from reaching the Room of Doors. We don't want them to make their way Upstairs.

I've contacted Craig about the issue, so hopefully he'll get back to me soon with what he's willing to do in order to help us out with this. Hopefully something good comes out of Banshee's End interfering, but I don't have my hopes high at the moment.

Take care, Chris. We all miss you and can't wait to hear from you again.

Ash.

CHAPTER SIX

Outpost Six

"Everyone, listen up!" Craig shouted, raising his voice to be heard above the noise his recruits were currently making. This always happened and he was sick of this outpost. He just wanted to move on to any other outpost, as long as it wasn't this one. He'd spent too much time here.

Everyone quietened down, knowing that when Craig raised his voice, he meant business. Most of the recruits at this outpost were newer than most at Banshee's End. They'd had some training but a lot of them were still rather green and nowhere near ready for field work.

It had taken a lot of work by Craig and there had been many issues the entire time he'd been here. Most of the recruits were intimidated by him and that had made things even harder, especially when trying to train everyone to be able to take on any threat they were likely to come into contact with.

It had gotten to the point where he'd had to leave most of the training to Arley and he'd only step in every so often when he was needed. Outpost Fourteen had not been a fun ride.

Craig looked around at everyone, glad they were all listening to him now. They were all looking in his direction and Arley stood off to his right.

"Outpost Six has gone down," he informed them, keeping his voice raised so that even the people furthest away from him were able to hear what he was saying. "We don't know the exact status of it just yet, so until we know, we just have to assume that no one made it out. Once we get confirmation on what's happened, that's when we'll decide on the best thing to do."

He looked around at everyone, hands on hips as he regarded his rather useless outpost crew. Only a few of them had shown any promise and even they were intimidated by him, and he sighed before continuing to speak.

"Banshee's End is sending out a field team to inspect the damage. So, with that said, everyone here who's under my division, you're coming with me. We're going over to Outpost Six to meet up with the field team. I'll also be taking a few of you who aren't in my team, so I need volunteers. If no one volunteers, I'll choose, and you won't have any say in the matter. So, anyone care to go for a nice walk to the Wonderland and Oz border?"

He waited, knowing it would take them a bit to volunteer themselves. Eventually, one of the younger recruits put his hand up, and Craig indicated for him to stand up. The recruit rose to his feet, staying quiet.

"Anyone else?"

Someone else reluctantly put their hand up, Craig indicating for him to stand as well. Arley shifted next to Craig, making eye contact with some of her trainees, which led to another two volunteers who also stood up at Craig's request.

"I need one more," Craig said. "This is going to be field experience. If you seriously want to be part of this movement, we need to be able to count on you when this kind of thing happens. If this is too much pressure or you think it's too dangerous, you shouldn't have signed up in the first place, so if you think that's the case, there's the door."

He pointed at the door, and several gazes followed his gesture, but the recruits all stayed seated.

Another quiet minute went by, then another hand went up and one more recruit stood up without being told, joining the others.

Craig looked around at the recruits who were now standing, making eye contact with each of them.

"I appreciate you all having the courage to volunteer and come out into the field with us," he said. "Thank you. We leave first thing in the morning, so be ready to go. We'll meet at the front gate of the outpost, so be there on time, else there'll be some serious issues. Is that clear?"

The volunteers nodded, and he looked around at everyone else.

"I want everyone else to seriously think about whether you should be here or not. While I'm not here, Sergeant Kay is in charge since Arley will be coming with me. I may not be coming back to this outpost after we find out the deal with Outpost Six, so don't expect me to be returning for some time, but think about what I've said. Dismissed."

Craig watched most of them leave, shaking his head, standing with his arms crossed now. A few stayed behind, gathering into a group to talk.

Arley looked at him. "Everything OK?"

Craig watched one of the recruits for a second, the only female who'd volunteered.

"Perfect," he said before heading for the door.

Arley quickly followed, catching up to him as he left the room. A few recruits were outside, and they all stepped back, moving out of his way and watching him pass.

Craig didn't even glance at Arley as he made his way outside, heading back to the lodgings he'd been living in for months.

"Can't wait to get out of this goddamned outpost," he said. "Fucking sick of this place."

"It's not that bad," Arley said.

Craig came to a halt out in the middle of the open area of the outpost. More recruits milled around here, pretending not to pay them any attention, even though it was obvious they were trying to listen in on Craig's private business.

"You can't be serious," he said. "Really? Not that bad? Honestly, Beckett, this is single-handedly the worst group I've had command over. Do you know how hard it is, being in my position?" Arley shook her head. "It's damned hard. Makes it worse that half the time with this outpost, I've been locked away in that damn room, trying to figure out where to hit next. I haven't been training people, and it's driving me to drinking again when I've been sober for nearly six years, and I sure as hell haven't had a decent conversation with anyone that isn't work talk. None of them want to talk to me because they're intimidated. They don't want to train under me because they're intimidated, and they know I have a high standard. I'd be surprised if they all didn't know my ability, too. You know how hard that is? Really?"

Arley continued to look at him, not sure what to say. She could now see just how frustrated this whole operation was making him.

"So, excuse me if I can't see the bright side to this outpost," he continued. "Because it's been a damn long time since I've been seen as *anything* but a commander. It'd be nice to be appreciated for being myself for once."

Without another word, he started walking again, the nearby recruits moving out of his way pretending they hadn't been listening as he strode past them.

Arley stayed where she was and watched him scan himself into one of the buildings, disappearing inside seconds later.

Hopefully this run to Outpost Six would make him feel a bit better, she thought, and hopefully it would be enough for him to be able to move on to another outpost.

He'd been at Outpost Fourteen for far too long.

Danny looked at the front of Outpost Six, hands on hips as he thought. The front looked more or less fine, except for the gate which was partially bent inwards.

He wasn't so sure about what they were going to find within the fence line.

He'd volunteered his group of recruits for the field team this time around, as he'd been sitting around at Banshee's End for weeks and he was bored. He was taking any excuse to get out of that place and do something that might be slightly more fun, even if this was going to be a devastating run.

His small group consisted of himself, Ted, Jordan, Shawn, Daniel, and three recruits whose names he'd literally picked out of Ted's hat.

"Whatcha think it looks like inside?" Jordan asked, standing slightly behind him, on his left.

Danny glanced back at him, seeing the slight worry on his face, even under the mask he was wearing. The bandits all still insisted on wearing their masks when doing field runs. It was something they'd been doing for years, and they weren't about to give it up any time soon.

"Your guess is as good as mine," Danny said, feeling the harsh sun beating down on all of them. He indicated for them all to move out. "Alright, let's go see the damage. Everyone keep alert and keep a thorough watch. Any signs of trouble, you know what to do. Let's go."

Danny didn't have high hopes for the inside of this outpost. It was right on the Wonderland border and, by the looks of it, the Legion had pushed through here and over the border.

There was a gap in the damaged gate big enough for them all to get through, and Danny went first, making sure he was being careful as he went through. His small group followed, with his usual crew seconds behind him and the recruits bringing up the rear.

"Aw man, this is bad," Ted said as they all looked around. "This isn't good at all."

What had once been housing for the recruits and the captains had been burned to the ground, leaving just bare dirt, ashes, and some still smoldering rubble.

"Jesus Christ," was all Danny found himself saying.

"What's the damage?"

Danny knew Craig's voice anywhere and he wasn't in the least bit pleased to hear it now. This was meant to be Danny's run, not Craig's. Why did he always have to show up and take over whenever Danny had a field run? It just wasn't fair.

He looked over his shoulder as Craig came through the gap in the gate. Craig slowed his pace as he also saw the devastation.

Danny gestured to it. "This is just the front, could be worse up the back."

Craig stopped off next to him, looking around at the rubble as he adjusted his sunglasses.

"Well." He looked at Danny, knowing there was a judgmental look on Danny's face even though his mask did a great job of hiding it. Craig knew how Danny reacted to certain people. "You guys just get here, I'll take it?"

Danny nodded. "Less than ten minutes ago. We were gonna keep looking around, see what we can find."

Craig gave a nod of agreement as the rest of his team joined him, staying back as Danny's group acknowledged their new companions.

"Sounds like a plan. Remington said that Cole's unit came through this outpost. We need to figure out who's missing and if they've turned anyone. If they have, we could be in serious trouble."

Danny frowned. "Cole's moved up the ranks?"

Craig nodded. "Unfortunately."

Danny sighed, messing his hair up a bit before mindlessly readjusting his mask as he tried to think of what to do. Craig was right about there being a problem if Cole had turned anyone. Although their recruits only knew basic information about what went on with the Banshee's End operation, they knew enough that it would cause an issue if they told the vampires.

Danny looked at his small group.

"We're gonna move around the perimeter. We're gonna take the right and Commander Taylor and his group are gonna take the left," he informed everyone, Craig not arguing. "Like I said before, keep alert and keep alive. No one is dying on my watch, got it? If anyone dies, I will personally resurrect you somehow and kill you myself for dying on one of my field runs." Everyone nodded, most of them used to Danny and his harsh attitude. "Good, now let's move out. We'll all meet up at the back of the outpost once we've scouted the area. Move."

If it was one thing Danny did well, it was make sure his words were obeyed. He didn't take too kindly to anyone below him back-chatting or disobeying his orders. He'd never asked to be a captain for Banshee's End, but he took his role seriously most days.

Without waiting for any kind of confirmation, he moved off, heading right like he'd said they were going to do. His group followed, as Craig directed his own group the opposite way.

Danny looked around at the damage the further into the outpost they got. Many of the structures were completely burned and now non-existent, except for rubble and ashes, and he wondered why the Legion had burned everything. They hated fire, so why wield it against the outpost? It made no sense.

Danny's group made it to the back of the outpost, where there were a few structures that were still more or less standing. The fence line was rather close to the only full building that had been left untouched.

"Captain," Daniel said, pulling Danny's attention away from the building he was looking at. Daniel pointed to a part of the fence where the wood and metal had been torn inwards, creating a gap large enough for anyone to pass through. "I think they got straight through here."

Danny moved over to the damaged fence, thinking as he looked it over. "Great."

"I'll take it this is how they got over the border?" Craig called.

Danny turned and watched Craig heading his way, stopping only a few paces away from him and the damaged fence.

Craig stood with him, observing the damage. "Well, then."

Danny put his hands on his hips as he watched Craig step through the gap. Craig turned back, studying the fence from Wonderland's side of the border, thinking.

"Any ideas, Commander?" Danny asked with a hint of sarcasm. Craig didn't take the bait and continued to look at the fence, before crouching down to examine something. Danny sighed. "Any ideas on what to do next, Taylor?"

Craig hesitated before looking at Danny who was expecting a response.

"We've got to track down Cole. We can't let him get too far into Wonderland," he said. Danny did not like this idea at all. "If he's gotten too far inland, we're going to have to take him out."

"I can't let you do that, Commander."

Everyone looked over at the one building that remained intact. Remington was watching them from the shade of the building, sunglasses on, hood up, and hands in his pockets.

"I can tell you where he is," Remington continued. "But I can't let you take him out just yet."

Remington watched the group of them, not trusting any of them right now, even Craig.

Craig stood up, looking directly at Remington as he addressed him. "I need to know where he is. I know you don't want them to make their way Upstairs either, Bell, so the best thing you can do to stop that, is tell me where Cole's going."

"Why won't you let us take him out?" Danny spoke up. "I don't know if you've noticed, but vampires are a bit of a problem around here."

Remington looked at Danny, hesitating before he answered.

"The why is not your problem, just know that you've got to keep him around for a bit," he said. Remington looked back to Craig. "Leave Cole to me, that's all I ask."

Danny crossed his arms, not liking that Remington was stopping him from doing his job.

Craig looked at Remington as he thought about what he'd just asked. Danny looked at him, everyone waiting to see what he was going to do. When it came down to it, Craig had the final say since Jacob wasn't here.

"If he's turned anyone from this outpost, his unit is all gone," Craig warned Remington, who nodded. "So, you'd better pray to God or whoever you pray to that he hasn't turned any of my recruits."

Danny looked at Craig who switched his gaze over to him. He gestured to Remington.

"You're seriously siding with him? He's a damned vampire, Craig! I don't know if you've noticed, but he's dead. He basically eats people for lunch and you're OK siding with him and not taking out a vampire who can turn people? You've got to be kidding me right now."

Craig's expression turned to annoyance.

"My say is final, you listen to me, or you get lost," he said harshly, Danny shaking his head in disagreement. "I get that you don't like it and, believe me, this is the last thing I want to do, but we have more important things to focus on right now. If Remington is going to take care of Cole, then I'm not about to stop him. I don't wish to risk anyone right now because we're low on recruits and the Legion is getting stronger. We can't afford to lose another lot of recruits like we have at this outpost."

Danny chose to stay silent, Craig taking it as his chance to talk again, addressing everyone this time.

"We're pushing forwards into Wonderland," he said, making sure everyone was listening, not just in his own group, either. "We're going to figure out with Ash where to put a couple of outposts and we're going to get on top of this situation before it gets too out of hand. Everyone who's here now, I need you all to listen to everything that is discussed when we get there. Clear?"

Everyone nodded.

"Good, let's get moving. It's going to take us a day or so to reach the castle."

CHAPTER SEVEN

Into Wonderland

Ash lazily looked over as the usual guard appeared in the doorway, disturbing the small now-blonde cat on the floor near her feet. She was lounging on the throne as she did most days.

"Someone here to see you," the guard informed her, getting the small cat's attention. The guard glanced at Alex before looking back at Ash. "Well, actually it's more than just one person."

The cat dashed out of the room, disappearing around the guard's feet and out of sight.

Ash sighed and rested her head on her hand. "Who is it?"

"Someone you've been desperately trying to avoid for the past twelve months," Craig said, moving around the guard to enter the room before stopping and crossing his arms as he looked at her. "Ash."

The cat trudged back into the room, going back to where he'd been lying before the interruption.

"Craig," Ash reluctantly greeted back, pushing herself up into a sitting position. "Surprised you trekked this far in. Thought it'd be too cold outside for you."

She pushed herself off the throne and headed over to him, followed by the cat, as Craig stayed in the same position just watching her. The guard stayed silent in the doorway.

"I just happened to be on the border. Wouldn't have stopped in, otherwise," Craig said. He looked her over when she stopped in front of him. "I'm surprised you actually asked for help."

Ash rolled her eyes, crossing her arms and mirroring his position as the cat sat down next to her, getting a glance from Craig.

"I wouldn't have if Alex hadn't pushed me to write to you," she said, glancing down at the cat. She looked back at Craig, summing him up with her usual unimpressed expression on her face. "But I guess now that you're here, you could be of some help."

Craig gave her a very slight, almost non-existent smile. "Well, then, it's lucky I didn't come alone."

Ash rolled her eyes again, and Craig smiled a bit more before he turned and headed back the way he'd come. Alex ran after him and Ash reluctantly followed.

She didn't understand why Alex liked Craig so much. She certainly didn't—at least, she'd never admit to it—and it was Alex's fault that he'd now shown up at her home. Hopefully he wouldn't be around for too long.

Ash followed Craig back through the hallways, hearing the blustery wind outside as they neared the massive front doors of the castle.

"Oh, wonderful, you brought thieves into my home," she commented as she saw who was waiting near the doors.

"Hey, Ash," Ted greeted cheerfully as Ash and Craig stopped a pace or so away from the medium-sized group.

The little cat went over to the group to inspect everyone, making his way around them all.

Ash gave Ted an unamused smile before turning her attention to Craig.

"You seriously thought I'd be OK with you bringing this many people here, especially bandits?" Ash asked harshly, keeping her voice down so only Craig could hear her. "Really?"

Craig shot her an annoyed look.

"You want to deal with this shit by yourself? Last time I checked, *you* were the one who asked *me* for help, so that's what's about to happen," he shot back, his voice down and equally as harsh. He straightened up, gesturing to his surroundings. "So be a good host and show us around."

Ash glared at him, looking back at the group, all of them waiting to be told what they were doing.

"Any of you break anything, you replace it," was the first thing she said, making Craig roll his eyes. Ash looked over to the guard who had followed them. "Show them to the spare rooms." She looked at Craig who just returned her look, still a bit of annoyance on her face. "Commander Taylor, here, has important things to discuss with me, don't you, Taylor?"

Craig couldn't help but smirk as he kept his arms crossed, looking directly at Ash. "If that's what we're referring to it as now, then, yeah, we do."

Ash hit him rather hard in the ribs, just making him laugh. Ash shook her head as the guard indicated for everyone else to follow him.

"You're such an idiot, you know that?" Ash said, crossing her arms as Craig regained his composure, the smile back on his face as the cat wandered over to Ash.

The group, including Danny and his bandits, followed the guard's instructions and headed past them.

Ash indicated for Craig to follow her. "Come on, let me show you around."

She managed a bit of a smile as she headed to the double doors that led outside, pulling one open. The harsh cold breeze and some snow blew in through the open door. Craig followed her outside, but the cat refused to venture out into the cold. The door shut behind them once they were both out.

"I don't know how Wonderland manages with this kind of weather all the time," Craig admitted as he pulled his jacket around himself, the wind feeling as if it was going right through him. "You're responsible for this, right?"

"Yes."

"Why?"

Ash sighed as they stood there looking out at the town, the snow rather deep in parts on the ground.

"Long, complicated story," she said.

Craig didn't bother pushing the matter and followed Ash as she walked down the snow-covered stone steps.

"How long do you plan on being here?" Ash asked when Craig caught up to her. "I assume you're here to work out where to put your outposts and then you're out of here again?"

"How long do you want me to be around?" he asked back, following her into the streets of the busy town close by the castle. "Because I can leave in the morning if that's what you'd prefer."

Ash came to a stop in the town square. The snow started to fall harder on the few people who had a reason to be out and about in this weather.

"Look, I don't want you to think I don't want you around," she said with a sigh. "Because that's not it at all."

"Honestly Ash, it seriously feels like you really don't want me here," Craig said. Ash crossed her arms and looked at the ground, as someone moved past them rather close. "It feels like you haven't really wanted me around for a while. You've been very adamant on avoiding me over the past twelve months. It's to do with Chris being gone, isn't it?"

Ash sighed again. "Craig, look..."

"No, it's fine, I get it," Craig interrupted, as a sad look now appeared on Ash's face. "Chris meant a lot to you, I get it. You might not believe it, but I do know what it's like to miss people you consider family."

The sad look stayed on Ash's face, Craig's expression mirroring it.

"I appreciate you coming over here to help out," she said, trying to change the subject. Craig's expression remained the same as she continued to avoid the reason why she hadn't wanted to talk to him over the past year. "Did you want to go back inside and see where's best to set up outposts to try and stop these vampires?"

"We can do that if you really want. The sooner we get that done, the sooner I'll be out of your home."

Not waiting for her to respond, he made his way back towards the castle, rather glad to be going back inside. It was too cold to be standing around in the snow for long.

Ash trailed him, back up the snow-covered steps and back inside the castle. Once they were inside, Ash walked faster, past Craig, heading further into the castle. Alex was nowhere to be seen.

"I'll show you to your room a bit later on," Ash said as she entered a room that looked much like the others. "Once we talk this over, you and your little clique can go and do whatever they want around town.

I don't care what they do, as long as they don't mess anything up too badly."

"Noted."

Ash gave a nod of approval, indicating for him to take a seat at the large round table. Craig obliged and Ash left the room. He heard her say something to someone, most likely a guard. A minute or two later, she reappeared, taking the seat on his left.

"I assume you want your whole party to join us so they know what's going on," she said, avoiding his gaze and looking at something over the other side of the room. "I've just sent the guard to go and get everyone."

Craig gave slight nod and reached into his jacket pocket, taking out the folded map he had with him. He got to his feet, pushing his chair back out of the way, and unfolded the map, placing it on the table.

Ash looked at it from where she was seated as Danny and his boys came into the room.

"What are we doing, Commander?" Danny asked, the slight sarcasm back in his tone. He halted at the table, interest on his face. "Strategy again?"

Craig gave him an unamused look as the remainder of their group came into the room. Arley stopped far enough away so there were a few people between herself and Craig.

"We're figuring out where we need to put outposts, where to start," Craig said. He looked around at everyone. "Those who can, find a seat, everyone else, you're just going to have to stand."

Danny grabbed the closest seat, and Ted pushed someone aside to sit next to him. Ash shook her head but didn't say a word as Jordan timidly moved past a few people to sit on Ted's right. Shawn stayed standing behind the three of them, arms crossed.

Arley took the seat on Jordan's right, and a few of the recruits took the remaining chairs. Once every chair was taken, the left-over recruits stood behind everyone else, waiting to hear what Craig had to say.

"We've established that Outpost Six has gone down completely, there's no rebuilding it, and there's no point trying," Craig said, getting straight into it as the little cat suddenly jumped up onto the table, walked across the map, and sat in front of Ash. "With that said, we still don't know who got out and who didn't. Hopefully if anyone survived it and didn't get turned, they'll head to the nearest outpost, but I don't think there's much chance of that."

He realized there was something he hadn't asked yet even though it was important He looked at Arley. "Who received the distress call about the outpost going down?"

Arley shrugged. "We just got told that Banshee's End received the call and that they were going to head out to check out the damage."

Craig raised his eyebrows as he looked at Danny.

"Yes?" Danny said, lazily returned his gaze.

"Who reported it?" Craig asked, getting a shrug from Danny. "You and your division have been at Banshee's End for weeks. Someone must've reported it."

"Whoever did it went straight to Cain," Danny said, sounding tired. "I don't know who it was because my division didn't deal with it, Cain's did. Contact him and find out."

Craig sighed. Why was Danny always so unhelpful?

"Alright, we'll worry about that later," he said. He turned his focus to the map, everyone following his gaze as he got a pen out of his pocket. The cat was now lying down, facing the map as well. "So, next question: where are we setting up?" He looked at Ash. "Is there anywhere in particular we're not allowed to go? Or anywhere you really want me to go?"

"Her bed," Ted said, his voice down and making Danny smile.

Craig and Ash both shot Ted a glare, getting a grin from him in return.

"What? We all know it happened," Danny said in Ted's defense. Ted, Jordan, and Shawn all nodded in confirmation. Danny looked at his crew. "Probably more than once."

Ted nodded in agreement, the annoyance on Craig's face still evident.

"If you guys don't shut it and actually take this seriously, you're all going back to Banshee's End and, I swear, I will make sure you're all gone for good by the time I get back," Craig threatened. Danny just looked at him, leaning his head on his hand. Craig gestured between himself and Ash. "This, is none of your fucking business."

"So, you're saying there's something there?" Ted dared to say, the amusement clear on Danny's face as everyone else stayed quiet, knowing not to challenge Craig.

"That's not what I said at all."

"But it's what you're implying," Danny said, getting nods of agreement from his usual three. Danny glanced at Ted before looking around Craig at Ash. "Honestly darlin', you could do a lot better than Taylor."

Ash decided against saying anything in return, knowing that it was only going to spur them on more. They just couldn't leave it alone.

"You'd better shut your mouth," Craig warned, not in the mood for Danny and his immaturity right now. "I get it, you don't want to be here. Well, guess what, none of us want to be here! You seriously think this is what I had in mind when I first came down here? You really think I wanted to be a commander in charge of an operation that hunts down and kills vampires? You really think this is how I want to spend my time?"

"You're still in the same position, Craig, so you tell me how you currently feel about your position because if you don't want to be commanding officer anymore, then by all means, step the fuck down," Danny said, shaking his head.

Craig growled and threw his hands up in frustration. "You'd all be dead without me, just remember that. Good luck."

Without another word, he threw the pen at Danny, left the map where it was on the table, and stalked out of the room.

Ash sighed, looking at Danny. "Really?"

Danny gave a lazy shrug. "Get out of the kitchen if you can't handle the heat."

CHAPTER EIGHT

Drunks Tell Truths

"Commander?"

"It's Craig," was the rather snappy response Arley received.

Craig stayed where he was, head on hand as he glanced over his shoulder. He went back to looking down at the wooden bar. "Don't call me Commander."

Arley hesitantly took a seat on the barstool next to him. There were quite a few people in the bar on this cold night. Craig glanced at her again but didn't say anything else. Arley awkwardly cleared her throat as Craig signaled for the bartender to bring him another drink.

"Ash marked down the places to put the outposts," she said, trying to get a bit of a conversation going as the bartender placed another glass in front of Craig who nodded his thanks.

Craig looked at Arley. He looked tired and done with everything.

"I really don't care," he admitted. "So, if you're only here to talk business then, please, take a fucking walk because I really don't wanna hear it."

He turned his focus back to whatever he'd been looking at behind the bar before the interruption and picked up the glass.

"I'm sick and tired of only talking business with everyone," Craig continued. He looked at her. "Am I seriously that hard to like as a person? Honestly, I wanna know."

Arley frowned. "I don't think I quite understand what you're talking about."

Craig looked at her for a few seconds before just shaking his head. "Never mind."

He fell silent, going back to looking at nothing behind the bar, taking a drink from the glass he was holding. Arley looked around the bar, watching people seated at the tables, talking and laughing about different things, and other bartenders placing drinks down on the tables and picking up empty glasses.

"You should go get some sleep, got a long day tomorrow," Craig said. Arley looked back at him to find him looking at her. "We'll head out in the morning. I'll take a look at the map before I go to bed tonight and decide where to hit up first."

"You sure you're going to be able to?" Arley asked hesitantly, watching him take another drink, the glass almost in need of a refill already. "How many of those have you had?"

"Not nearly enough."

Arley didn't say anything more, giving Craig a nod before standing up and walking away, leaving him there by himself.

Craig signaled for the bartender to refill his glass before taking his phone out of his pocket and looking at it.

It had been quite a while since he'd really done much with his phone, but he knew that if he wanted to, he could easily contact anyone back Upstairs. The few of them at Banshee's End had the same 'upgrade' to their phones as did the others who frequented these Underground Worlds. It was something they'd worked on quite early in the campaign, at least since Banshee's End had become their home of operations.

Craig stared at his phone for a minute or so before a notification came through, causing him to unlock it to see what it was about. He'd had alerts set for certain things and now something had finally shown up. He mindlessly pressed the notification, seeing that it was for a live stream, watching as the video loaded before it played. It had only just started by the looks of it.

"Ladies and gentlemen, thank you all for joining me today," the woman in the video said.

Craig turned the sound up a bit so he could hear it before he turned his phone sideways to make the video fill the entire screen.

The woman looked at the man next to her, and Craig recognized him straight off.

"I'm here right now with Astin Short, former bassist for the rock band Alcazar," the woman said.

Craig felt his heart sink a bit upon hearing the words. Had his disappearance caused the band to split?

He took a drink from his recently refilled glass.

The woman in the video continued to talk. "Astin, thank you for joining me. I know this time of year probably isn't the best for you and the other members, so thank you for coming down here to have a chat with me."

"Thanks for having me down here," was Astin's uneasy response. "It's never easy when this time comes around, but we've all managed to more or less push forwards."

The woman nodded, Craig rather interested in what he was seeing now. The woman looked at the camera, speaking again.

"For those of you out there right now that don't know what we're talking about, today marks five years since Alcazar's lead vocalist, Craig Taylor, disappeared without a trace," she said, Craig feeling that sinking feeling again. He took another drink. "We wanted to have a chat with Astin about this mystery and, thankfully, he agreed, so here we are."

She switched her gaze back to Astin.

"So, Astin, if you wouldn't mind, can you tell us how you and the others have managed to move on?"

Astin shifted awkwardly, looking uncomfortable now.

"Well, it's no secret that the band broke up not long after Craig disappeared," he began. Craig nodded to himself. He was right. His disappearance *had* caused the band to split. "We all still keep in contact, but we've also all now moved onto different things. I play with a new band now, so that's something for me to focus on. Obviously, it's not the same as before, but it's still something I get to do, and I'm grateful for that."

The woman nodded. Craig could tell that she was only pretending to be interested and most likely didn't care either way. He wondered if she even knew who he was.

"Why did you all decide to break up the band?" she asked. "Craig wasn't even your original singer. Was there any thought of replacing him?"

That made Craig a little annoyed, and he signalled the bartender again as he watched Astin shake his head.

"Never crossed our minds. We talked about what to do and we never once brought up the thought of replacing him. It was either he showed up or we broke up. There was no in between."

"Even though he's been gone for five years now, is there still hope that he's out there somewhere and might still come back?"

Craig watched as Astin hesitated, clearly not too sure how to answer.

After a minute or so, a sad look appeared on Astin's face and he spoke, looking directly at the camera.

"In all honesty, I do believe he's still out there somewhere, whether he wants us to know or not. And, I'd like to say, Craig, if you *are* somewhere out there and if you, for some reason, happen to see this, please, please, come home. We miss you and we want you back."

Craig locked his phone and put it face down on the bar. He finished off his drink and grabbed the next one the bartender had left for him.

"Has it really been five years?"

Ash sat on the vacant seat next to him.

"What do you want?" Craig asked tiredly, glancing at her but not looking at her properly. "You here to drag my ass back to the castle? Can't I, just for once, get fucked up without anyone trying to convince me otherwise?"

Ash looked him over as he leaned his arms on the bar, gaze on something behind the bar again.

"I'm sorry about what Danny said."

Craig scoffed. "Sure, you are."

Ash looked at him sadly as he shifted, now resting his chin on his hand as he watched someone off to his right.

"Those recruits look up to you, you know," she said.

Craig looked at her. "Those recruits are scared of me. They don't look up to me, at all." He gestured to himself. "I don't blame them for being scared. I'm scared of me."

He shook his head and went back to looking behind the bar again, arms back on the wooden top. Ash continued to look at him sadly as he spoke again, refusing to look at her.

"I just want to go home," he said, feeling a few tears run down his face. He shook his head as he looked down at the wooden top of the bar. "That was my life, all I ever wanted to do. I don't want to be stuck down here anymore. I want to go home."

"Then go home."

Craig gave an unamused laugh, shaking his head again.

"Yeah, right," he said, grabbing his glass and taking a drink again before placing it back down in front of himself. "Like I can just up and leave." He looked at her, and Ash saw the tiredness on his face. "You're all done without me. At least, that's what I like to believe, whether it's true or not. It's the only way someone like me can feel important down here. I hate this world, but those vampires are not getting Upstairs. Not on my watch."

Ash stayed silent, having nothing more to say on the matter. She figured it was no use arguing with Craig, especially since she was sure he'd had a bit too much to drink. He'd disappeared from the castle hours ago and Ash had followed Arley to find out where he was.

Craig ran a hand through his hair, finishing off his drink and putting the empty glass back down.

"Alright, I'm out," he said, placing both hands flat against the bar. He looked at Ash. "I will see you later."

He got up and felt his head spin. Ash got to her feet, glad that Craig had a slight hold on the bar.

She sighed. "Let's get you back to your room."

CHAPTER NINE

Vampires are a Vampire's Best Friend

R emington enjoyed minding his own business. If there was one thing he enjoyed about being a vampire, it was that he was left alone by other vampires, for the most part.

He had his few vampire friends whom he hung out with on occasion but, for most of his time in the headquarters where he lived whilst he was infiltrating the Legion, he was left to himself.

He even had his own room. The perks of being a high-ranking vampire within the Underground Worlds. It came with its privileges and some of them, Remington enjoyed.

"Yo, Rem, you in?"

"Cole," Remington greeted without turning around or abandoning his task.

He glanced over his shoulder and saw Cole standing in the doorway, arms crossed as he leaned against the doorframe.

Cole was roughly six feet tall, but his build was intimidating. Remington couldn't hold a candle to his friend, even if he tried. Most days, Cole had his light brown hair tied back off his face and today was no different.

"Didn't think you'd be back from your Wonderland crusade for another few weeks," Remington said, continuing to organize a few things on his desk.

He could hear some of the newer vampires down the hall. It never stopped with them, and it had been going on for days, now.

"Got word Taylor had moved into town, so we pulled the operation before we ended up in the line of fire," Cole said in his clear British accent as he wandered into the room. He looked around. "I'm waiting for further instructions from Graith. Once he decides on what we're doing next, we'll get moving again."

"Any ideas on what he wants to do exactly?" Remington asked, not paying Cole much attention. He wrote a note for himself about something he needed to remember later on in the week.

Cole gave a shrug and stopped in front of one of the few art pieces on the wall, appraising it.

"Don't know just yet," he admitted. He looked over at Remington, who was busy thinking as he stared at the wall. "There's been rumors that he wants to take out Taylor soon."

That made Remington stop. He turned and looked at Cole, raising his eyebrows in interest. This was something that Craig probably needed to know. "Is that so?"

Cole nodded.

"Any ideas on how he's going to achieve this task?" Remington asked.

Cole shrugged again, and Remington thought a bit more before turning his attention back to the desk and what he'd been doing.

"It's only speculation at the moment," Cole said, going back to looking around Remington's room. He went over to the bedside table.

Remington always found it strange that every room had beds, even though none of them ever slept. Maybe it was just to make it feel homier.

"The thing I don't get is why Graith thinks that taking out Taylor will do anything," Cole continued. "He's not even the one in charge of Banshee's End and their stupid movement. I don't get why he's not going straight for the head of operations, you know?"

Remington sighed, shuffling a few pieces of paper, his back still to Cole. "Your guess is as good as mine."

Cole grunted in response as he opened the top drawer of the bedside table. Remington froze. Cole frowned as he reached in and took something out.

"Dude, what the hell?"

Remington quickly turned around and saw what Cole had found. No one was meant to find that. He was over there in a flash, putting his hand over Cole's mouth and getting a surprised look in return.

"Keep it down," Remington hissed, the surprise still on Cole's face. "You know how much trouble I'm gonna be in if anyone finds out about this?"

He removed his hand from Cole's mouth, roughly grabbing his Banshee's End ID card and the two badges that accompanied it. Cole indicated to the two badges.

"That's the head of operations badge and also the one for Taylor's division," Cole said, his voice very low. Remington prayed that no one else was listening to their conversation. Hopefully the new vampires down the hall were too busy partying to hear what was being said a few doors down the hallway. "What the hell, man? You been workin' for them this whole time?"

Remington looked at him for a few seconds before going back over to the desk and putting the ID card and badges in the top drawer. He grabbed the key and locked it. Why hadn't he done that in the first place?

"It's not what you think," Remington said, looking over to Cole who was looking incredibly betrayed. Remington sighed. "At least let me explain?"

Cole seemed reluctant but gave a nod. "Alright then, explain."

"Thank you," Remington said with a sigh. "Look, Cole, if I could have told you, I would have, you know that right? I just couldn't risk anyone finding out because if they did, I'm as good as dead. Graith will have my damn head."

"But Banshee's End? Come on, Rem, I thought you were better than that."

An annoyed look crossed Remington's face.

"I got them off your fucking back, so don't you give me that attitude," he said harshly. Cole stayed quiet. "You've no idea how long I've kept you out of the damn way and now you go into Wonderland, possibly turning people as you go! Do you know how hard it was to convince Craig not to immediately hunt you down? Because that's what he was going to do, and I deterred him from it. So right now, you have me to thank for you being alive. Well, living dead."

Cole didn't seem to have anything more to say, still looking shocked about what he'd just found out.

Remington gave him a bit of a sad look. "Nothing to say?"

Cole looked at him for a few seconds before he managed to make himself sigh and actually give him an answer.

"I think we need to go for a walk, somewhere we can talk," he said. He indicated over his shoulder to the half-open door. "Come on."

Not waiting for an answer, Cole left the room, leaving the door fully open. Remington sighed and trudged over to the doorway. He shut the door after himself, making sure it was locked, before he headed off after Cole.

The last thing he wanted was for anyone within the facility to get into his room and find what Cole had just stumbled across.

Cole was almost out of sight as Remington walked along the metal grated floor towards the loud party. One of the newer vampires—for the life of him, Remington couldn't remember his name—watched him approach.

The closer he got, the louder the music seemed. One of the cons of having great hearing was that everything sounded too loud all the time.

"Going for a walk, Rem?" the vampire asked. Remington gave him an unamused look as he got closer to him. The vampire indicated down the hallway, the way Cole had gone. "Somewhere to be?"

"Not really your business," Remington said back with a hint of annoyance as he passed. He came to a stop a few paces away from the door, turning back to face the vampire. "Also, think you could keep the partying down a bit? Some of us actually have things to do, unlike some of you."

The vampire wasn't impressed with his words, but he knew he had no power or authority when it came down to it. He knew that Remington was ranks above him and he had to do what he was told.

Remington continued on his way. He wondered where Cole was going. He was sure it wasn't dark outside yet and the entire facility was crawling with vampires, so there weren't really many places they could go and talk where someone couldn't hear them.

Unless it was down to the lower levels.

Sure enough, Cole was waiting for him at the stairwell. Cole opened the door and went through, not bothering to hold it for Remington. Remington followed and made sure the door was closed properly behind him.

Remington tried to avoid the lower levels as much as possible. It was too far underground, and it made him uncomfortable. It was where the highest-ranking vampires hung out in their spare time.

Luckily for Remington and Cole, no one was present today, as they were all out on their own crusades. All of them, apart from the vampire who actually ran the Legion's operations, the one Remington still didn't know. He never left the facility, and Remington had never seen his face and probably never would.

He'd been trying for months, ever since he'd first joined Banshee's End, to find out who ran things and yet, here he was, over a year and a half later and still with no idea who was in charge.

The two of them continued to descend the stairs, going deeper and deeper underground. The further they went, the more uncomfortable Remington felt. This wasn't how he'd wanted this to go down.

Cole eventually stopped on one of the levels, clearly feeling like this was far enough down and far enough away from everyone else lurking throughout the facility. He opened a door and went out of the stairwell, stepping into an area with a few lights near the door.

Though it was dimly lit, it didn't make much difference to Remington, and he knew Cole wasn't fazed either.

"Alright, tell me what's going on," Cole said, still making sure his voice was down just in case someone happened to be within hearing range.

Remington sighed. Cole just watched him, not offering anything more in the way of words.

"I work for Banshee's End, I have for the past year and a half," Remington admitted. "Craig's my superior officer. I work under both him and Jacob."

"Why? I'm failing to see the point of basically double-crossing your own kind."

That annoyed Remington and he gave an unamused laugh and crossed his arms.

"Excuse me? *My* kind?" He laughed again. "I'm sorry, Cole, I seem to somehow keep forgetting that I'm dead. My bad, how could I possibly have ill will against *my* kind."

Cole's expression saddened, but Remington continued to speak.

"You know better than anyone that I never wanted to be a vampire," he said, all jokes aside. He pointed at himself. "I'm dead, Cole. I'm dead and my family don't even know. They don't know what happened to me; they don't know anything! I've been gone for seven years and, because of this damn Legion, I can never go back home. I can never see my family again. I have two brothers Upstairs that I won't ever see again. I may still be walking around but, boy, do I feel dead."

The sad look remained on Cole's face, but he stayed silent, allowing Remington to continue.

"I don't know if you ever had any family before you got turned, what your human life was like, but I can tell you for sure, mine was just fine. I never wanted to be a vampire. My life got ripped away from me the moment I got turned. Makes matters worse that now, since he died, I can turn people, too. I'd only been a vampire for two years and I could already turn people. Do you know how hard it's been for me since that happened? Do you have any idea?"

Cole shook his head.

"No, of course you don't. You haven't had that issue until recently," Remington continued. "You're lucky, Cole, you're damn lucky it's only just happened to you, and you can only just now turn people. I've been able to for the past five years, and it's a huge burden. I never wanted to be a vampire, let alone be able to turn anyone!

"This is the thing, Cole, you asked me why I decided to go and join Banshee's End? Has what I've just said been enough to make you understand? I never wanted to be in this position and when I heard about Banshee's End when they started up nearly two years ago, I wanted to help because I don't want someone else to have their life ripped right out of their hands because of the damned undead. I am not letting the Legion make it through Wonderland and Upstairs. Even if it kills me for good, I will not let that happen."

Cole sighed, running his hand through his hair as he looked down at the floor for a minute or so. Remington just watched him with irritation and a serious expression on his face.

"Graith's put me in charge of the Wonderland operation," Cole said, putting his hands behind his head as he looked up to meet Remington's cold gaze. He shook his head. "There's no way I can get around it."

"I'm sorry, Cole, but either you find a way to stall it until Craig can work something out and block it all off for good, or you're gonna have to deal with me and we both know that neither of us want that to happen."

Cole sighed again. "I know, Rem, that's the last thing I want. I just … I don't know what I can do. This is Graith we're talking about. You and I both know he won't relent and he's doing what the boss has ordered."

Remington scoffed. "'The Boss', Cole? Please, if Graith wasn't the one in charge of this entire thing, we'd know by now. We're both high enough in the ranks to know who runs shit around here and this so called 'boss' of ours hasn't ever shown his face. Until I see him with my own two vampire eyes, he's a myth and Graith's the one in charge."

Cole just shrugged, not saying anything.

Remington sighed, the irritation disappearing from his face as he glanced down at the floor.

"I need you to keep this between the two of us, I can't have anyone else know," he said, noting the unsure look on Cole's face. "I need you to stand by me with this. Please, man."

Cole seemed incredibly reluctant, and Remington saw the hesitation on his face. Eventually, Cole sighed in defeat and put his hands up.

"Alright, fine, your secret's safe with me," he said. Remington gave him a grateful smile. "Just ... figure out how to persuade Graith to take me off the Wonderland team and we'll be fine."

Remington nodded and Cole walked past him, back to the stairwell.

"Cole," Remington called. Cole turned slightly to look at him as he held the stairwell door open. Remington gave him a bit of a smile again. "Thank you. I'm glad I can count on you as a friend."

CHAPTER TEN

Plans aren't Easy

Craig jerked awake as he felt someone, or something, move across the bed. He groaned, feeling his head pounding as whoever, or whatever, was now on the bed stayed where it was next to him. Craig was lying on his front and he turned his head to the side, trying to make heads or tails of what was going on.

Ash was looking at something on what looked like Craig's phone, casually lying on what had been the vacant side of the double bed. She glanced over at him when she realized he was awake, then looked back at his phone again.

"Afternoon, Commander," she greeted.

Craig shut his eyes and wished that his head would stop hurting. He couldn't even remember what had happened overnight.

He opened his eyes again as his brain caught up with what Ash had said, a bit of panic rising in his chest as he realized he'd overslept. He moved, sitting up rather quickly, but all it did was make his head spin and make him feel sick.

Ash got bored of playing with his phone, and she tossed it onto his side of the bed and looked at him. Craig shifted until he was sitting on the edge of the bed, his head now in his hands as he willed his head to stop pounding.

"Anyone would think you'd been out drinking heavily last night if they saw you like this," Ash commented, sitting up. "Also, the fact that it's nearly three in the afternoon and you possibly told your cute girlfriend that you were all headed out in the morning? Not the best impression you're giving off here, Commander."

"Oh, get fucked, Ash," Craig snapped, wincing at the sound of his own voice, instantly regretting how loud it had been.

Ash couldn't help but smile. "How do you know I didn't last night?"

Craig removed his head from his hands, trying to ignore the pain in his head as much as possible as he looked over his shoulder. Ash was sitting on the other side of the bed with a smile on her face.

Craig looked at her for a couple of seconds before shaking his head, instantly regretting it, and going back to his original position. "I don't wanna know."

The smile stayed on Ash's face as she moved across the bed. She stopped behind him, draped her arms around his shoulders from behind, and leaned on him.

"You should probably head out and inform everyone what they're meant to be doing," she said, trying not to talk too loudly. She knew Craig wasn't feeling the best this afternoon, even though it was his own fault. She rested her chin on his shoulder, Craig doing a very good job of ignoring her. "Because I'm sure you'd rather be ordering those idiots around instead of Danny doing it. He'll mess up your entire operation if you let him run things. You know that."

Craig dared to remove his head from his hands and look at her as best he could, which was difficult because of the position Ash was currently in.

"Does this face really look like it cares this afternoon?" Craig asked. "Because, believe me, Ash, the only thing I wanna do right now is be sick, so please, don't start. Danny's the least of my worries, right now."

Ash rolled her eyes and removed her chin from his shoulder. She shifted and placed her hands on his shoulders instead, while Craig sighed and wished she'd just go away and leave him to his misery.

"I expect you down in the briefing room in ten minutes," she said, finally removing her hands from his shoulders. "So, get a move on, Commander."

"Would you stop calling me that?" Craig sighed in annoyance.

"Sorry, Taylor," was all she said before getting off the bed, leaving him sitting on the edge. She stopped at the door to the bedroom, and Craig reluctantly looked over at her. "Better get a move on, eight minutes."

Ash left the room.

Craig knew that if he didn't force himself to get moving, he'd be here for the rest of the day. He'd already missed his morning deadline. This was the first time in a very long time that this had happened and, right now, he wished he was still asleep.

He pushed himself to his feet, his head once again not agreeing with his action, making him wince and truly wish that proper painkillers were a thing down here in the Underground Worlds. Sadly, he was just going to have to deal with this hangover the hard way.

He grabbed his shirt from where it had ended up on the floor and shrugged it on. By the looks of it, he'd been too drunk to bother with anything else, having slept in what he'd been wearing the previous night.

It was not going to be a good day.

Craig left the room and headed for the winding staircase that led down to the ground floor. Luckily, it was quiet around the castle at this time of day, and Craig found himself rather thankful for that.

He remembered now why he'd given up drinking for good.

The closer he got to the ground floor, though, the more voices he heard. He sighed, trudging down the last few steps before heading towards all the obnoxiously loud voices, knowing they would lead him to the briefing room where Ash had said everyone was going to be waiting.

The noise died down a bit as Craig appeared in the doorway, and an amused smile appeared on Danny's face the moment he saw him.

"Well, good afternoon, Taylor, overslept a bit, did we?"

"Don't start with me, I'm far from the mood, yeah?" was Craig's half-hearted response as he went over and sat next to Ash. Everyone watched him as he looked at the map which was still where he'd left it yesterday. "Alright, where are we at with this shit?"

"Well, since you were a no-show this morning, we started discussing the best thing to do," Danny said, as Craig rested his head on his hand and regarded him tiredly. Danny looked at the map, and Craig followed his gaze as Danny pointed out individual places, taking it seriously now. "We figured that you'd wanna have final say on everything, so we did a base plan of where to put up outposts after you disappeared on us all yesterday. We figured the Room of Doors was our number one priority since that's where we're sure the Legion's hitting up next."

"Graith's pulled the operation," they heard from the doorway.

Everyone looked over and saw their friendly neighborhood vampire. Remington wandered into the room, joining them, and coming to a stop behind Craig's chair. He placed his hands on Craig's shoulders. "You, my friend, are a bit the worse for wear, if I do say so myself, which ... I do."

"Don't mention it," Craig sighed, as far from the planning mood as he could get.

"I think we should just address the issue," Danny said, Remington nodding in agreement. Danny cleared his throat, looking directly at Craig who just returned his gaze, having no effort whatsoever at the current time. "Commander Taylor, we all think you should take a couple of days off and let us figure this out. You're clearly not in the right mind frame and we all just want what's best for you and this world."

Craig's expression turned to slight annoyance.

"You're the one who drove me out last night!" he exclaimed, wincing at the sound of his own voice again, having somehow forgotten that everything was loud and his head hurt. He sighed, trying to calm himself down. "Look, if I want to occasionally go out and get completely fucked up, I'm going to do it. Get off my back and let's get back to this shit."

Danny rolled his eyes, chin on his hand now as Remington spoke again, keeping his hands where they were on Craig's shoulders, much to Craig's discomfort.

"As I was saying upon dramatically entering the room," Remington began, not looking at anyone in particular. "Graith pulled the operation. I'm currently the only undead being within this beautiful county." He looked at Ash and winked. "Love what you've done with the place, by the way."

Ash gave him a smile, and Remington turned his attention back to everyone else in the room.

"Why has he pulled the operation?" Craig asked with a frown as he stared at the map. He felt a bit more alert now and was trying to make his mind work.

"Well, Craig, I'm glad you asked," Remington said. He cleared his throat, slightly increasing his grip on Craig's shoulders. "Someone knew you were coming, which sent them right off and back to their hidey-hole, which I still won't tell you the location of, so don't bother asking."

Craig rolled his eyes. "So, what's their plan from here?"

"Well, you see, Mister Taylor, sir, here's where the problem lies," Remington said, sounding awkward about having to explain it all. "I may have run into an issue, but I've also gotten some information that I think you might be entitled to hear."

That got Craig's attention properly. "What did you do?"

Remington removed his hands from Craig's shoulders, crossing his arms and giving him an unimpressed look as Craig looked around at him.

"Always assuming I've done something," Remington said, shaking his head. He paused. "OK, well, I may have done something this time, but usually it's not my fault."

"Remington," Craig warned, making Remington shift uncomfortably.

"OK, so Cole might know that I'm a double-agent," was his rushed response. Craig's expression fell and Remington held his hands up. "But, but, hear me out here, Taylor. I also got a bit of info from him before he found out and promised to keep my secret."

Ash frowned. "Why's this Cole guy, of all people, willing to keep your double-agent status a secret?"

"Yeah, wait a second," Danny spoke up, Remington looking to him, now caught in the middle of everything. "What's the deal with that?

You mentioned at Outpost Six yesterday that you weren't going to let us take him out. Spill, vampire."

Remington sighed. "Ugh, fine, seeing as you're all so damn pushy." He sighed again. "Cole's my friend."

Danny rolled his eyes. "Of course, he is."

Remington shot him an annoyed look.

"You wouldn't get it, bandit. You don't have any friends," he snapped. "You've no idea of what I've been through these past seven years, OK? So, keep your mouth shut and don't be judging me so hard. Vampires bond too, yeah?"

"Cole got something to do with your turning?" Craig asked, interested now but not really showing it. He sounded bored and completely unfazed.

"It's a long story," said Remington

"We've got time," Ted said, and Danny nodded as Remington's now cold gaze flickered over to them.

"We sure do," Danny said. "Because the commander here is too fucked up from his night of drinking to go anywhere today, so we have nowhere to be whatsoever. So, talk."

"My afterlife isn't exactly your business," Remington said, feeling offended. What was Danny's deal these past few days? "All you need to know, is that I got a bit of interesting info before Cole found out I was back-staking."

"Have you ever actually staked another vampire?" one of the recruits spoke up.

Remington switched his gaze away from Danny and over to the recruit who'd spoken. "Maybe. You don't know what I do in my spare time."

The recruit didn't dare say anything else, and Craig sighed once more, shifting in his chair to rest his arm on the back of it as he looked at Remington.

"Alright, what'd you get from Cole?" he asked, briefly shutting his eyes before opening them again to see Remington returning his look, just nowhere near as tired or unenthused.

Remington hesitated before speaking.

"Ah, well," he began, awkwardly clearing his throat again. "He was saying how they're just waiting to be told what to do next with this movement into Wonderland. Cole's been appointed the head vamp for this journey. But, ah, he said that Graith's possibly planning on taking *you* out before they move fully across the border back into Wonderland."

Craig raised an eyebrow in interest. "That so?" Remington gave a nod. "And how exactly do they plan on doing that?"

"I don't know that bit."

"Not much of an informant if you can't get all the relevant information," Danny muttered, drawing Remington's glare.

"Vampire hearing," was the response he got from the rather annoyed vampire in the room. "You keep teasing the dog, you're gonna get bitten."

Danny once again rolled his eyes, taking Remington's threat as hollow.

"Alright, you two, settle down," Craig said. "Don't go antagonizing the dead, Danny."

"Living dead," they all heard, the few people who knew the voice frowning. Matt stopped next to Remington. "Sorry, am I crashing the party?"

CHAPTER ELEVEN

Planning the Way Out

C hris tapped the pen continuously on the blank piece of paper in front of himself, thinking as he did so. As usual, he was in his regular place at the bar.

The windows blocked a lot of the daylight from coming in, always making the bar dimly lit, even when the lights were on. They really needed to replace the lighting, Chris had thought more than once.

It wasn't evening yet, but it was late in the day. Chris hoped Maddie would show up soon. He needed to talk to her about what they were going to do about getting this binding spell broken so he could free himself from Marion and leave her behind when he left.

He was not going back to his correct dimension with her, no matter what.

He figured Maddie wouldn't show up until the sun had completely gone down, but he had nothing better to do than wait in the almost empty bar. The usual bartender leaned against the wooden bar top a few feet away from where Chris was currently sitting, on the same side as him.

Chris switched his gaze back to the piece of paper, trying to decide whether he should write another letter to Ash and inform her of what was going on. Or should he wait to write the letter until he'd spoken with Maddie? He didn't know how long Maddie would be, but he didn't want to write a letter and miss out important details.

Maybe it was best to wait.

"You're awfully quiet."

Chris jumped and looked up. Maddie was now stationed where the usual bartender had been, but she was the only one there now. He looked around but the other bartender was nowhere to be seen.

"Did I scare you?" she asked, an amused smile on her face as she rested both of her elbows against the bar behind herself.

"You startled me, big difference," Chris responded with annoyance.

Maddie's smile stayed on her face as she slid herself across the top of the bar, jumping down and standing on the opposite side to Chris now.

"If you don't drink, why do you hang around the bar?" Maddie asked, grabbing a clean glass and observing the different forms of alcohol on the wall.

"I'm pretty sure you asked me that yesterday," Chris said.

Maddie shrugged. "Can't keep track of everything I ask everyone."

Chris watched as she decided on one of the bottles and poured herself half a glass. A frown crossed Chris's face.

"I thought vampires couldn't stomach real food."

Maddie looked over her shoulder as she put the bottle back on the shelf and turned to face him fully.

"Your cute little vampire friends might not be able to, but I can," she said before downing the contents of the glass, wincing a bit at the taste. "Boy, I do not feel sorry for vampires that can't taste this."

"How? How come you can, but the one I know can't?" Chris queried.

Did this kind of thing differ from dimension to dimension? Was it only the vampires in his dimension that couldn't eat real food?

Maddie grabbed a different bottle off the shelf, pouring herself another half-glass.

"I might be a vampire, but I still have part of my ability from when I was human, therefore, some of my humanity is left," she explained. She gave him a grin, lifting the glass up slightly into the air. "Which means more alcohol for me!"

Chris watched her down that glass too, clearly enjoying the taste of this one, as she poured herself another.

"So, you still have parts of your humanity left," Chris stated, getting a nod from Maddie as she took another drink, pouring herself yet another. "Yet you've lost your ability."

"Mmhm," was the attempted beginning of the response. Maddie placed the empty glass down and leaned against the bar. "The part of my ability that's left, the part where I can sense auras and everything, is all I have left of my humanity. Just so happens to be enough to allow me to drink excessively, not get drunk, and also eat real food if I so wish to. Obviously, I can't live on real food, but it's a nice treat every now and then."

Chris didn't say anything in return, and Maddie pushed off the bar and poured herself more alcohol. She indicated to the diary Chris had on the bar in front of him.

"What's the deal with that?" she asked, filling the glass completely this time. "You've always got it here and I see you write in it occasionally. What're you writing? Anything exciting?"

Chris gave a shrug, looking down at the blank page and still holding onto the pen.

"Been writing letters back home to someone," he said.

Maddie raised her eyebrows in interest as she took a drink from the full glass. "Girlfriend?"

"Friend."

Maddie's expression showed that she didn't believe his statement, but she let it slide.

"What do you guys talk about? You write to her often?"

Chris shrugged, resting both of his arms on the wooden bar top.

"Just keeping her informed of what's been going on. They're trying to keep a vampire problem in check back home while also trying to get me back there," he said, the interest still on Maddie's face. Chris looked her over. "Are you from this dimension?"

"No sir," she said with a shake of her head, emptying the rest of the liquid from the bottle into her glass. "I'm actually from the same dimension as you. Dimension One holds all the Dimension Walkers."

"Thought that'd be something I'd needed to know before now."

Maddie gave a shrug. "Never asked."

Chris sighed, watching Maddie finish off the contents of her glass. She carelessly tossed the empty bottle into the bin off to her right.

"So, if the Dimension Walkers are all from Dimension One, that means someone back home could potentially track one down for us," Chris said, his mind working over the beginning of a plan. He looked at Maddie. "Do you know who else can cross dimensions and get back?"

Maddie shook her head, and Chris felt his heart sink a bit.

"Unfortunately, not," she admitted. "The Dimensions Council talks to us all separately. We don't get linked or told who's who because it puts everyone at risk. Complicated, but at risk."

Chris sighed. "Wonderful."

Maddie indicated to the blank piece of paper in Chris's diary.

"Maybe write to your girl and ask her to scope out some info on Dimension Walkers in your dimension, see if she can get one tracked down somehow," she suggested, Chris agreeing that that was a good idea. "She writes back, right?"

Chris nodded. "Never fails."

Maddie's expression turned to a grin. "Perfect! Looks like we're on our way to getting you back home before this place goes to Hell!"

Chris shook his head a bit upon her wording, trying to decide what to ask Ash to do in this letter he was about to start.

"What about you?" he asked, a bit of a frown appearing on Maddie's face. "You said you're from Dimension One as well. Are you going to come back with me or stay here while this whole place collapses?"

Maddie looked a bit thrown off by the question and it took her a minute or so to answer.

"Oh, I don't know. It hadn't really crossed my mind. I mean, I haven't been back there for years. I got stuck here when I got turned into a vampire. I wouldn't even know where to start if I went back to my right dimension."

"Well, it's got to be better than sitting back and just waiting for this dimension to cave in on itself."

"True," Maddie mused, resting her chin on her hand. "I'll consider your proposal. I'll also try to figure out how to get you unlinked from whoever you're currently spell-bound to. May need some outside help for that, though, but I'll look into it and as soon as your missus gets back to us, we should be as good as gold."

"Ash is not my girlfriend."

Maddie grinned at him again, Chris shaking his head.

"If you say so," she said with a shrug. She indicated to the paper again. "Also, if you care to take notes, I have an easier way for you to contact your girl."

CHAPTER TWELVE

Making Decisions and Finding Surprises

"Mail! Chris! Mail!"

Everyone in the room looked up at the sudden disruption. Alex ran into the room, sliding to a very quick stop and nearly running straight into Matt who raised his eyebrows in interest. Alex's expression changed to surprise as he stared at Matt.

"Hello!" Alex greeted him cheerfully, still quite out of breath. He looked past Matt and saw Remington. "Hello!"

"Alex?" Ash said, getting his attention away from the two new arrivals. Ash pointed at the white envelope in Alex's right hand. "Mail? Chris?"

Realization crossed Alex's face, and he held the envelope out to Ash.

"Dare I ask what this is?" Matt asked, seeing Chris's signature on the back as he watched Ash open the letter.

"Ash and Chris have been sending letters back and forth all year!" Alex said, his cheerful tone not going away any time soon.

He was happy to see Matt, even if he didn't know why he was here.

"How?" Matt asked with a frown.

Ash ignored him as she read through the letter.

Ash,

Letting you know that I did receive your last response and so this is a return letter from that one. I might also have a bit more important information to tell you and everyone else back home this time around. This might be worth sharing...

"Chris worked out how to send mail from one dimension to another," Alex informed Matt who blinked at him briefly before returning his gaze to Ash. "It's been very useful."

"Care to share?" Matt asked as Ash looked up from the letter.

"Only because he says there's important information for everyone in here."

Craig looked at her, interest back on his face now. All the recruits stayed quiet and just listened as they'd been instructed to do a few days before.

"Go for it," Craig said, indicating to the letter. "We're all waiting."

Ash turned her focus back to the letter and began reading it out loud.

At the end of this letter, I'm going to put instructions for a different and better way we can communicate back and forth, but until you reach the end of the letter, please read everything I say carefully.

I ran into someone yesterday, a vampire by the name of Maddie...

"Wait, Maddie?" Remington interrupted. "Is that what you just said? Maddie?"

Ash nodded. "That's right. It's what Chris has written."

Remington shook his head. "No, no, it can't be the same person. That can't be right." He looked over Ash's shoulder at the letter. "That is what he said, right?"

"Yes, it says exactly what I read out *'a vampire by the name of Maddie'*. What's the big deal?"

"That can't be right," Remington said. "Maddie's a Dimension Walker."

The frown on his face was matched by everyone else's because of his words, not the contents of the letter.

"I'm sorry, a what?" Ted asked, feeling rather confused.

Remington looked at him. Ted was confused easily, same as Jordan. It wasn't unusual.

"Dimension Walker, they can go from one dimension to another," he explained, clear interest on Craig's and Matt's faces now. Remington shook his head once again. "This can't be right."

Craig indicated for Ash to continue reading, so that's what she did.

She's informed me that there's been a problem with this dimension (wouldn't explain what exactly); all I could get from her information-wise was that Dimension Four is coming down and going to collapse rather soon. She didn't have a timeframe or anything, but the sooner I get out of here, the better.

We got talking and she mentioned that there may be a way to get me back home. She mentioned something called a 'Dimension Walker'; someone with a very rare ability that can allow access throughout dimensions willingly. She mentioned that she used to be able to perform such a task, but since becoming a vampire over here in Dimension Four, her ability has been lost.

"See! I wasn't lying!" Remington exclaimed, happy that he'd been right and hadn't been imagining things. He paused. "Wait, did he just say she's been turned into a vampire?"

Ash rolled her eyes. "Keep up, Rem."

Remington crossed his arms and allowed Ash to continue.

Maddie said that there are only a total of six Dimension Walkers across every dimension, of which there are thousands. She said that all six originate from Dimension One, the one that you all reside in, the one I'm from. If this is true, then there may be a chance for you to help me out from over there.

If someone over there can track down another Dimension Walker before it's too late over here, there's a chance I can get back home before this entire place collapses and I'm gone for good. Please work on this as quickly as you can. Maddie and I are working on getting me untied from Marion so that I don't have to bring her back there with me.

I've written the instructions for better contact on the back of this letter.

Please reply as soon as you can.
Chris.

Ash refolded the letter, planning on looking at what Chris had written on the back a bit later when she was by herself. It wasn't anyone else's business but hers.

"How in the world are we meant to track down one of these Dimension Walkers?" Danny asked. Everyone looked at him. "If there're supposedly only six in the entire span of dimensions, where's that leave us? All of them could be in a dimension thousands of dimensions away!"

"When you think about it, there's really only five," Matt commented, everyone looking at him now. He indicated to the letter that Ash was still holding. "If this Maddie girl is now a vampire and she was one of the six Dimension Walkers, that leaves the possibility that there are only five left out there. So, in reality, we only have five choices."

Danny sighed, knowing Matt was correct. If Maddie had been able to get Chris back into his right dimension, he'd already be back by now and they wouldn't have been so concerned.

"So, what do we do to track someone like that down? Where do we even begin?" Arley spoke up.

Craig was the one to answer. "I know where we can start, but you're not gonna like it."

When he didn't elaborate, Ash spoke up.

"Well? What is it?" she asked, seeing the hesitation on Craig's face as he returned her gaze, clearly still feeling the effects of his hangover.

Craig sighed.

"Hunter's a Dimension Walker," he said. Most people around the table showed surprise at that news, but others had an uncomfortable look instead. "If we can find him and persuade him to help us, we might be able to make this work."

"I don't like our chances," Matt said. "Hunter's probably long gone. We'd have a better chance and luck at finding someone else."

Craig nodded in agreement. "I know, but if I hadn't mentioned it then someone would've found out and then gotten annoyed at me for not saying anything." He glanced at Ash as he said the final part before he returned his gaze back to Matt. "Which is why I brought it up. I haven't seen any sign of him since the Funeral Masquerade last year, he's gone, M.I.A."

"So, what are we going to do?" Ash asked, looking between Craig and Matt, ignoring everyone else. "If we can't get to Hunter and get his help, who do we look for?"

Craig shrugged, and Matt was the one to answer her question.

"I'll see what info I can find on this whole thing, see if there's something or someone who can shed a bit more light on this topic," he said. He looked around at everyone. "So, we're looking for five Dimension Walkers. Brilliant."

"Ah, maybe possibly four," Remington said awkwardly, everyone looking to the now timid vampire.

"Meaning?"

Remington cleared his throat. "Um, well, I may know a thing or two when it comes to Dimension Walkers," he admitted. "And so, I can tell you all that if you include Hunter in this equation, you're down to four."

"Care to elaborate?" Craig asked, the look on his face making Remington uncomfortable.

Remington sighed, looking down briefly before explaining.

"Cole was one of the six," he said, noting that Craig glanced at Matt before returning his gaze to Remington. "But since he's a vampire, he's out of the question. He has no ability anymore so you're only looking for four out of six. If Maddie's a vampire as well, that makes it that much harder to figure out who's who and where they are."

Remington looked at Matt with a bit of sadness on his face, while Matt crossed his arms as he thought about what Remington had just told them.

"Alright, then, four it is," he said. He looked at Craig, giving him a slight smile. "I'll let you know what I find."

Without another word, Matt stepped back a pace into the closest shadow, disappearing from sight.

Remington sighed. "I wish I was able to disappear like that."

CHAPTER THIRTEEN

Battle Strategy

"We head out in the morning," Craig informed everyone in the room, whether they were recruits or not.

"That's what you said yesterday but it didn't happen," Arley said.

Craig switched his gaze over to her with evident annoyance.

"I had a rough night, get off my back," he said harshly.

Arley realized she'd spoken out of line, and she looked away. The last thing she wanted was to make Craig any angrier than he had been over the past few days.

Craig stood over the map and looked down at it, indicating to one of the areas that had been marked overnight, most likely by Ash.

"This is the area we're hitting, it's outside the Room of Doors and the exit that leads back Upstairs. Right now, it's our number one priority because that's where the Legion is looking at getting to. I don't care about anywhere else at the moment, just this particular spot."

Ash had left the room half an hour ago, saying she had more important things to work on than Craig's strategy. She was leaving the battle tactics up to him. It was what he did, and it was his area, not hers. As long as he helped defend Wonderland, she didn't care how he did it anymore.

Remington now sat in the seat she'd vacated, with his feet up on the table close to Craig, and he watched the little blonde cat suddenly jump up onto the table, startling one of the recruits. The cat walked over the map and lay down on the table in front of him. Remington reached out a hand and patted the cat, who closed his eyes and relaxed.

Arley cautiously raised her hand to ask a question, not wanting to speak again without permission, as she was bound to mess it up and say the wrong thing.

Craig sighed and carelessly sat back down on his chair, resting his arms on the table before resting his head on his right hand. His head still hurt, but he was somehow coping. "Yes?"

Arley shifted awkwardly. "How exactly are we going about setting up at this place?"

Craig pointed to the map again.

"We're going to put up a major outpost on the perimeter," he explained, kind of glad that she'd asked, as he was going to explain it all eventually anyway. He just hadn't had the chance yet. "I'm going to stay down here for a bit to plan it all out, but in the end, it'll probably the second biggest outpost we'll have control over, Banshee's End being the biggest."

Arley gave a nod, more on board now. She was glad that Craig was more or less back to being himself, and she hadn't seen him this focused in months. Sure, he was still incredibly hungover, but his mind was somehow in the right place now, and he was thinking about their best move against the Legion. This was what she'd signed up for.

"With that being said, I still want a few of you out in the field and in the towns, in pairs," Craig continued, not missing a beat. "We need eyes everywhere at the moment. You'll all be assigned a partner and a town. Keep a low profile. We don't want people questioning everything and word getting out to the Legion. We want to do this as quietly as possible and get this outpost up and running, at least for the basics right now." He looked around at everyone. "If any of you stationed in a town see any sign of the Legion whatsoever, you abandon your post, you come straight to the outpost, and you let me know. We need to know when and where they're moving into Wonderland, so we know what our timeframe is for this outpost."

Remington looked at Craig. "If I hear anything new, I'll come find you," he said, getting a nod from Craig. "I assume you'll be stationed at this new outpost from now on?"

Craig nodded again, back to resting his head on his hand. "You assume correctly."

Remington nodded in return and swung his feet down off the table. "Well, alrighty then, Commander. I should probably disappear for a while. Been out too much this past week or so. Might arouse suspicion and I have some new vampires to straighten up back home."

He gave the cat one last pat and Alex meowed in protest, but Remington ignored him and got to his feet.

"Tell us straight away if you find out anything that might help us," Craig said, Remington giving him the thumbs up. "You have my number."

Arley looked at Remington, the vampire sensing it and returning the look with a curious one of his own.

"You said you're going back home," she stated. "Where exactly is that for you?"

Remington gave her a ghost of a smile. "If I told you, I'd have to kill you, m'dear."

Arley wasn't impressed with his attempt at humor, but Remington wasn't about to share his usual whereabouts. It was his business, and he figured that if anyone else knew, they'd either get themselves into trouble and get killed, or they'd ruin the entire operation and mess things up for him.

"Get out of here." Craig waved him away, knowing that Remington needed to get a move on to get back to his vampire buddies. "Saunter back to your lair and come back when you have information."

Remington rolled his eyes. "Would have thought that'd be more something that Danny would say. You continue to surprise me, Taylor. You really do."

Craig just waved him away again, Remington once again rolling his eyes before taking his leave without another word or any form of gesture, disappearing out through the doorway and out of sight.

Arley looked at Craig who now just looked bored. She gestured at the rest of the people in the room.

"What do you want us to do for the rest of the afternoon and night?" she asked, knowing that none of the other recruits were about to ask. "If we're not leaving until the morning?"

Craig gave a shrug.

"Free rein, your decision on what you want to do between now and when we leave in the morning," he said, some of the recruits looking rather pleased with that statement. "As long as you don't break any of Ashley's rules, you should be fine. Go out and enjoy yourselves, if you so wish. Otherwise, sit around the castle and do nothing. I don't care. As long as you're not in this room while I'm figuring things out, we won't have any problems. You're all dismissed until called upon again or until the morning. Now, get out of here."

Not needing to be told twice, Danny and his usual crew were first on their feet, all of them out the doorway within seconds.

Craig shook his head, his gaze automatically going back to the map as the little cat moved a bit closer to the map's edge, lying down rather close to it.

The recruits all took their leave, Arley staying where she was for a minute or so before she spoke, her voice down in case any of the other recruits were still hanging around and once again trying to listen in on Craig's private business.

"Are you sure this is going to work?" she asked. Craig looked at her as the cat got to his feet again and peered at the map. "Because we may not have time to get this outpost up and running if the Legion knows that's what we're doing."

Craig looked at her for a second and thought before responding.

"We're going to do the best we can and establish at least a normal outpost," he said. Seeing the uncertainty on her face, he sighed and ran his hands down his face. "You don't have a lot of faith in me, do you?"

"Right now? No," Arley admitted, figuring she may as well tell her commander what she thought.

"Well, you're going to have to start believing that I know what I'm doing," Craig said. He gave her a tired smile. "Have I ever let you down before?"

Arley still looked uncertain, but she gave a slight nod and got to her feet, pushing her chair back under the table. "I'll leave you to it, then."

Craig watched her leave the room and disappear around the corner, gone.

He sighed, turning his focus to the cat who was now lying down again, watching him. "Well, guess we get this shit done and we can both call it a day."

⊷⬥⊶

"Didn't take you as the reading type."

Matt rolled his eyes, mildly insulted as one of Craig's recruits joined him in the library, sitting down opposite him. He looked her over, not remembering her from the last time he'd been down to Banshee's End.

"Excuse me for being well read," he said, turning his focus back to the book he'd been mindlessly flicking through. "Won't attract men with that kind of attitude, y'know."

The young woman gave a shrug, watching Matt as he turned the page, scanned down it, and found nothing of use.

"I have more important things to worry about than men," she said.

"That's what all the single girls say. I'm sure you've got your eye on someone, whether you want to admit it or not."

The young woman had nothing to say on that, and Matt turned another page.

"It's Matt, right?" the woman asked. Matt gave a nod, never breaking his concentration on the book. "I'm Arley Beckett, I work under Craig."

"That so?" Matt said, turning another page and getting a nod from Arley. "Interesting."

"You don't sound too interested," Arley commented, leaning forward a bit to try and see what he was reading.

Matt moved it out of her line of sight, looking up and meeting her gaze.

"I know you work for Craig, your division badge tells me everything I need to know," he said. Arley looked down at the badge on her jacket. He looked back at the book. "Just be grateful you don't work under the bandit."

"Danny?"

Matt nodded. "Yeah, the thief."

Arley continued to watch Matt as she responded.

"He took my position, you know," she said, getting a glance from Matt before he turned the page again. "I would have been in the captain's position if Danny hadn't needed a home."

"That so? Who'd you hear that from?" Arley gave a bit of an awkward shrug, and Matt looked at her and raised an eyebrow. "You hear it from Craig?"

"I may have overheard him at one point when he was talking to Jacob about needing a few more captains to run divisions," she admitted, looking down at the table as someone went past. "But he gave the vacant position to Danny for some reason. I know Danny doesn't care for that position. He doesn't ever seem interested in it, whatsoever. Does nothing but complain."

Matt shifted and leaned back in his chair.

"One thing you've got to understand about Danny is that he looks out for himself and his little clique of thieves," he said, Arley looking at him and listening to what he was saying. "He just gets to order people around. Craig does everything strategy-wise and whatnot, while Danny sits back and reports to whoever tells him he needs to listen, whether he likes it or not." He looked her over with thought. "How long have you been with Banshee's End, Miss Beckett?"

"Since I first heard about it, about a month after they started up," she said. "I was there before Craig even showed up. I don't know why Jacob took such a liking to him straight off. Well, I do get it, I guess, but when it comes down to it, some of us have been there longer than he has and he's pretty well second-in-charge. I feel like I'd do alright as a captain, I just need to be given the chance." She sighed, looking down. "I don't know if Craig wants me in that position anymore, though. He hasn't brought it up with me."

"Why do you keep calling him by his first name and not Commander Taylor?" Matt suddenly asked with a frown, Arley looking back up at him, a bit confused. "None of his other recruits would ever dream of calling him by his first name. You're not all on a first name basis. Something going on between the two of you?"

Arley scoffed and looked down at her hands.

"No, definitely not," she said, and Matt actually believed her. Arley gave a bit of a sigh and looked at him again. "He's not interested."

"But you are," Matt stated bluntly, watching as she awkwardly looked away, rather embarrassed. Matt shrugged and turned his gaze back to the book. "Your choice on what you do. Now, if you'll excuse me, I have research to do."

"You're from Upstairs, aren't you?" Arley asked.

Matt reluctantly looked up with no amusement on his face. "Yes."

Arley nodded, watching Matt go back to vaguely reading.

"Why did you choose to come down here?" she asked, making Matt sigh and look at her again.

"Why does anyone choose to come down here?" he asked back. "Most times it's accidental and you don't know until you're here." He paused as something occurred to him. "Craig talk about himself much?"

Arley shook her head. "No. Why?"

Matt shrugged, turning his focus back to the book once more. "Just curious."

CHAPTER FOURTEEN

The Vampire Ranks

"No need to knock, I heard you approach."

Remington turned slightly to look at Cole who was standing in the doorway to Remington's room. He didn't say anything else, then turned back to reading the piece of paper he was holding.

Cole shifted awkwardly, clearing his throat a bit before he crossed his arms. "You, ah, wanted to talk?"

Remington stopped what he was doing and turned to look at him properly before nodding.

"Think we should get outta here and away from prying eyes and ears," he suggested.

An uncertain look appeared on Cole's face. "Look, Rem, if this is some Banshee's End shit..."

"I need you to put aside your hatred for them and help me out," Remington interrupted with annoyance clear in his tone. "Please?"

Cole sighed, knowing he didn't have much choice. Remington outranked him and he knew it.

"Alright, what do you need from me?"

Remington looked at him for a couple of seconds, seeing that he wasn't about to leave the room and take the conversation elsewhere.

"I need to know about Dimension Walkers," he said, bringing a slight frown to Cole's face.

"Why?"

Remington sighed this time. "A friend's been stuck in a different dimension for the past year and, apparently, the dimension he's stuck in is collapsing."

"He's in Dimension Four?"

Remington frowned. "How'd you know which one I was talking about?"

Cole shrugged. "I hear things. I'm still in the loop, like the other five. Might be a vampire, but just because I'm dead doesn't mean I'm not informed."

Remington gave a bit of a nod before continuing.

"I, ah, also have something else I need you to do for me, in amongst the information about the Dimension Walkers," he said awkwardly.

"Which is ... what?" Cole asked, interest now on his face.

Remington sighed, knowing there was no way around this and that he just had to go ahead and ask.

"I need a list of everyone you turned when you went through Outpost Six," he said.

"What? Why?"

"Because I can vouch for you!" Remington exclaimed, hoping no one else was listening in to their conversation right now. "If you show you're willing to help, you might have a chance at getting Craig to change his mind about taking you down. Please, Cole, if you show that you're willing to help, you won't be such a big target."

Cole was reluctant, and Remington could see that he wasn't sure what to do. If he wasn't about to cooperate, there was really only one other thing that Remington could do to ensure this went the right way.

"Look, Cole, I'm asking you this as your friend," he said. "But if you don't do this for me as a friend, I'm going to have to invoke my right as a higher rank and you'll have no choice but to do what I ask. I don't want to do that, but I need you to help me out here, as a friend."

Cole sighed in defeat. "C'mon, Rem," he said, sadness in his tone. "Don't be like that."

"Cole, please. I don't want to have to ask again. We both know what happens if you deny a direct order from a higher rank."

Cole shook his head, moving properly into the room. He went over to the desk, grabbed some paper and a pen, and started to write. A few minutes later, Cole tossed the pen back onto the desk and turned to face Remington, holding the paper out for him.

"Give me twenty-four hours and I'll get as much info on Dimension Walkers as I can," Cole said. "Don't say I never help you."

Remington hesitantly took the piece of paper and Cole stalked out of the room, leaving the door wide open.

Remington sighed and moved over to the desk. He sat down and grabbed a blank envelope, picking up the pen from where Cole had left it. Just as he was about to address the envelope, a slight sound made him stop.

"In the letter writing business now, Remington?"

Graith made his way into the room, strolling casually with his hands behind his back, and Remington felt panic start to rise in his chest.

He turned in his chair, hoping that Graith hadn't heard the previous conversation.

"Can I help you with something, Graith?" Remington tried to keep his tone steady, fighting back the fear.

Graith was a much higher rank than Remington, and ten times more intimidating, for that matter. Remington didn't want to think about what would happen to him if Graith knew that he'd been conspiring against the Legion for the past year and a half.

Graith stopped at the end of the bed. "Always thought it was a bit strange to have beds in these rooms. It's not like anyone can use them for anything but ... just lying there, you know?" he said, Remington watching him the entire time. Graith looked away from the bed and at him. "You think it's a bit strange, too?"

"Yessir."

Graith gave an unenthusiastic nod, looking Remington over as he stayed at the end of the bed, hands still behind his back.

"So, who are you writing to?" he queried, nodding at the envelope Remington had just been about to address. "Friend?"

Remington hesitated but managed to respond, so it didn't seem too awkward.

"I guess you could say that," he said, turning his attention back to the envelope. He was hoping Graith wouldn't notice the paper Cole had given him with the names on it, still sitting face up on the table. "Just someone I hadn't heard from in a while, thought I'd check up with them and see how they're doing."

"That right?"

"Yes."

Remington took the piece of paper, folded it and slid it into the envelope, hoping it wouldn't look suspicious if he just went about doing things he was already in the middle of.

"Who's this ... friend of yours?" was Graith's next question.

Remington turned around in the chair, staring him down.

"Why does it matter so much to you?" he dared to say, seeing a hint of amusement on Graith's face. "My personal business is not your issue."

"I just like to know that all my vampires are working to make the Legion a better, stronger, place, that's all," Graith said. "That we don't have any ... conspirators in our walls, especially in the higher ranks."

An unamused look appeared on Remington's face as he crossed his arms. "Is that an accusation?"

Graith gave a slow shrug before linking his fingers together.

"Take it how you will," he said. He gave Remington a bit of a smile, indicating to the letter. "Haven't addressed it yet?"

Remington narrowed his eyes, turning his attention back to the envelope, scribbling something onto it, Graith watching him the entire time. Remington reluctantly sealed the envelope, stood up, and looked at Graith.

"If you'll excuse me, I have a letter to send."

He headed past Graith.

"I'd watch your back if I were you, Bell." That forced Remington to stop in the doorway, not even looking back at Graith who spoke again. "The higher ranks don't take too kindly to traitors." Graith moved from where he was, stopping next to Remington in the doorway, lowering his voice as Remington looked at him. "I'd be sleeping with one eye open if I were you."

Graith gave him a bit of an amused smile again before leaving. Remington stood and watched him disappear down the corridor heading to the stairwell.

CHAPTER FIFTEEN

The Past

"I got a letter this morning."

Chris jumped as Maddie sat down next to him on the grass in the shade. She had sunglasses and a jacket on, making sure she wasn't about to feel the sunlight in any way. She held the envelope out to Chris who hesitantly took it, not sure why she was showing him if it was addressed to her.

"What's this got to do with me?" he asked, frowning as Maddie moved a bit closer to make sure she was definitely out of the sunlight.

She shrugged but the smile remained on her face. "Turn it over and see who sent it."

Chris turned the envelope over. It was from Remington Bell, Dimension One.

"I don't get it. Why did Remington send this to you?" he asked, looking at Maddie who shifted her position to face him a bit more.

"Maybe take the letter out and see what he had to say?"

Chris took the pieces of paper out and unfolded them.

Sorry about the abrupt and out of nowhere request, but the second piece of paper needs to be sent over to Craig. I was going to send it directly but got caught up with Graith and had to rethink what I was doing. I only had time to quickly add this actual letter in, so please, send it over to Craig because he needs to see what I've written.

I hope you understand, and I may have to send more through you soon because, by the looks of it, I need to lay low for a bit. My cover may have been compromised by someone or by my own carelessness. Either way, this is important and I need you to make sure it gets to Craig.

Remington xx

Chris put the letter down and looked at the second piece of paper, the one that Remington had asked to be sent onto Craig. It was about half a page, just a list of names, not a lot on there, and it also wasn't in the same handwriting as the letter.

"I assume you know more about this than I do," Maddie said.

"I don't know what this list is for, but if Remington needs it sent over to Craig, then I'm going to do it because it's clearly important enough that he didn't want anyone else to know about it," Chris said, still looking at the list. He pushed himself up off the grass, back to his feet. "You coming?"

Maddie sighed, getting up and putting her hood on to make sure she wasn't about to burn in the light. Not waiting for any word of protest, Chris headed down the small hill, planning on going back to his residence to sort this out.

"By the way, how did Remington know to send this to you?" Chris asked.

Maddie didn't answer at first, just hurried past him at a quick pace to get out of the sunlight as fast as possible. Once she was in the shade again, this time on the street, she waited and watched him until he caught up to her.

Chris came to a stop in front of her, a few people passing them but not acknowledging them in any way whatsoever.

"I've known Remington for a while, met him just after he got turned," she said. "He wasn't doing too well when we met, let me tell you."

"I know he mentioned that he hadn't really had the best time as a vampire, especially when he was first turned."

Maddie nodded. "He's always struggled with the vampirism. It's such a shame because he's one of the nicest people I've ever met. He's been wronged by being turned."

"He told me he didn't have much of a choice."

Maddie frowned. "I don't really know too much about that, but when I met him he'd only been a vampire for about four months."

September 21st, 2012

The rain pounded the ground as Maddie left the bar, glad her shift was over for this miserable Friday night.

If she'd had just one more creepy older man try and get her to go back to his place, she seriously would have snapped.

She began her walk home just like every work night, the streetlights lighting up the surrounding areas. Maddie was glad there weren't many people around due to the miserable weather. It made her walk home a bit less worrying. Though, you never could tell if something was going to happen.

It rained a lot in Waterwall Incline and a few of the areas close by. It hadn't ever really bothered Maddie much. In fact, she rather enjoyed the cold.

Passing by an alleyway close to her residence, someone caught her attention. She hesitated, then backtracked a pace or so to stop in the alleyway's entrance.

From what she could see, a young man was sitting, leaning against the wall of a building underneath one of the dim lights.

She couldn't really see many of his features, as he had his head down. His hair was dark, his dark jeans were ripped slightly in a place or two, and he had a neat looking jacket on.

It was rather unusual to see people out on the streets during the night, with nowhere to go and nowhere to stay. It was a rare occurrence, indeed, to see someone homeless in Waterwall Incline.

"Um, excuse me?" Maddie asked quietly. "Is everything OK?"

She wasn't sure what to do. The young man hadn't moved at all or showed any signs of hearing her. What if something was wrong? She decided to try again, against her better judgement.

"Are you alright? Do you need help at all?"

Still nothing. Starting to feel uncomfortable and uneasy, Maddie decided to leave. She'd worry about it tomorrow if he was still there when she went to work her next shift.

She continued on her way, leaving the alleyway behind, still feeling rather uneasy. She glanced over her shoulder a few times as she walked but didn't see anyone.

Glancing into another alleyway, the last one before her house, Maddie felt panic start to rise when she saw the same figure of the same young man. Again, he was underneath one of the lights, halfway down the alleyway, in the same position as the previous one.

Trying very hard to ignore it, Maddie got her keys out of her pocket, picked up her pace, and finally made it to the front door of her house. Fear made her fumble with her keys, resulting in a rising panic and taking too long to find the right key to unlock the door.

Why did she have so many keys?

Someone suddenly hit the front door just off to Maddie's right, making her jump, a slight scream escaping her from the sudden shock, and she dropped her keys.

"Bit late to be outside, isn't it?"

The voice was male, and Maddie had a decent idea of who it was. She looked to her right with just her eyes, seeing the man's hand flat against the door, the light from the closest streetlight reflecting off one of the silver rings he had on.

He was very close to her. She tried to calm herself down so she could think clearly.

Deciding that her best course of action was to see who her potential attacker was, Maddie turned slowly. The young man who looked back at her was, without a doubt, the one she'd already seen in two different alleyways in that ten-minute time span.

Even though there wasn't a lot of light in front of her house, she could still see determination and what looked to be a hint of sadness in his dark brown eyes.

The young man looked at the ground briefly before returning his cold gaze back to her, still uncomfortably close.

"You dropped your keys," he noted. "It would be a shame if you lost them, best you pick them up."

Maddie felt her panic increase again, as the young man just watched her, clearly not bothered by the rain or anything else. He indicated to the keys on the ground again, and Maddie knew she had no other choice at the moment but to pick them up off the wet ground.

The young man watched without a word as she cautiously crouched down. She tried to keep watching him while feeling around in the dark for her keys.

"Remington!" a deeper, British male voice suddenly snapped. Maddie froze for a second. "No."

The young man behind her took a rather annoyed breath.

Maddie's hand finally found her keys, and she looked up, a frown appearing on her face. The young man was completely gone. There was no sign of him and no sign that he was ever there to begin with.

She got to her feet and looked around, wondering what had just happened.

Not wanting to wait and find out what was going on, she unlocked the door quickly, went inside, and shut it, immediately locking it. She put her back against the door, trying to breathe properly and calm her nerves.

Still not too sure of what had just happened, Maddie went straight to her bedroom, just wanting to forget about the confusing and scary encounter.

September 22nd, 2012

Maddie sighed as she made sure that she had everything and headed out to work.

The rain had eased off a bit, and there were a few more people outside today. She walked at a faster pace than usual, still rather shaken up after the previous night's events.

Surely it had all just been a misunderstanding. Whoever that young man was, he'd backed off rather quickly after he'd been called off. It was enough to send a chill up Maddie's spine.

Hopefully that was the last time something like that happened to her.

Like every Saturday afternoon, the bar was packed. Maddie sighed. It was going to be another night of being asked if she was single.

She headed around behind the bar, and one of her co-workers saw her.

"Oh, hey!" she greeted, Maddie giving her an unenthusiastic smile in return. Her co-worker grabbed something from behind the bar, placing it in front of Maddie. "This was left for you. It was here when I got in."

Maddie frowned as she looked at the small vase of flowers, a small envelope attached to the front of it. She carefully detached the envelope, opened it, took the small note out, and read it.

'Sorry about the scare last night – Remington xx'

Maddie couldn't help but smile slightly, shaking her head as she did so. It had to be from the young man from the night before, there was no doubt. It was the name he'd responded to when the second, unknown, man had intervened.

She shook her head again, putting the note back into the envelope and moving the vase off to the side of the bar, so she could begin her job for the night.

"I hope you know my intention wasn't to scare you," someone suddenly spoke, making her jump.

The young man, Remington, was sitting at the very end of the bar on the opposite side to Maddie, watching her. He was dressed very similarly to the previous night, except that this time he had on a different jacket and his hair was properly styled, not drenched from the rain.

He spoke again, seeing he had her attention.

"I thought I should at least apologize in person, as well. That wasn't meant to happen, and I promise it won't ever happen again," he said, the sincerity in his voice very clear. He gave her a rather nice smile, extending his hand in a friendly, non-threatening manner. "I'm Remington, sorry for the scare."

Maddie sighed internally, reluctantly taking his hand and shaking it in greeting. She noticed some rings on his fingers and a couple of bracelets on his wrist underneath the jacket, then she frowned as she felt how deathly cold he was. That certainly wasn't normal.

"Maddie," she introduced herself, letting his hand go.

Remington grinned at her, the frown staying on Maddie's face as she pieced together what was going on. She'd only ever heard of vampires being a myth around Oz and the other counties, but she was now sure that she'd just shaken hands with one.

"You're very lucky, y'know," Remington said, crossing his arms and leaning them against the bar, focus on the vase of flowers, admiring them.

"Why, because I was going to end up as your dinner last night before you got called off?"

Remington rolled his eyes. "I was going to say because I actually went out before the sun went down to buy you the prettiest flowers I could find to apologize, but, I mean, yeah, that too."

Maddie looked him over as he observed the flowers, still admiring them, a hint of a smile on his face. As handsome as he was, she wasn't about to excuse the fact that he'd scared her senseless and had been going to make a meal out of her.

"Why didn't you do it?" she dared ask. "Someone called you off, why?"

Remington looked her over before responding, interest on his face.

"Because he knows your worth, what you can do that others can't," he said. He sighed. "Look, I'm really sorry about what happened. We're both lucky that Cole called me off because, truth be told, I probably would've killed you last night."

Maddie crossed her arms and Remington shifted, resting his chin on his arms which were still on the bar, gaze ahead.

"I just ... I'm new to this shit, OK?" he said, sadness clear in his voice. "Four months isn't that long and it's hard trying to get the hang of everything. Vampires suck."

Maddie couldn't help but laugh a bit. Remington looked at her, a bit of a smile appearing on his face again. He looked happier. He shifted again, moving from where he was sitting.

"I should let you get back to what you're doing," he said, messing his hair up. He gave her a nice smile again, Maddie managing to give him one in return. "I guess I'll see you whenever I'm lurking in the streets around here. Keep yourself safe."

With those words, a wink, and another smile, he was gone.

CHAPTER SIXTEEN

Maddie's Friends

Chris glanced over his shoulder, sighing and coming to a stop as he saw that Maddie wasn't following him. She'd stopped in the shade to look at some flowers outside a shop.

"You coming or what?" he called. Maddie picked up a tulip and looked at it, sadness on her face. Chris sighed again. "I guess not."

He walked back and stood next to her as she gazed at the flower. A couple stopped next to them to also look at the assortment of flowers.

"You OK?" Chris asked, seeing that this particular type of flower had made her remember something that was making her sad.

"Yeah," she said with an unconvincing nod, not looking away from the flower. Chris knew she was lying, then she sighed. "I mean, no, not really." She looked at Chris before showing him the flower she was holding, a sad smile on her face now. "Remington used to leave these for me by the window in my kitchen whenever I'd had a hard day at work. I don't know how he knew, but he always did, and I'd always come home to three different coloured tulips and a note that always said, 'I hope tomorrow is better'. I never found out why he did it, but he did it for years until I disappeared."

The smile disappeared from her face, her gaze back on the flower. A tear ran down her cheek, although she quickly got rid of it.

Chris couldn't help but feel bad for her. Her whole life had disappeared.

"How long have you been here?"

"Three years or so, roughly thereabouts, I think," she said. She shook her head. "You lose track after a while." She sighed. "I don't know Chris, I just ... I actually really miss him."

Chris looked at her sadly, not too sure what to say. Nothing he could say would make this situation any better for her. Maddie sighed again, finally looking away from the flower, putting it back where she'd initially picked it up from.

"We should get a move on!" she said, a smile on her face now. Chris could tell it was fake and very forced. "Where are we going, again?"

"Back to my place so we can sort this letter out," Chris explained, Maddie giving a nod of approval. "Once we do this, we can decide on what our next move is."

Maddie gave an enthusiastic nod, once again rather forced from what Chris could see. It was very clear that she missed Remington a lot. Maybe that would be enough to convince her to come back to her proper dimension with him. If it wasn't, then Chris didn't know what would make her go with him.

He started walking again, Maddie making sure she was following him this time, trying to stay in the shade as much as possible. The sun was still very bright, and Chris was sure she wasn't too happy with being outside.

It had been her own decision to come with him, though, and there was nothing Chris could say to convince her to stay indoors. She must have realized that the letter was important enough to risk coming out during the daylight.

"Where do you normally hide out during the day?" Chris asked, trying to get a conversation started that would hopefully take Maddie's mind off everything that was making her sad, mainly Remington.

Maddie looked at him, giving him a grin. "I'll show you tonight if you want."

Chris raised his eyebrow at her as they stopped outside his current residence.

"Is that an invitation?"

"Sure," she said, Chris shaking his head in disbelief. Maddie looked him over. "We should head over there tonight, anyway. I need to talk to a couple of people either way, so looks like tonight is the night for it."

"Talk to them about what?"

Maddie gave him a normal smile this time. "Getting you out of here and back to Dimension One."

It took Chris a second or two to register what she'd said, but then he nodded and unlocked his front door. He held the door open for Maddie who went in first, taking off her sunglasses and hood once she was in.

The curtains near the table in the front room were open, letting light into the small residence, and Maddie looked around as Chris headed through the door on the left into his bedroom.

"So, this is where you've been living?" Maddie called, staying in the front room.

"For the past year, yeah, unfortunately," he answered, opening the drawer of his bedside table and taking out his journal. He picked up the pen from the bedside table and headed back out.

Maddie watched him take a seat at the table, but she stayed where she was in the middle of the room.

"You really hate it here, don't you?" Maddie asked, making Chris sigh as he started writing a brief letter to send with the list Remington had sent their way.

Chris stopped writing and looked up at her. "I shouldn't even be here," he said. Maddie put her hands in her pockets as she listened. "I've been here for at least twelve months. My family back home have absolutely no idea where I am or why I haven't contacted them. I wouldn't even be here if everything had gone according to plan but, as always, it didn't and I'm the one who had to suffer the consequences, yet again."

He turned his attention back to what he'd been writing, and Maddie decided to stay quiet this time. Once he finished, he tore the page out of the journal, folded it, and stood up.

"I'm going to send this off, so feel free to join me if you want to," he said. "Otherwise, I guess I'll see you later tonight to go and meet these … people you want to talk with."

Maddie nodded and Chris walked past her to the front door.

"Will you be here later tonight?" she asked as Chris held the door for her.

"Sure."

"It's quite out of the way, so it'll be a bit of a walk."

Chris didn't bother saying anything in response. He followed Maddie down the dark road that headed away from town. It wasn't that late, but the sun had disappeared quickly and it was now cloudy, so there was no sign of the moon tonight.

There were no words spoken between the two of them as Maddie stayed a pace in front. Chris watched her back, hoping she wasn't playing for the opposing team this entire time and leading him into some elaborate trap or something. Knowing his luck, though, that would be the outcome.

Maddie checked over her shoulder a few times to make sure he was still there as they walked. The track had turned to dirt and the woods on either side now cut off any more light that may have snuck through the clouds.

Eventually, Maddie switched direction, turning right and heading into the woods. Chris had no other choice but to follow along. He'd already come this far.

The woods weren't as dense as they looked from the outside. Maddie walked along the almost invisible track, going deep into the forest. There was hardly any sound as they walked, and it wasn't long before a clearing with a small house in the middle of it came into view.

Maddie glanced over her shoulder again, giving Chris a bit of a smile as she headed for the house. There was a mailbox near the front of the clearing, and a gravel pathway led up to the front door. Everything just got stranger and stranger in this dimension, Chris thought.

When Maddie reached the front door, she tried the handle and found it unlocked. She went inside, not bothering to hold the door open for Chris who made sure it was closed behind him once he was in.

"Come on," Maddie said, keeping her voice low. Chris heard people talking in a nearby room. "Don't want to disturb the house owners."

Chris frowned, following her over to the staircase. Maddie opened the small door underneath the staircase and turned the light on inside. Steep stairs led downwards.

"Is this where we're going?" he asked.

Maddie gave him an excited smile but didn't answer. She went in first, heading down the stairs without a care. Chris sighed and stepped onto the first wooden step, shutting the door before following Maddie down. There weren't a lot of stairs, but the air got noticeably colder the lower they went.

Chris, again, heard people talking, probably from another room. How many people lived in this place?

Maddie was waiting at the bottom of the stairs, and Chris finally joined her on solid ground. They were in what he assumed was the basement, as it was all concrete and stone, with a few miscellaneous pieces of furniture and boxes scattered around.

"This way!" Maddie said, that same cheer still in her tone as she headed across the basement towards a wooden door at the other end.

Chris followed without a word, and this time Maddie held the door open for him, indicating for him to go through. Chris stepped through hesitantly, and Maddie quickly followed and shut the door.

The three people within the well-lit room looked up at the disturbance.

"Chris, this is Mason, Amber, and Emmie," Maddie introduced everyone. "Guys, this is Chris."

The girl with dyed dark red hair gave Chris a rather enthusiastic wave of greeting. She couldn't have been older than about twenty-three. The other girl looked to be the same age, with similar features as the red-haired girl, but her hair was emerald green in color. She also gave Chris an enthusiastic wave.

The only other male in the room, who Chris assumed was Mason, gave Chris a lazy wave of greeting. He had short blonde hair that kept falling over his face, only to be brushed off to the left every time it happened. His facial structure was also similar to the girls'.

Maddie looked at Chris, indicating to the two girls.

"The one with the red hair is Amber," she explained, Amber grinning at him. "Emmie's the other one, they're twins. Well, I mean, technically triplets because Mason's their brother."

Chris raised his eyebrows. That made sense as to why they all looked like they were related.

"So, would I be right in assuming that I'm the only one in the room right now who isn't a vampire?" Chris said, his gaze on Maddie the entire time.

Maddie smiled. "Yup!"

Chris sighed. "Awesome."

Mason pushed himself up from where he'd been lounging on the sofa, stretching a bit as the two girls just watched Chris.

"Maddie said she was bringing you here tonight," Mason said. He glanced at Maddie before returning his gaze to Chris. "Said you were in need of some help."

"That all she's said?"

Maddie crossed her arms as she looked at Mason who returned her look with one of his own.

"Pretty sure I elaborated the entire situation and spelt it out for you," she said. "You, mister, just need to listen more!"

Mason ignored Maddie, looking back at Chris. "We're more than happy to help you out. We just need to know what you need."

Chris looked directly at him, Maddie waiting to hear what he had to say. Mason looked like he was interested in hearing the situation from Chris himself.

"Well, first off, I'm sure Maddie's mentioned that I'm trying to get home," Chris began explaining. "I'm currently spell-bound to someone who I don't really want to take back home with me, so that's the first thing on the list: getting myself separated from her. Then, the second thing is to figure out how I'm going to get back home."

"Spell-bound, hey?" Mason said, Chris giving a defeated nod. "Well, that's unfortunate."

Chris gave an unamused laugh. "You've no idea."

Mason smiled before speaking again. "Maddie mentioned that she thinks you've had someone following you for a while."

Chris glanced at Maddie. "She mentioned it to me, but I haven't seen any sign of it."

Mason pursed his lips in thought, Maddie giving him a shrug as he looked at her. He switched his gaze back to Chris.

"Do you know much about the witch who did this spell? Because, depending on how powerful they are, we may not be able to find someone to break you out of it," he said, which wasn't something Chris wanted to hear.

"I don't know a whole lot about Carmen, but she's got quite the knack for the mystics."

Mason's expression changed and Chris didn't like it.

"Carmen?" Chris gave a nod and Mason sighed. "Man, that makes things hard. If she's the one who's done this, you may have to just deal with the spell-bind until you get home."

"Oh no, I am not going back with Marion, she stays here," Chris said, watching Mason bite his lower lip a bit as he thought. Chris frowned. "Also, wait, how do you know about Carmen?"

Mason looked back at his sisters who prompted him to keep speaking, seeing as he'd already started.

"The three of us are from the same dimension as you guys, Dimension One," he explained. Chris felt his heart sink. "Carmen's always been a big problem. A lot of people tried to take her and Heather out multiple times but never managed to."

"Please, for the love of God, don't tell me you guys were Dimension Walkers." Mason awkwardly looked at his sisters who also stayed quiet. Chris sighed. "You're kidding me. What the fuck?"

Mason cleared his throat awkwardly, feeling the tension in the room now.

Chris looked at Maddie who returned his look, just a bit more worried.

"You never thought to mention to me that there are four out of six of you in this dimension? And to make it worse, you're all vampires! You think you should have said something to me?"

"Look, Chris, don't be mad, OK?" she said, Chris shaking his head as he put his hands on his hips and looked down, trying to calm himself a bit. "I didn't want to dash your hopes of getting home, OK? Look, please trust me when I say that we're working together to get you back home."

Chris looked back up at her.

"I can't believe this," he said, shaking his head again. He indicated to the other three vampires in the room. "They could've gotten me home, and now we're down to two Dimension Walkers left within thousands of dimensions, and we're on very limited time! I needed to know this!"

"We'll get you out before anything happens," Maddie reassured him, but Chris wasn't sure how much more to believe now.

"I'm starting to find that very hard to believe."

Maddie looked at him sadly, before Mason spoke again, getting Chris's attention.

"We get it, you're mad," he said, Chris giving him a bit of a look. "But we're doing our best down here to try and work things out. You've just got to give us a bit more time."

"We don't really have much more time, do we?" Chris said bitterly. "We need to start working this whole thing out now because otherwise we're all dead and, I swear to God, I will not die here, and I am never going back to Hell."

CHAPTER SEVENTEEN

Traitor in the Ranks

"Why are you going back?" Arley asked, watching Craig fold up the map. "You said you were going to be setting up the new outpost!"

"Danny's in charge until I get back," Craig said, putting the map in his jacket pocket and looking at her. "So, I need you to do what you're told and help get it running until I get back."

"You can't go back by yourself, what if something happens?" Arley tried, Craig putting his hands on his hips as he regarded her. "At least let me go back with you, just in case."

"It's OK, I'll go back with him." Ash surprised them both as she walked into the room.

She stopped close to Craig on his left, slipping her hand into his back pocket, making sure Arley saw her do it, much to his annoyance. Ash looked at Arley with a disapproving look as the little cat sat down on the floor next to her.

"Probably a good idea for you to stay back and keep Danny in line," Ash said.

Arley shot her a glare, hating the smug look now on Ash's face as she moved closer to Craig who chose to ignore the suggestive gesture. Ash knew Craig wanted Arley to stay back, and that he trusted her more than he trusted Danny.

Craig looked at Arley. "I need you to stay back here, make sure Danny doesn't fuck it all up," he said much to the disbelief on Arley's face.

"Seriously? You want me to stay back here while *she* goes with you?" she argued back. She indicated to Ash. "*Her?*"

"I need you to do what you're told, Beckett," Craig said, his tone harsher now, not liking her arguing his direct order. "If Danny messes something up, I know you can fix it. I trust you, Arley, you know that. I need you to go with Danny. Ash will go back with me in case something happens."

Ash gave Arley a smile, though Arley saw right through it. She didn't like Ash very much. She was too manipulative and Arley knew Craig was better than that, deserved better than that.

Craig sighed. "Please, I need you to go with Danny."

"Why, when Matt's going with him as well?" Arley argued.

Craig sighed again. "Matt does his own thing. We have no say in what he does. Please, listen to what I'm telling you to do and just do it."

Arley didn't like it, but she eventually nodded, knowing she'd get a demotion or possibly be released altogether if she kept arguing back to her commander. She had enough respect for Craig to do as he said, but she'd had to voice her concerns.

"Yes sir."

Begrudgingly, Arley left, and Craig looked at Ash once she was out of sight.

"Why do you have to be like that?" he asked.

Ash raised an eyebrow, and shifted, linking her arm with his. She looked him over before responding.

"I'm sure we both know why, Commander," she said. Craig was not impressed. She looked him over again. "She's been vying for your attention for what I assume has been quite a while. As you said, best she stays here to keep Danny out of trouble."

Craig sighed. "Whatever. Come on, let's go."

Remington heard the noise before he even got anywhere close to his room. A frown crossed his face and he picked up his pace.

He didn't even glance at the vampires in the room a few doors down from him, the ones that wouldn't stop partying. They were crowding the doorway, not game to step out, but wanting to know what was going on.

All eyes were on Remington as he ran past, seeing the door to his room wide open. There was a reason he always kept it locked and now it looked like someone had broken in.

He stopped abruptly in the doorway, the dread hitting hard.

The entire room had been turned upside down. Graith was at the desk, all drawers open as he leaned against it, turning something over in his hands. There were at least six other vampires in the room, all below Remington in the ranks.

"I want to know who it was that you were writing to," Graith said, focused on what he had in his hands, inspecting it closely. He looked up and met Remington's cold gaze. "Wouldn't happen to be someone in Banshee's End, would it?"

Graith held up Remington's small Banshee's End badge, then reached into the open drawer on his left.

"Wouldn't have been Craig Taylor, would it?" was his next question, holding up the second badge, the division one.

It was too late now. Graith had everything he needed to convict Remington of treachery, and Remington knew that was exactly what he was going to do. Graith threw both badges at Remington who caught them with ease, keeping a firm hold on them.

"You see, Remington, I've been onto you for a while," Graith explained, reaching into the drawer again, carelessly tossing the ID card over to him as well. Remington caught it and put it in his pocket. "You really thought I wouldn't find out?"

"Truthfully, I thought you'd find out sooner. It took you a while."

Graith's smile looked amused as he crossed his arms, still leaning on the edge of the desk. The other vampires in the room all just watched Remington.

"It's always the nice ones," Graith said.

Remington glanced around the room at where everyone was stationed, just in case he needed to move quickly. His gaze flickered over to Graith.

"When did you figure it out?" he asked, wanting to know how long he'd truly been keeping tabs on him.

Graith pretended to think. "Funeral Masquerade," he said.

Remington tried not to show that he was kicking himself for not being more careful.

Graith pushed off the desk, linking his fingers together as he walked slowly over to where Remington was standing in the doorway. He stopped directly in front of him, but Remington didn't show any intimidation whatsoever.

Graith looked him over before speaking. "Lowest level."

The two closest vampires moved, roughly grabbing Remington and holding onto him with a very strong grip.

Remington scowled. "You going to kill me?" he dared ask, knowing this was always going to happen.

Graith looked him over, thinking.

"No, I don't think so. Not yet, at least," he said, looking him dead in the eyes. "I'll let the higher ranks decide what to do with you, what they think is best." He looked at the other four vampires in the room. "Escort him to the lowest level. Make sure he's locked down there."

The two vampires who were holding Remington started to drag him away and the other four followed.

"I'll be seeing you soon, Bell," Graith called after them.

Vampires in the other rooms all watched from the doorways as Remington was dragged past them, down the corridor.

Remington stayed silent, letting Graith's lackeys direct him to the stairwell and push him through the door. The stairway was narrow, so they headed down the stairs, two vampires in front and the rest behind in case he tried anything.

The stairs wound around and around, going down each level of the hideout, past closed doors on each level. Remington kept walking, knowing it would take a few minutes to hit the lowest level. That was where traitors and prisoners ended up and now it was his turn.

The lowest level finally came into view, and the vampire in the lead opened the door at the bottom of the stairwell. The other vampires directed Remington through, dragging him again once they were clear.

Remington knew it was no use fighting back. He knew he wouldn't be able to overpower six vampires.

Seeing the large holding cells up ahead, a scowl appeared on Remington's face when he saw someone occupying one of the usually empty cells. The vampires threw Remington into the holding cell, locked the door, and left.

Remington hated it down here. The cells were impenetrable, even for vampires, which was why they'd been built in the first place. Whatever the cells were made of, it stopped anything and everyone from breaking through.

Remington looked through the bars on his right, and Cole looked back at him from the other side.

"I thought we had a deal!" Remington shouted, his voice echoing off the walls, through the blank space and dim light. He was beyond angry. "You sold me out!"

"I didn't say anything!" Cole snapped back. He gestured to his surroundings. "Why the hell do you think I'm in here if I so willingly gave you up?"

The bitter look stayed on Remington's face.

"Then how did Graith know to raid my room?" he snapped. He held up one of the badges. "This? How'd he know this was in my room?"

"I don't know," Cole said through clenched teeth. "He asked me, and I didn't say anything." Remington just looked at him, his stare cold. Cole sighed. "Please, Rem, you've got to believe me here. You know I wouldn't tell Graith anything, no matter what."

Remington looked him over, trying to decide what to say. His anger suddenly dissipated and he sighed as he put the two badges in his pocket next to his ID card.

"I'm sorry, Cole, I know you wouldn't do that," he said, Cole giving a single nod. Remington sighed again, going to the back of the cell and leaning against the solid back wall. He slid down it until he was sitting on the floor. "Goddamn it."

Cole moved over to the bars that separated the two cells. He gripped the bars and leaned against them.

"Any idea how we get out of here?" he asked.

Remington looked at him. He was tired but he knew there was nothing he could do about it now. He shook his head, taking one of the rings off his finger and turning it over as he looked at it, trying to think.

"Honestly, no," he admitted. "Graith said he was going to take it up with the higher ranks, so we're basically screwed." He sighed once more, looking at Cole again who was watching him turn the ring over in his hands. "What did Graith do to try get you to rat me out?"

Cole gave a slight shrug, moving and sitting down where he was at the bars, hand flat against the floor behind him.

"Asked me, pushed me around, threatened me. Anything he could think of to try to force me to talk," he said. "Doesn't matter, though. Son of a bitch could do whatever he wanted to. I wasn't about to sell you out no matter the stakes."

Remington couldn't help but smile at his word choice, and Cole smiled back.

CHAPTER EIGHTEEN

On the Trail

The little blonde cat ran on ahead as the front gates to Banshee's End opened, creaking a bit as the recruits kept their post, making sure they were only letting in authorized people.

Craig and Ash weren't far behind the cat but, by the time they'd made it through the gates and onto Banshee's End territory, he was well gone.

"Wonderful," Ash sighed, seeing absolutely no sign of Alex. She looked at Craig, who was already heading to his destination. "Where are you going?"

Craig didn't bother responding, so Ash quickly followed him to make sure he didn't disappear on her. Some of the recruits they passed greeted Craig, as most hadn't seen him since he'd left for Outpost Fourteen months ago. Craig greeted them back as he passed, heading towards the barracks.

He scanned himself in and Ash quickened her pace to make sure the door didn't close on her. Craig was a few paces ahead, heading for his room. The cat was lying on the floor in front of the door, chewing on a piece of paper.

Craig sighed and crouched down, taking the paper from the protesting cat. Craig stood back up and looked at what he'd taken from Alex.

A frown appeared on his face when he realized it was a letter addressed to him. He turned it over and saw Chris's signature on the back, their sign of authenticity.

"What is it?" Ash asked, moving closer to see what he was looking at.

Craig waved the envelope at her before he opened it. "It's from Chris."

Craig began to read the letter and Ash frowned. Why would Chris be writing to Craig of all people?

Craig,

The second piece of paper in the envelope was sent over to me from Remington, asking me to send it on to you. I don't know what it's about or what it's for, but I figure you'll have more of an idea than me.

He mentioned in his letter that he was going to send it directly to you, but Graith was onto him and he didn't want it getting intercepted and marked as suspicious. He said he was going to lay low for a bit, so it might be worth trying to check in with him to make sure he's still alive.

Hopefully this is of use to you.

Chris

Craig looked at the second piece of paper, his eyes scanning over the page.

"Shit," he said before he turned and headed back the way they'd come at a fast pace.

Ash rushed after him, the cat right on her heels. Craig was already quite a way ahead as they left the barracks. Unable to catch up, Ash saw him go into the church up ahead, disappearing inside.

Whatever had been on that piece of paper must have been very important and urgent.

Reaching the church doors, Ash scanned herself in, and Alex dashed in ahead to wait at the next door.

Down in the underground room, Craig went straight over to one of the boards at the opposite end of the room, the few other people in there looking rather surprised to see him.

They were even more surprised when Ash and Alex, no longer a cat, came through the door.

"What's going on?" Jacob asked with a frown, looking between the three of them.

Craig didn't say anything, just grabbed a red marker and looked between the list Chris had sent and the list on the wall in front of him.

Jacob joined Craig at the board and Ash stopped at the closest table. Alex sat on the edge of the table, close to Ash.

"Craig?" Jacob said, but Craig's focus was solely on the lists of names on the board and the paper.

Everyone watched as Craig put red crosses next to multiple names on the board, going through the list several times to make sure he hadn't missed any. Once done, he sighed, looking at the board.

"Damn," he said, shaking his head.

"Care to let us in on what's happening?" Ash asked.

Craig finally acknowledged her and Jacob.

"We're fucked is what's going on," he said. He indicated to the board and then the piece of paper. "If I'm right, Remington has sent me, via Chris, a list of names of people from Outpost Six." He looked at the board. "My guess is that these are the ones who are now part of the Legion."

Ash didn't know what to say.

Jacob broke the silence. "You think they were turned?"

Craig nodded, holding up the paper list.

"This isn't anyone's writing that I recognize," he said. Ash, Alex, and Jacob all looked at it. "It's not Remington's but, if what Chris said is true and he was going to send it straight to me, I think this is Cole's writing. Remington said they're friends. He's a higher rank than Cole so he could get this kind of thing from him."

Craig placed the paper on the table, and Alex picked it up to have a closer look at it.

"Wait up, just a minute," Jacob said, holding up a hand. "Did you just say that Remington's a higher rank than Cole?"

Realizing he'd slipped up, Craig stayed silent. Jacob indicated for him to speak, waiting for an explanation.

"Yes, yes I did say that," Craig admitted, Jacob unable to believe what he was hearing. "Remington's done a lot for us, so I didn't think it was something I needed to tell people about. It could cause a lot of tension, especially if Danny found out about his ranking in the vampire hierarchy."

"How high of a rank are we talking about here?"

"From my understanding, at least a twelve."

Jacob raised his eyebrows. "I'm sorry, a fucking twelve? You thought you shouldn't tell anyone about a damn rank twelve? Not even me?"

"I know, I should have said something," Craig said, trying to justify himself. He indicated to Ash. "She knew he could turn people as well."

Ash looked at him in disbelief.

"He can turn people and is at least a rank twelve," Jacob stated, also in disbelief, but for a different reason than Ash. "Oh my God."

Craig gave an awkward shrug, and Jacob stared at him as he tried to figure out what to say.

Alex was the one to break the silence. "Um, so, how bad's a rank twelve...?"

They all looked at him and no one spoke for a few seconds.

"That's very high in the hierarchy," Jacob explained. "Graith's a thirteen, put it that way." Alex's eyes widened and he stayed quiet now. Jacob glared at Craig. "How long have you known?"

"We found out he was able to turn people when we were at the Funeral Masquerade," he said reluctantly. Jacob shook his head and sighed. "He told me his rank a couple of months ago when we were putting the list together at Outpost Fourteen."

"Yet, you clearly left him off the list."

"Because I didn't want anyone to find out!" Craig snapped, finally having had enough. "He's gotten us more information than we could ever have hoped to get and if anyone knew what he was capable of, the entire operation would have been compromised because someone would have tried to take him down, either out of fear or because we try to get the higher ranks before they turn anyone to kill off their bloodline. I wasn't about to risk that."

"And now he's most likely been caught out trying to get that list to you," Ash input, Craig looking at her.

Jacob looked between the two of them. "Someone better tell me what the hell you're talking about."

Craig was the one to speak again, knowing that Ash wasn't about to do any of the explaining, even though, right now, Craig had a lot more to lose than she did.

"Chris sent me this list. Remington was getting grilled by Graith and apparently had to take precautions in getting it to me," he explained, crossing his arms. "Chris thinks Remington may have been caught out."

Jacob sighed and ran his fingers through his hair as he tried to think about what to do.

"This isn't good," he said. "If they kill him, our whole operation goes down. Even though they're most likely aware he's double-crossing them, we can't let them kill him."

"Agreed," Craig said, sounding very tired now.

"So, what do we do?" Ash asked, not really wanting anything to happen to the vampire.

Over the past twelve months, Remington had been back and forth, in and out with every piece of information he could provide, even when it wasn't much to go on. He'd been risking himself every time he'd left, and Ash, for some strange reason, now saw him as part of their dysfunctional family.

"We don't even know where he goes when he isn't with us," Craig said, looking at her. "I don't know if there's really much we can do."

"We can't send people into a full-on vampire habitat," Jacob said seriously.

"But we can't sit back and do nothing!" Ash stressed, looking between Craig and Jacob.

"I know, but we don't have a lot of options."

Alex jumped off the table, feet firmly on the ground as they all looked at him, wondering what he was doing.

"I can try and track him down," he suggested.

"Alex, no," Ash said, not happy with him volunteering himself. "Please don't."

"Uh, how exactly?" Craig asked.

Alex stood a bit straighter.

"Well, Craig, I don't know how much you know about me, but I can assure you, I'm more than just a pretty face," he said. He noted the unsure look on Craig's face, so he put his arms out to his sides, a slight grin on his face. "I'm not just a cat. Ya boy here is a shapeshifter. I just like being a cat more than anything else."

Craig wasn't convinced, but he didn't say anything. Jacob looked at Alex who put his arms down and returned his look.

"Alright, what do you need?" he asked.

A grin lit up Alex's face. "Anything that can help me find him!"

CHAPTER NINETEEN

Unbound

H e was going to say something, but decided against it, unlocking the door to go inside.

"I'm sorry, Chris," Maddie suddenly apologized, touching his shoulder and making him stop in the middle of opening the door. "I know tonight wasn't what you wanted to hear, and I should have told you before now."

Chris stayed where he was for a few seconds before going inside, shutting and locking the door behind himself. He heard Maddie sigh outside, and heard her leave seconds later.

The house was quiet and dark, as usual. Marion pretty well never left the residence and whenever Chris got back, it was always the same: dark and quiet, the curtain next to the table always open from when he opened it before leaving earlier in the day. She never moved anything or even showed herself very often anymore.

While that was good for the most part, there were times when it would have been nice to have someone else around to talk to, even if that person was Marion.

He was about to head to his bedroom, when a slight noise made him stop, a frown appearing on his face. It was too dark to see anything, making him even more unsure. Moving back over to the front door, as the light switch was next to it, he heard the sound again.

Suddenly, someone roughly pushed him up against the wall, holding him there as the light switched on. Once Chris's eyes adjusted, he felt his heart sink as he saw who was in front of him.

Hunter kept him up against the wall as Carmen walked over to join them.

"You're a hard man to find, Chris," Carmen said, stopping next to Hunter who didn't relent his grip at all. Carmen looked Chris over. "Nothing's changed, I see."

"What do you want, Carmen?" Chris asked, wishing Hunter would back off.

How they'd managed to find him in this dimension, let alone get to the right place was beyond him. There had to be some easy explanation for this that he wasn't seeing.

"I'm sure you can figure out why I'm here," Carmen said, drawing Chris's attention back to her. Carmen glanced at Hunter, then looked back at Chris. "We've been looking for you for a while."

"Whatever you want, I don't have it," Chris said, Carmen looking him over as she thought about what he said. "So, you have to take your business elsewhere."

There was a sudden, urgent knock on the front door, right next to where they were all standing. Maddie called Chris's name, and Carmen shook her head at him.

"Don't say a word," she threatened, keeping her voice down.

The urgent knock came again. Chris knew Maddie had figured out something was wrong if she was back so soon. He stared at Carmen.

"What do you want?" he asked again, not bothering to keep his voice down now. The knocking had stopped, and he hoped Maddie realized there was a back door. "Because I don't have a whole lot of time and it's late."

Carmen looked him over again, crossing her arms. "I'm not impressed at how royally you screwed me over with your little ... stunt."

"Craig's the one you should be mad at," Chris said. "He threw the piece of paper through the damn portal, not me. I wouldn't even be here if it wasn't for you."

"Oh, don't worry, Craig will get what's coming to him. It's only a matter of time," Carmen assured him. Chris didn't like the sound of that, but there was nothing he could do about it right now. "As of now, you're the only one who knows how to bring Heather back and I want you to hold up your end of the deal."

"She wrote it down for me, that piece of paper is all I knew about it. I didn't exactly memorize it!" Chris snapped, hoping Marion wasn't hearing any of this from the other room.

Out of the corner of his eye, he saw someone move in the dark. It looked like Maddie had found the back door after all, but she was trying to stay out of sight until she got into position. Chris kept his focus fully on Carmen, not wanting to risk giving Maddie away. He knew what Carmen was capable of when it came down to it.

"Well, then, we have a bit of a problem, don't we?" Carmen said.

"Hey!" Maddie called from the middle of the room. She held up a folded piece of paper as Hunter and Carmen both turned to look at her. "This what you're after?"

Maddie glanced at Chris, while Carmen glared at her.

"Who are you?" she asked.

"Doesn't matter who I am, just know that I have what you're after," Maddie said, staring fully at Carmen, not wavering in the slightest.

Carmen summed her up before she spoke again. "Well, that's mine either way, so best you be a good girl and bring it over."

She held her hand out in front of her, expecting Maddie to bring the piece of paper over to her.

Maddie crossed her arms, keeping hold of the paper. "You have to do something for us first."

Chris hoped she knew what she was doing.

Carmen sighed. "What?"

Maddie indicated to Chris. "Remove the binding spell and you can have this."

Carmen narrowed her eyes, looking back at Chris who was still being held against the wall by Hunter. Chris could see her thinking and considering her options. Eventually, she sighed in annoyance.

"Alright, fine," she said. She looked at Chris again. "Where's Marion?"

"Bedroom at the back of the house," he said, using his head to indicate down the hallway.

Carmen gave Maddie a bitter glare as she passed by her, disappearing down the hallway into the darkness.

Chris glanced over at Maddie, seeing her watching the hallway and quickly put the hand that was holding the piece of paper into her pocket. What was she up to?

Minutes ticked by, dragging on, but eventually Carmen reappeared, walking over to Maddie and standing in front of her. Maddie was not intimidated and showed no sign of backing down.

Carmen raised her eyebrows and held her hand out.

"Prove you did it," Maddie said, arms once again crossed. "How do we know you've actually removed it and haven't just pretended to?"

Carmen gave another annoyed sigh. "How? How do you want me to prove it?"

Maddie gave a shrug. "Hm, I dunno. Maybe take her somewhere else, like maybe a completely different dimension? If Chris ends up gone as well, we'll know you're lying. If nothing happens, you can have the paper."

Carmen narrowed her eyes again before she looked at Hunter, indicating for him to go and get Marion. Chris looked at Maddie as Hunter let him go without a word and headed down the hallway.

"Go with him," Chris said. "Make sure he's not trying to play you."

Maddie followed Hunter down the dark hallway, leaving Carmen and Chris alone in the front room. Carmen looked at Chris who just returned her gaze.

"If any of this is wrong, I hope you know I'm coming straight back for you," she said.

"Well, you'd better make sure it's quick because this entire dimension is coming down and if I don't get out, I'm as good as dead, Carmen."

Carmen didn't say anything, and they stood there glaring at each other in silence.

After a long wait, Maddie and Hunter joined them in the room again. Maddie went straight to Chris and Hunter stopped next to Carmen.

Carmen looked between them all.

"Well, I think that clears your test," she said. She looked directly at Maddie and held her hand out again. "Paper, now."

Maddie rolled her eyes, carelessly throwing her the piece of paper, Carmen catching it with a smile. Without another word, she and

Hunter disappeared back into the house, out of sight and hopefully gone for good.

Waiting a few more minutes before speaking, just in case they were still lurking around the corner, Chris looked at Maddie.

"Want to tell me what just happened?"

"I changed one little part in the instructions, it won't work," Maddie said, Chris giving a bit of a nod. "Also … he was probably our only way out of here."

Chris had already gathered that. Now they had no way of leaving this dimension and would most likely be going down with it. He shook his head slightly.

"Surely there's got to be some other way we can work this and get back home," he said, thinking as he went over to the table and took a seat. "What did you do with Marion?"

Maddie followed and sat opposite him. She shrugged, resting her head on her hand as she looked at the table. "Left her in whichever random dimension we ended up in."

Chris gave a bit of a nod, glad to hear it.

"OK, so we now know for sure that Hunter's one of the six," he stated, Maddie nodding. "Which leaves one more out there."

"Hopefully," was Maddie's response. "We're just assuming that there are two that are still alive."

Chris frowned, Maddie not looking at him at all. "What do you mean?"

There was a minute of hesitation, but then Maddie sighed.

"I think he's possibly the last one," she admitted. She sighed again, finally looking at him. "Dimension Walkers can tell when they're in the presence of another one. It's hard to explain, but we know. When I met Remington, someone named Cole called him off. I never saw him, but I felt it. I think he's one of them and, if I'm right, he's a vampire because vampires don't usually back off when humans tell them too. I think we're down to one, and that one just left."

Chris sat there for a minute or two as what she'd said sunk in. This wasn't good. They'd just let their only chance of getting home go and now they had no other options.

"Look, we'll make something work, no matter what it is," Maddie tried to reassure him, reaching out but not quite touching his hand.

Chris slouched in his chair, shaking his head, unable to make himself say anything.

"I promise you, Chris, even if it's just you, I will make sure you get home."

Chapter Twenty

The Vampire Habitat

This was, without a doubt, the scariest thing Alex had ever attempted to do in his life. Why he'd volunteered himself in the first place was beyond him, but it was too late now and here he was.

The little brown mouse slipped in through a small crack in the wall next to the door, carefully making his way down the steep stairs, descending further and further underground. There was not a lot of light around for him to see.

It was still daylight above the surface, which meant there was going to be many vampires roaming the halls in this scary underground lair Alex had tracked Remington back to. Why was he doing this?

The stairs kept going down, and Alex wondered if it was ever going to end. Hopefully, he'd get to the bottom soon, as he didn't wish to be going too far underground in case something happened and he couldn't get back out. He told himself he was going to get out no matter what.

As long as all the vampires assumed he was just another mouse scampering around in their lair, he would be fine. An unpleasant thought crossed his mind. What if they tried to eat the occasional small creature that managed to find its way down here? That wouldn't be good.

He could finally see the end of the stairs, and he dashed down the final few and through the large entrance way that led onto a metal grate. It was rather quiet, which made him uneasy. Was this normal for a vampire hideout?

He dared to venture out onto the metal grate a bit more, seeing the layout in front of him. There was a stairwell in the middle of the open structure, stairs only leading down. Did he dare venture down there first, or try and see if Remington was somewhere else within the facility?

Deciding to try his luck on this level, Alex dashed off to his right, hoping to find something of use that would tell him where Remington was. He didn't know what he was going to do if he couldn't find him anywhere. If he wasn't here, did that mean that he was OK and just outside somewhere, or would it mean they'd already done something to him and he was long gone?

The possibilities were endless, and Alex didn't wish to think about what may have happened.

The few vampires who were around didn't pay Alex any attention as he ran past them along the metal grate. That was a very good sign. Passing a few rooms, one in particular got his attention.

The door was wide open, and the little mouse cautiously entered the room, seeing things thrown around everywhere. Without a doubt, this was Remington's room. But where was Remington? Alex looked around the room a bit more, trying to figure out what they would have done with him.

There had clearly been a raid on the room which, in Alex's mind, meant they'd taken him elsewhere. But where? He moved around the room, trying to find any sign of what the vampires would have done with Remington.

"Leave him down there for a few days," he suddenly heard, the voice very close. The small mouse ran underneath the bed, hoping he hadn't been seen. "We'll let the higher ranks figure it out. The last thing we need is word getting out about traitors in the ranks."

Alex didn't know who was speaking, but the speaker entered the room, with two other people not far behind him. From his position under the bed, Alex watched the back of the first person as he went over to the desk and picked something up.

"I need someone to track that letter down, the one he sent yesterday," the speaker said. Surely, he had to be someone in charge of something. "We can't let it get back to Craig Taylor, no matter what. Kill anyone who tries to stop you, unless it's Bell. We need him alive until we can get enough information on how far ahead Banshee's End are and how much they know about us."

The other two vampires left the room, and Alex cautiously moved forwards to try and see a bit better. The only vampire left in the room was Graith. Alex recognized him from the Funeral Masquerade and didn't like him very much.

Graith stayed at the desk, leafing through the pieces of paper strewn across the surface before he grabbed something else off the desk.

It was a framed picture and Alex watched Graith look it over for a minute before carelessly tossing it onto the ground, the glass shattering when it hit the floor. Graith then turned and left the room.

Alex waited a few minutes to make sure he was actually gone before daring to venture out from underneath the bed.

It looked like Remington was somewhere in the facility and, judging by what Graith had just said, Alex had a bad feeling that he had to go even further underground.

The little mouse ran over to the doorway, looking out and seeing nothing. No vampires lurking in the hallways for the time being. He went back into the room, going over to where Graith had dropped the framed picture.

Alex carefully nudged bits of glass out of the way, dragged the picture out of the broken frame, and looked at it. It was an older picture, by the looks of it, of Remington with two other young men. If Alex had to guess, the three of them were possibly related.

Dragging the picture, Alex made his way to the door again. He double-checked that he still had a clear path before he moved out onto the metal grate, continuing to drag the picture with him towards the stairwell.

It was going to take him a bit longer to get down to whatever level Remington was on, but Alex was determined to take the picture with him.

Somehow managing to avoid any undead beings, Alex made it to the stairwell door. It had been left open. Was that a normal thing?

Not wanting to dwell on it for too long in case someone came along and realized he wasn't just some ordinary mouse dragging a picture down the hallway, he headed down the stairs, hating how far apart they all were for a creature his size.

How many levels were there in this facility? What level would be logical for them to have their prisoners on? How had he gotten this far without being caught?

Alex tried not to think of it all as he continued down the stairs. He decided that he was going to go down the entire way and leave this picture somewhere safe. Once he'd found where Remington was, he'd go back for the picture.

It took a while but, eventually, Alex saw the end of the stairs, picking up his pace as he neared the end, glad to see it. It was rather dark on the lowest level, but Alex's mouse eyes were able to see well enough as he slipped through the open doorway at the bottom of the stairwell.

Looking around, it was clear he was in the right place. There were countless numbers of cells lining the walls on every side of the large room, people—some possibly vampires—in many of them. There were multiple parts separating the front and the back of the room, and Alex felt his heart sink as he couldn't see Remington straight off in any of the front cells.

He had to be here somewhere. He'd managed to track him this far, and he wasn't about to give in now.

He started moving again, determined to find the correct cell, dragging the picture with him as he began his search.

Many of the cell occupants watched as he went past, confused and curious. It wasn't every day that a mouse dragging a picture appeared on the lowest level of a vampire habitat.

After looking at each cell in the first three rows individually, Alex saw Remington in the fourth row. He picked up his pace, dragging the picture with him over to the cell.

Remington was sitting up against the back wall of the cell, eyes closed, and arms crossed. The person in the cell directly next to him frowned as Alex stopped in front of Remington's cell.

"Rem," the guy said, staring at Alex.

"Mm?" was Remington's lazy response, but he didn't open his eyes or move at all.

"I think you have a visitor…"

Remington frowned before opening his eyes. He looked to the front of his cell and saw the small mouse on the other side next to the picture.

Remington crawled over to the front of the cell and stopped at the bars. He took the picture from the mouse who just watched him.

Remington sat back on his heels, holding onto the picture with both hands as he looked at it. Alex saw the sadness in his eyes, then Remington switched his gaze back to the mouse.

"I appreciate the gesture, Alex, but I don't think this is going to unlock that door," he said, already knowing what was going on. It wasn't every day a mouse came to the rescue. Remington sighed, shifting to sit on the floor properly. The guy in the other cell just watched and listened. "Even if you got that door unlocked, I can't get out of here. They'd stop me before I reached the top floor."

The mouse squeaked at Remington who just rolled his eyes, not saying anything to him.

The guy in the next cell looked at Remington. "Can you maybe explain to me what's going on?"

"Cole, this is Alex. Alex, this is Cole." Remington introduced them to each other.

The mouse squeaked at Cole who just gave a confused nod in return.

Remington looked at Alex again as Alex slipped through the bars into the cell.

"Look, man, I appreciate you coming down here to help, but there's not really anything you can do right now. Did Craig get my letter?"

Another squeak.

"I'll take that as a yes," Remington said.

Cole looked at Remington who hadn't moved from where he was sitting on the floor, but his gaze was back on the picture Alex had brought him.

"What are we going to do?" Cole asked. Remington's gaze never left the picture. "We can't stay here. They're going to kill both of us, especially you, Rem. Seriously, we don't know how long they're going to sit there before they decide to off you."

"There's nothing I can do, Cole!" Remington snapped. Cole sighed and sat down while Alex wandered around the cell, looking for any possible way to get Remington out. "I'm a Twelve, Cole! Graith outranks me, which is why he gets to make all these decisions! He's got a lot of influence on the rest of the higher ranks because he does whatever they want him to do. Even if I wanted to, I can't do anything because no one's gonna listen to a damn Twelve when they have a Thirteen in their ears all the time."

Alex came back over, squeaking at Remington who looked at him.

"I appreciate it, Alex, but I've no idea what you want."

The little mouse dashed out of the cell and back into the darkness of the room. A minute or so later, Alex, no longer the mouse, came to a sudden stop in front of the cell, looking at where Remington was sitting on the floor.

"You're seriously gonna get yourself killed doing that," Remington commented.

"I don't care, as long as it helps you get out," Alex said.

Remington pushed himself up off the floor, Cole following suit and trying to figure out what was going on. Alex ignored the look he was getting from Cole as Remington moved forwards, leaning his head against the front bars of the cell.

"Look, are you sure you're a rank Twelve?" Alex asked.

Remington looked up at him, a confused look on his face now. "Of course, I'm sure. Why wouldn't I be?"

Cole listened in on their conversation as Alex shifted uncomfortably, not wanting to be easily seen for too much longer.

Alex gave a rushed shrug. "I don't know. Graith was talking about not wanting word to get out about you."

"Probably about my traitorous ways," Remington said sarcastically, waving his hands in front of Alex's face before he turned and moved back into the cell. "Everyone would know about that by now, though, so who even cares?"

Alex put his hands on his hips as he watched Remington begin pacing the length of his cell, picture in hand the entire time. He wasn't about to let that go.

"Why does Graith hate you so much?" Alex asked.

Cole just looked between Alex and Remington, trying to keep track of what was happening.

Remington stopped pacing and looked at Alex with an annoyed expression.

"He just does!" he exclaimed, a few other cell occupants looking over at the sudden outburst. "He doesn't have to have a reason to hate me, he just does, Alex! Why does Graith hate anyone? Because he's a prick."

"But he's trying to get rid of you for good," Alex said, trying to get his theory across to the annoyed vampire who was luckily on the opposite side of the bars to him. "He's clearly threatened by you!"

"Look, he pushes me around all the time because he knows he can, because he's a higher rank, and that's it," Remington snapped. "You're going to get yourself killed if you keep this up."

Alex was not convinced there wasn't more to this. "Is that a threat?"

Remington didn't say anything in response, moving to the back of his cell again, and going back to his original position sitting on the floor, leaning back against the wall.

Alex sighed. "What rank was the vampire who turned you?"

Remington shut his eyes. "Twelve."

"Was he, though?"

Remington sighed, eyes still closed and arms back to being crossed. "I don't see why they'd lie about a high rank, Alex."

"Because they're vampires! They're evil!" Alex exclaimed. Cole rolled his eyes and sat down where he was in the front corner of his cell. "Come on, Rem, there's clearly some kind of conspiracy going on here."

"You think what you want, Alex," Remington said in defeat. Alex was not impressed with his attitude. "At the end of the day, I have no rights because there are higher ranks than me and there's nothing I can do about it."

Alex looked between Remington and Cole, Cole returning his gaze as Remington stayed where he was.

"What's the highest rank in this place?"

Cole glanced over at Remington who didn't move before he looked back to the determined Alex. "Twenty."

Alex nodded. "And who turned Remington?"

Cole gave a bit of a shrug, and Alex looked at Remington. He didn't respond straight off, but eventually he sighed, not opening his eyes or uncrossing his arms.

"His name was Bailey Adams," he said, knowing that Alex wasn't about to let this go.

"And they tell you he was a Twelve," Alex stated.

"He was!" Remington suddenly shouted, eyes open and anger on his face now. He was sick of Alex and his idiot theories. "Drop it, Alex!

They're not about to lie about ranks just because they don't like me, just because they don't want me in the upper class, alright? Bailey was a Twelve, he turned me first and I took that position when he got killed. The higher ranks don't like me because I'm independent, because I don't fit their 'vampire criteria', alright? You happy?"

Alex looked at him sadly, and Remington spoke again, but more softly.

"If you keep pushing this, I'm never getting out of here," he said. He held the picture up for Alex to see. "I'm never going home to this no matter what, so really, does it matter? I'm already dead, Alex. I've been dead for seven years and this..." He indicated to the picture. "This is all I have of my life before all of this. This is the only thing my brothers have left of me back home, pictures from before I disappeared.

"They don't know I'm dead. They don't know what happened to me seven years ago and they never will. My younger brother was only sixteen when I disappeared, and I never came home. He's grown up without me now and, truth be told, I'm honestly just so damn close to giving up because I have nothing down here like everyone else, so why even bother trying anymore?"

Remington put the picture on the floor, crossed his arms again, and turned his head to look out the side of the cell.

"You can go home, Alex. I can't ever leave," Remington continued, even quieter this time. "My hopes of ever going home died on the same day I did."

"I can't go home," Alex said. Remington continued to look away at something across the room. "Until last year, I didn't even know I was from Upstairs. I don't remember any of it, so how can I go home?"

"You've got more chance than I have, man."

CHAPTER TWENTY-ONE

Building Bases

"I'm not about to give up on this. I hope you know that."

"Well, you should," Remington snapped, eyes on Alex again. "You don't get it, Alex. You can't do anything about this. You don't understand the vampire hierarchy, how it works."

"Then explain it to me, tell me who runs this joint."

"If I knew, I'd tell you," Remington said seriously, shifting how he was sitting. "I've been trying to find that out since Banshee's End recruited me, and I still haven't found out. Only vampires Thirteen and up are in the inner circle, because there aren't many of them. I don't think we even have any Fourteens or Fifteens at the moment. They know who runs the place." He indicated between himself and Cole. "We aren't high enough in the ranks to know who's in charge. We're not in the inner circle, we don't get a vote on anything. We do as we're told, and we deal with it."

Alex looked at him for a few more seconds before he left his post at the front of the cell, disappearing back into the darkness. Remington rolled his eyes, while Cole watched the darkness, Alex no longer in sight.

"Where's he going?" Cole asked when he saw the small mouse running back up the stairs.

Remington shrugged, staying where he was, looking at the picture on the ground off to his left. "Who knows?"

Alex continued on his way back up the staircase. He had no idea where he was going, but he was sure he'd find the right place. Surely the vampire council, or the 'higher ranks' as they were referred to, would lurk in the lower levels somewhere. He highly doubted they'd stay any closer to the surface than they had to.

It was going to be a slow process, but Alex was going to find out the truth. If Remington was right, and he really was only a rank Twelve, Alex would apologize and leave it be, but there was something inside him that was truly convinced it wasn't that simple, that there was a conspiracy going on here.

It wouldn't surprise him. They were vampires, after all, and he didn't feel they were overly trustworthy when it came down to it. Nonetheless, Alex was going to find out the truth, and he was going to somehow get Remington out of his cage and back into society.

He would do whatever it took to make sure that happened.

Danny turned the blueprints the other way, confusion on his face the entire time as everyone around him continued to work on the construction of the latest outpost. Ted, Jordan, and Shawn all peered over Danny's shoulder as he tried to interpret the layout.

Matt put his feet up on the box in front of where he'd conveniently placed himself, hands behind his head as Danny readjusted his sunglasses. Matt observed Arley making her way over to where they were.

"How does this make any sense?" Danny said, annoyance evident in his tone as he stared at the blueprints in his hands. He lowered the papers and looked at Matt. "You right there? Plan on helping any time soon?"

Matt gave a lazy shrug, watching someone who was in the middle of putting up part of a wall. Everything had somehow already been marked out, even under Danny's bad knowledge of construction.

"Not really," Matt said as Arley stopped in front of Danny and his crew.

Danny shook his head and glared at Arley, who Craig had annoyingly placed in his care. He didn't much like her. Maybe it was her attitude towards him, the way she presented herself, carried herself around like she was the best thing to ever happen to this dysfunctional Banshee's End group.

He was sure she didn't like him much either. From his understanding, he'd been given the captain position that she'd been after and would have gotten if he hadn't managed to weasel his way into the rankings that he hadn't ever wanted to be in in the first place.

But for now, she had to report to him, and so she was going to have to deal with it until Danny got promoted, demoted, died, or Craig came back.

Snow was falling around them lightly, the sunlight somehow still out, even with the cold weather. He'd come to despise the stupid snow.

"Yes?" Danny said, finally addressing her presence.

Arley regained her composure as she crossed her arms, looking directly at him, trying to keep the bitter look off her face as she addressed him.

"A few people up the back are wondering what's next with the plans," she said. "The whole back is marked out, and they want to know what's next. Do you want to come check it all before they move onto actually building the buildings?"

Danny straightened up a bit to try and look more sure of his job than he really was. He stared at her as he thought.

Arley waited patiently. She could tell he had no idea what he was doing. He usually stayed back at Banshee's End while Craig and other crews went out to do the outposts, so it was evident that he was incredibly lost.

"Well, of course I want to know what's happening and to make sure it's all good back there," Danny said with a bit of annoyance and a lot of arrogance. He looked at Shawn and Jordan. "Go check it over to make sure it's actually right."

Jordan and Shawn exchanged looks before looking back at Danny, who was giving them an unimpressed look.

"Uhhh, how do we know it's right, exactly?" Jordan asked.

Danny rolled his eyes, though his sunglasses masked it for the most part. He held up the blueprints, rolling them up.

"Make sure it matches!" he exclaimed, using the blueprint to hit Jordan upside the head, much to Jordan's annoyance. "Go!"

Danny looked back at Arley, waving his hand to dismiss her. Arley rolled her eyes and reluctantly followed Shawn and Jordan.

Matt watched on with amusement as Danny's crew wandered away. He looked at Danny, noting Ted off to his side, arms crossed as he looked around at who was where and what everyone was doing.

The sun was slowly disappearing as the low, dark clouds took over, the snow starting to get heavier.

"You've no idea what you're doing, do you?" Matt asked, the amusement clear as Danny switched his gaze to him.

"Um, of course I know what I'm doing. I obviously do this all the time, *Matthew*," Danny shot back at him, which just made Matt smile more. Danny shifted, crossing his arms, the blueprints still in his grasp. "How about you get up from there and go find something to do to help? What's the point of you being here unless you're actually doing something, hm?"

Matt watched two people walk past, chatting about something. Danny stared Matt down, his gaze never wavering as the construction continued around them.

"I am helping, just not with this ... issue," Matt said. Danny shook his head. Matt looked at him, the sun completely gone now. "Someone has to figure out how to get Chris back to his right dimension. Ain't gonna work itself out."

"And how's that going for you?" Danny asked sarcastically. He looked around. "I mean, I don't seem to see Chris anywhere! Boy, Matt, you're being so productive! I'm so glad we can count on you to get our friend back."

Matt shrugged, back to watching someone else. "You are incredibly rude sometimes, Daniel, you know that?"

Deciding to leave it alone for the time being, Danny took a deep breath and unrolled the blueprints again, needing to at least try and make it look like he knew what he was looking at. It would make sense eventually. When it did, that was when things would really take off.

No one would be laughing once this outpost was built to perfection.

"I don't know why I even bother with this bullshit," Danny sighed. He looked at Ted who was looking over his shoulder. "Can we go home yet?"

Ted shook his head, and Danny sighed again, pulling his jacket around himself a bit more, really feeling the cold as the wind picked up.

A recruit he didn't recognize stopped in front of them.

"Captain," the recruit greeted. When Danny didn't move, just looked at him, the recruit cleared his throat. "We just got word that there's been a disturbance in the next town over. We thought you needed to know."

Danny stared at him for a few seconds.

"Wonderful," he said in a dead-pan tone. "Just fucking wonderful." He looked at Ted, rolled the blueprints up and held them out to Matt who took them without a word. "Let's go get the boys and see what's going on."

"Don't worry, I'll make sure things get done according to plan," Matt said as Danny stalked off with Ted in tow. "Have fun!"

Danny gave him a slight wave to signal that he'd heard him.

CHAPTER TWENTY-TWO

Disturbance in the Town

"We're gonna split into two groups," Danny explained as they stayed near the entrance to the town. He looked around the group in front of him. "Ted, you and Jordan take half the group, Shawn and I will take the other."

He switched his gaze to his favorite recruit, Daniel. "Kid, you're with me. Make sure you stay close."

Danny raised his voice, speaking to the rest of the group. "I want even groups, so everyone pick a side and let's go."

Not waiting for any sort of complaint or backtalk, Danny turned his back and headed towards the town, a few others in tow. He'd left most of the Banshee's End people at the outpost being built, but he'd taken his usual crew since he trusted them to know what they were doing, as they'd been under his instruction for a while now.

The town was busy with people everywhere, walking the streets and talking like any other normal day. If there had indeed been some sort of disturbance, it wasn't obvious at first glance.

Danny shoved his hands in the pockets of his jacket, wishing he'd grabbed a slightly warmer one before the vampires had taken over their hideout. He missed that hideout.

"Any idea about what this so called 'disturbance' might be?" Shawn asked, having caught up as the others trailed along behind, on alert as always.

"No idea," Danny said, looking around. He'd taken his sunglasses off because of how dark it now was.

He stopped suddenly, Shawn coming to a stop as well. Everyone behind also halted, seeing there was something Danny wanted to say.

He looked solely at Shawn who returned his look with a curious gaze of his own. "It's not just me, is it? Something is definitely off in this town?"

Shawn gave a nod, and Danny looked around again, the snow obscuring his view somewhat.

"I just don't know what it is," Danny continued. He watched a few townspeople pass by, not paying any attention to them. "What is it?"

"Vampires?" Daniel asked, stepping forward and inserting himself into the conversation.

Danny slowly shook his head. "I don't think so. If they're here, they're not the main issue." He looked back at his group. "Let's keep moving. Keep a lookout and at the first sign of trouble, call for backup."

All the recruits nodded, and Danny continued on his way. The further into the town they went, the more uneasy Danny felt. Something was definitely off and, whatever it was that was causing the uneasy feeling, it wasn't good.

Halfway through the town, Danny came to a stop again, putting his hand up to signal his group to stop moving.

"Do you hear that?" he asked, tilting his head.

Shawn frowned and strained to hear whatever it was that Danny had heard.

Everyone stayed silent, no one daring to speak or move. Sure enough, in the distance, they all heard what Danny had previously heard: a chorus of terrified screams. Not waiting any longer, Danny ran, the urgency clear as the others followed, narrowly avoiding a few of the townsfolk who had been in the way.

The further they went, the clearer the screams got. Danny slowed his pace as they reached a small courtyard, arriving at almost the same time as Ted and Jordan's team.

The courtyard contained a multitude of slain bodies, presumably the people who'd been screaming. But the killers were long gone.

"Keep your guard up. Do not wander off by yourself," Danny ordered. "Pairs at all times, now move in."

Not needing to be told twice, the recruits cautiously moved into the courtyard and fanned out to check the bodies and for any survivors. Danny and his usual crew stayed back near the entrance.

A few curious civilians stopped nearby, trying to see past them, but Jordan was quick to try and handle the situation. He and Ted tried to get the civilians to move out of the way to stop them from seeing the terror in the courtyard.

"Vampires?" Danny called to his team. "What are we dealing with?"

Daniel was the one to respond and Danny was glad he was starting to get more confidence in himself since he'd been dragged onto the field team.

"Looks like vampires," Daniel said, looking over at Danny. Danny sighed and put his hands on his hips. "We need to handle this, though.

Some locals working on the outpost mentioned the presence of ghouls here after the sun goes down."

"Fuck me," Danny sighed, rubbing his temples as he shut his eyes. Ghouls were the last thing he needed.

The vampires that had ravaged the courtyard would be long gone by now. They could be anywhere, and it was already too dark to even bother trying to track them down.

"What do we need to do about the ghoul situation?" Shawn asked reluctantly, seeing that Danny was far from the mood to ask.

"Have to bury them in the graveyard, it keeps them out of the town itself," one of the recruits spoke up, Shawn looking to her. "Graveyards are on the outskirts to keep them out of town, makes it safer to walk the streets after dark."

"It's never safe to walk the fucking streets," Danny muttered to himself. He sighed. "Alright, alright, let's get this mess sorted. We'll keep a patrol here tonight in case they come back."

"Are you sure that's a good idea?" Shawn asked as the recruits got to work with their task. Danny turned his unimpressed look on him. "You really want our guys out here tonight?"

"Well, I'd rather have them here than have to run back and find vampires again. They could do a lot more damage than this." Shawn couldn't argue his point. "So, we'll clean this up and go from there."

Shawn still seemed unsure about the whole thing, but when Danny said to do something, he knew it would probably work out for the best.

"Alright, you heard the man, let's get this dealt with now!" he called out, Danny looking around as all the recruits listened to what was being said. "Move this out so we have one less thing to deal with. We'll put someone on patrol tonight to make sure this doesn't happen again. Let's get a move on!"

"Matt?"

Matt looked up from the blueprints. Arley had stopped in front of him, a bit of uncertainty on her face.

"Arley," he greeted. He shifted, looking her over as he removed his feet from the box he'd had them up on. "Can I help you?"

"Danny's not back yet," she stated. Matt already knew that. She cleared her throat. "There's apparently been another disturbance in the opposite direction."

"Another town?" Matt sighed as Arley nodded. "Alright, I'll go check it out."

"Did you need someone to go with you?" Arley asked, as Matt got up and put the blueprints down on the chair. "Surely you can't go by yourself?"

Matt shrugged, looking at her as he put his hands in his jacket pockets, feeling the cold.

"You're more than welcome to join me," he offered. He looked around. "Think everyone here'll be fine for a couple of minutes?"

Before she could respond, Matt put his hand on her shoulder and yanked her back into the darker spot behind them.

Arley blinked a few times, her head spinning as she tried to figure out what had just happened. She'd forgotten that Matt could shadow-step. How she'd forgotten that was beyond her.

Matt looked around as he waited for Arley to get her bearings back. They were on the outskirts of a town.

"This the right place?" he asked, as Arley finally looked at him, clearly feeling a bit less confused.

"This is it," she confirmed, clearing her throat. Matt gave a mindless nod as he looked around again. "One of the recruits said there was a disturbance here as well."

"Guess we should go check it out then, hey?" Matt gave her a smile before heading towards the town entrance which was lit by streetlights.

Arley quickly followed, not wanting to be left behind in the dark when it was possible there were vampires lurking. At least she knew she was with someone who wouldn't let anything happen to her and who was more than capable of defending both her and himself if it came down to it.

Matt slowed his pace as they got closer to the town. Arley took the hint and stayed back a step, not wanting to cause any trouble or get in the way. To her understanding, they were only here to scout the area, not to take care of any actual issues.

Sure, Arley was trained and had been very persistent. She was not someone who just backed off when the going got tough, but the thought of being out here in the dark with just one other person, and possibly a bunch of vampires, was terrifying. She trusted Matt not to take things too far, but she was still on edge.

They reached the town and the lack of anyone moving about the well-lit streets made Matt uneasy. Sure, most towns weren't too populated after dark. Most people stayed indoors and, especially in all this snow, it made a lot of sense. But Matt could feel there was definitely something wrong here.

Arley followed Matt through a few streets, noting the interest on Matt's face as the snow kept falling around them.

They turned a corner, and Matt quickly grabbed her arm, dragging her behind one of the houses. Arley tried to keep her breathing steady as she heard someone pass close by, the snow crunching under their feet.

Matt signaled for her to keep quiet. He moved around the house as whoever was in the street stopped moving. Matt looked around the corner, shaking his head, and Arley moved closer, trying to see what was going on.

"We've had word that Commander Taylor has gone back to Banshee's End," said an unknown male voice.

Arley and Matt both watched a large group standing in the open street, one of them uncomfortably close to them. Arley didn't like this at all.

"So, for now he's out of reach and we'll have to take him out when he's not so protected."

There was a pause as the speaker looked around at his group. There was no doubt in Matt's mind that these guys were vampires and, if that was the case, they were in a bit of trouble.

"Our move right now is against the construction of their next outpost," the leader said, voice raised so everyone would hear him. "Take them all out. Leave no survivors. Turn that entire operation upside down. We need a clear path up."

Not needing to hear any more, Matt grabbed Arley. The next second, they were back at the partially-constructed outpost, Arley's head spinning again.

"We need to get everyone out of here," Matt said.

Arley looked at him as a few people moved past them, continuing on with their jobs, unaware of the impending threat headed their way.

"We can't just up and leave," Arley insisted. "Craig ordered..."

"Fuck what Craig ordered!" Matt snapped, making Arley jump at the tone of his voice. "Right now, one man's orders are the least of my worries. We need to get everyone out of here, now. Anyone who's here when they get here is going to die."

Arley looked at him, not wanting to defy a direct order from her commander, but she knew Matt was right. She'd heard everything that had been said as well, and if they didn't act fast then there was no way any of them here would survive. The worst thing to do would be to sit around and wait.

"OK, so how are we getting everyone out?"

CHAPTER TWENTY-THREE

True Identities

Alex scurried through the underground lair, not liking this one bit. This entire idea he'd had, to prove what he'd thought for a while, was insane and now he was thinking that maybe Remington had been right and there was nothing more to it.

Ever since Craig had said that Remington was only a rank Twelve 'at the least', it had made him think there might be a chance that he was a bit higher up than that. Why else would Graith hate him so much? Besides the fact of him being a double-agent, of course.

To Alex's knowledge, Graith, as a commander, was a rank Thirteen. He didn't quite understand the vampire hierarchy, but he'd have more time to learn about it once he'd gotten Remington—and himself, and also maybe Cole—out of this wretched place.

Finding a new set of stairs against the very far wall of the level he was on, he went down them, figuring there was a reason they were so out of the way.

There were no other floor levels; the stairs just kept going down and down and down. Alex highly considered abandoning all hope and going back, but he couldn't turn back now and leave Remington stuck in that cage. He had no idea how he was going to get him out, but he'd figure that out once he'd broken this conspiracy wide open.

Eventually, the end of the winding staircase was in sight, a heavy looking door now blocking his path. Reluctantly, Alex shifted from the mouse, back to his usual human self. He looked around, taking a breath as he stopped in front of the door.

He couldn't hear a sound from the other side, which made him more uncomfortable. He pushed against the door and felt it give slightly. That was a good sign. He pushed a bit harder, wincing at the noise it made as it scraped across the concrete floor, echoing around the small landing he was on.

He held his breath and listened. Hopefully, no one had heard that.

He pushed again, a bit more aggressively this time, and the door moved enough for him to slip through. He left it open, knowing he'd need a way out quickly if something happened.

He moved in, looking around at the surprisingly nicely lit room. Luckily, no one else was in the room. The round table in the middle was solid and large, surrounded by thirteen chairs in total. The walls were, as expected, solid concrete, with multiple papers attached to certain walls.

Alex moved over to the table, seeing papers set in front of some of the chairs. He grabbed the closest ones and looked them over, feeling dread when he saw what looked like the current vampire battle strategy.

There were pictures of the outposts, a few pictures of Banshee's End, and a few outposts that were currently under construction.

Alex put the papers back where he'd found them, got his phone out and quickly snapped some pictures of the strategy before moving around the room to look at the papers stuck to the walls. Most of it was the same kind of layout as the ones on the table but, as he moved around, one of the walls in particular got his attention.

There were many pictures on the walls, all lined up with names on the pictures and ranks underneath. Alex counted twenty lines in total, from rank One, all the way up to rank Twenty. This had to be all the high ranked vampires, every single one. There was another wall of pictures, the heading above them all labelled as 'REDECEASED'.

Taking the chance, Alex snapped a picture with his phone, immediately messaging Craig's number since he'd need to know. If Alex never made it out of here, Craig wouldn't have any way of finding out this information himself.

Another group of papers on the wall next to it had the heading 'UNDERGROUND'. It took a minute or two for it to register what that meant, but upon closer inspection, Alex saw Cole's picture up there, and he realized it was a list of the vampires in the cells below. Alex quickly scanned the pictures, hoping this was going to be his proof.

Alex grabbed one of the pictures, feeling rather triumphant as he read the ranking under the name.

'REMINGTON BELL; RANK 18'

This was exactly what he'd been after. Alex held onto the picture, looking around at everything in the room. There was so much information here. There was no way he was going to get pictures of everything in such a short time.

Thinking quickly, Alex dashed back to the door, running straight back to the dungeons.

Remington was exactly where he'd left him, and Alex quickly halted in front of the cell door.

"Find what you were after?" Remington asked, sounding bored.

Alex nodded and slipped the picture through the bars, and it fell face down. Remington frowned and crawled over to see what it was, picking it up and turning it over.

Remington stayed on his knees and stared at the picture. When he didn't say anything, Alex cleared his throat, getting Remington's attention.

Remington's gaze went back to the picture seconds later. "Surely this isn't right."

"What is it?" Cole asked, curious.

"It's exactly what I thought the case was," Alex said. "They've lied this entire time. You're an Eighteen, not a Twelve."

"I don't understand why," Remington said, very confused as he continued to stare at the picture.

"Because they're vampires!" Alex exclaimed a bit too loudly, Remington signaling for him to keep his voice down. "They lie. They know when they don't want certain people on their little vampire committee, know who is and isn't fit enough, and they lie so there are no questions. Why else would Graith have such an issue with you? You're a higher rank than him."

Remington had nothing to say. Alex gave him a shrug, not knowing what else to say.

Remington suddenly looked past Alex. "They're coming downstairs. You need to move, get out of sight."

Alex nodded, not about to doubt Remington's hearing. He moved off into the darkness, while Remington stayed where he was at the front of the cell. Cole stayed next to the bars in his cell, too.

A minute or two passed before a small group of vampires stopped in front of Remington's cell, one that Remington didn't recognize at the head of the pack.

"We've been instructed to bring you to the courtroom," he said, as Remington stared him down.

"Of course you have."

The door was unlocked, and Remington quickly slipped the picture into his back pocket, the vampires not seeming to notice. The door to Cole's cell was unlocked as well. Two vampires grabbed Remington, another two grabbed Cole, and dragged them both out.

Out of the corner of his eye, Remington saw the small mouse running along behind them as they were hauled up the stairs back to the upper level.

Once on the upper level, the two of them were dragged to an open door near the end of the landing. Remington and Cole were both shoved inside, and the little mouse managed to slip inside as well before the door was shut and locked.

Remington and Cole were forced to stand in the middle of the circle of white marble flooring. Multiple people stood around the edges of the room, with a committee of six at the front. Alex saw Graith on the lower section of the committee.

"I'm sure we all know why we're here," the vampire at the very head of the committee said, his voice echoing off the walls. Remington could see the smug look on Graith's face. "We have two traitors among our ranks, and we need to decide what to do with them."

There was a chorus of shouting, displeased vampires sharing their opinions all around. Cole looked around as Remington just stared at Graith with a bitter look on his face.

"Bury them!"

"Don't let them leave!"

"Lock them up for eternity!"

Those were the most common phrases that Cole and Alex were hearing as Alex stayed near the door in case he needed to disappear quickly.

"Silence!" the head vampire shouted, and everyone quietened down. "I understand that we're all displeased with the situation, but we need to make this fair and we need to hear them out, see what they have to say before we make any sort of decision."

"No decisions made here are ever fair!" Remington shouted, his voice echoing off the white walls. He looked directly at Graith. "With him here, there's never a fair trial."

Graith kept the smug look on his face as the main vampire spoke again.

"There's been a lot of discussion over the last few hours on what to do in this situation, and the worst possible outcome is execution," he said. "The One in Charge has also agreed to this."

Remington grabbed the picture out of his back pocket, holding it up. Cole and Alex saw Graith's expression fall.

"And you can't execute an Eighteen."

There was a shocked silence, until a few vampires began talking quietly amongst themselves.

Graith glared at Remington. "How did you get that?"

"Why was I lied to this whole time?" Remington shot back. He looked at the committee members. "You're all fucking liars."

Alex was glad that Remington knew his vampire hierarchy and what was what because, if it was up to him, he wouldn't have known any of this. But he guessed that since Remington had been a vampire for so long and he'd been working as a double agent, he'd needed to know his rights in case this kind of thing happened.

"We might not be able to execute an Eighteen, but we can execute someone of Cole's ranking," Graith responded.

"Not if I say you can't," Remington said forcefully. "It doesn't matter what either of us have done, my ranking stands. You idiots made the laws, so you have to abide by them, just as we do."

The silence dragged on for what felt like forever before the main vampire spoke again.

"Unfortunately, he's correct," he announced, bringing a displeased sound from the crowd. The vampire tried to calm it down. "I know and I understand the frustrations, but rules are rules. We can't do anything against someone of that rank. The protection laws are in place for a reason and, unfortunately, we have to abide by them." He looked at Remington. "You tell us what you want to happen and we'll make it happen."

"You let me grab whatever I need from my room and you let me and Cole walk out of here," Remington said. "I know there's no possibility of you stopping anything else, any of the plans, so that's the least I can ask. You let us walk and we won't come back here unless it's to take you out."

Another frustrated murmur rippled through the crowd.

After another few minutes, the main vampire nodded. "Thirty minutes to be out."

Remington gave a nod of agreement. "That's all I need."

CHAPTER TWENTY-FOUR

A Possible Way Back

Chris sat up, messing his hair up and trying to get his vision to focus. Out of the corner of his eye, something moved, getting his attention.

Maddie gave him a smile from where she was sitting at the desk, mindlessly turning through the pages of his notebook.

"Good morning," she greeted, focus back on the notebook, chin on hand.

Chris frowned, looking around the bedroom before subconsciously pulling the blanket up a bit.

"Have you been sitting there all night?" he asked hesitantly. Maddie turned the page, not paying him any attention. "Have you been watching me sleep?"

Maddie rolled her eyes but never looked away from the notebook.

"I'm not a creep, Chris," she said defensively. She looked at him, giving him a bit of a smile. "But I may have been lurking in the corner for a few hours."

Chris gave her an unimpressed look but didn't push the matter. He pushed the blankets back, got out of bed, and went over to where she was at the desk. She turned another page, and Chris roughly grabbed the notebook out of her hands, slamming it shut and making Maddie jump.

"Hey, I was reading that!" she exclaimed as Chris left the room, notebook in hand.

"Have you ever heard of privacy?" Chris called as he went into the small kitchen, needing to find somewhere to hide the notebook so she couldn't keep reading it.

It wasn't her business, and she had no right to invade his privacy like that.

"You left it on your desk," Maddie said in her defense as she stood in the doorway, watching Chris with crossed arms.

Chris held the notebook up. "This is none of your business. For one, you shouldn't have even been in my bedroom. I'm still a bit unsettled about that, and two, you shouldn't be touching what isn't yours." He put the notebook on the dining table, right in the middle. "Don't touch."

Maddie didn't say anything or move.

"So, what's the plan for today?" she asked eventually as Chris went past her and back into the bedroom. She turned to watch Chris grab his jacket and a shirt from the small closet space on the other side of the room. "Anything fun?"

"You mean besides the end of the world?" Chris asked, pulling the shirt on, followed closely by his jacket. He adjusted his jacket as he spoke, moving over to where she was in the doorway. "I don't know about you, but I'm going out to do some reading."

Maddie frowned and watched Chris go past, put his shoes on quickly, grab the notebook off the table, then head to the front door.

"Reading for what?" she called.

Chris was already out the front door, and Maddie sighed and ran after him. She made sure to shut the door, before pulling her hood up and jogging after him. He was already quite a few paces ahead of her down the sidewalk.

She caught up and walked beside him at the same pace. They walked in silence for a few minutes.

"Are you still mad about the whole 'Hunter might be the only Dimension Walker left in existence' thing?" Maddie dared to say, getting a sidelong glance but no words from Chris. She sighed, putting her hands in her jacket pockets. "Of course you are."

"Well, what do you expect?" Chris asked. "You seriously think that's something I can just get over in a few days? No, it doesn't work like that. Unlike some people, I'm not happy here and I want to go home."

Maddie grabbed his arm, roughly pulling him to a stop. Chris gave her an annoyed look, and someone walked past, heading in the other direction, glancing at them as they passed.

"You seriously think I'm happy here?" she asked, raising her eyebrows.

Chris forced her to let go so he could cross his arms disapprovingly.

"When I first met you, you had no desire to go back home," he said. "Maybe that's the reason I think that." He looked her over. "Something's obviously changed your mind, though."

Maddie just looked at him, not offering any words on her reasoning. He was right, there was something now that had made her rethink going back to her correct dimension but, for now, that wasn't his business.

When she refused to answer him, Chris uncrossed his arms and continued on his way. Maddie stayed where she was for a few seconds before she followed along, not bothering to keep at his pace this time. Turning down a street, Chris saw his destination up ahead.

The town's library loomed above them as Chris headed up the stone steps. He pushed the door open and stepped inside, Maddie right behind him.

"So, what are we looking for, exactly?" Maddie asked as Chris stopped and looked around the large library. There were quite a few people here today.

"Anything and everything."

Maddie crossed her arms as she regarded him and someone pushed past them to get into the library properly.

"Anything that could possibly lead us back home," Chris said. "Anything on dimensions, abilities, travel, anything. Anything that might help."

Maddie seemed a bit unsure, but gave a nod, nonetheless.

"Well, OK," she said before moving past him. "Let's get to it then."

"You can't just pull the whole operation!"

"We don't have a choice!" Matt snapped, Craig shaking his head before taking a seat. "You seriously think that leaving your entire division out there to be swept up by vampires, sorry, *killed* by vampires, is going to do your movement any good? Please, tell me I'm wrong."

Craig tapped on the table as he tried to think. Matt was right, he couldn't let this happen. It was pretty well Craig's entire division out there, and he couldn't lose that.

"How long's it going to take to move them out?" he asked eventually.

"Depends where you want them and how long you want them gone for," Matt said, leaning against the table. "Because if it's down to me, I can do it in one swift hit, but if you don't want it done by me, they walk, and they won't get far."

This certainly was a predicament and Craig swore to himself, not sure what to do.

"Matt's right, you can't leave everyone there," Ash spoke up.

Craig looked between her and Matt.

"Well, what do you propose we do once they get Upstairs? What happens then?" He indicated to Matt. "Matt said that's what he and Arley heard them say. That's their next move. The whole point of the outpost near the Room of Doors is to stop this exact thing, and now I'm being told to pull the operation because they'll kill my division. Part of the reason people signed up for this movement is for this exact thing."

"It's not just your whole division, it's Danny's as well," Matt said, Craig looking at him again. "Danny's still over at one of the other towns, handling a situation over there with his guys, and the majority of his division is also down there with him. None of them know about the threat headed their way just yet."

"Danny doesn't know?"

Matt shook his head. "No. Like I said, he's been busy a town over."

Craig sighed, linking his hands together and resting them on the table, trying to think of what to do. In a sense, Matt was right, but then, so was he.

"How far in are they with the outpost?" he asked, thinking as he looked at Matt.

"Not far enough to stop anything getting through. The wall's not even up yet."

"Well, we can't just leave it unattended," Craig said. "If we do, the vampires will get straight through. We can't leave it without a fight. If they get through, they get through, but we need to at least try to stop them."

"What do you propose?" Matt asked back, his tone just as serious as Craig's. "Because I don't know how many are going to be willing enough to stay back and, most likely, die for the cause."

Another good point. Craig sighed. This time, though, he sounded defeated.

"Alright, pull the operation," he said reluctantly, Matt nodding. "Bring them back here to regroup. But anyone who wants to stay and defend can do so."

Matt gave another nod, not needing to be told twice. He headed past Craig and Ash, disappearing the moment he hit the dark shadows of the room.

Arley looked up as Matt walked over to her, the outpost still under slow construction.

"How'd it go?" she asked, arms crossed and held close to try and keep the cold out.

"As good as we'd have hoped," Matt said. "He said to pull the operation and regroup back at Banshee's End. Anyone who wants to stay back and protect the Room of Doors is more than welcome to because otherwise they're waltzing right through and Upstairs."

"Let's hope that's not the case."

Matt nodded in agreement, looking at Arley again.

"I need to go find Danny and his group and let them know what's happening. You round everyone up, explain the situation and tell them they can stay back if they want, otherwise they have to follow orders and get back to Banshee's End. I'll be back in a couple of minutes to get everyone back, so make sure everyone who's going is ready to leave."

Arley nodded, and Matt disappeared back into the shadows.

Danny was watching his crew drag bodies out of the courtyard when Matt stopped next to him. Danny glanced at him before looking back at his crew.

"We've got vampires heading towards the outpost construction," Matt informed him. "Craig's called for everyone to regroup back at Banshee's End, so we're leaving in a few minutes. Anyone who wants to is more than welcome to stay back if they want to try and stop them getting Upstairs."

"Well, unfortunately, we can't go anywhere until this is done," Danny said, watching the last body being moved out. "Gotta deal with this shit before we can even consider leaving."

"So, what are you planning on doing?"

Danny shrugged, gaze on the now empty, quiet courtyard.

"Not sure," he sighed, shifting how he was standing. "Guess we're just gonna have to make a stand."

Matt frowned. It was unlike Danny to sacrifice himself and his crew for anything other than their own benefit.

"You're staying behind?" Matt asked, confused.

Danny shrugged, glancing at him as a few of his crew came back into the courtyard.

"I don't think we have much choice," he admitted. He looked at Matt fully. "We'll do what we can, keep 'em off your back for as long as we can. We're not done here yet, and we can't have you waiting all night for us. Just get everyone else out and if we make it, you'll know."

Matt was unsure but gave a nod anyway. "Just be careful."

Danny smiled slightly. "Always."

Chris mindlessly turned the page of the book on the table in front of him, his mind not taking in as much information as it had earlier. They'd been here for hours and, so far, nothing had come from it.

Maddie was much the same, sitting across the table from him, head on hand as she turned page after page. It had been a very slow day.

"Shame you don't know any shadow-steppers," she noted out of nowhere, getting Chris's attention. "Shame."

"Wait, why?" Chris asked, interest piqued now.

Maddie looked up from the book. She didn't speak straight off, but indicated to the book she'd been mindlessly leafing through.

"It says here there's an unproven theory that some might be able to stretch their abilities over dimensions," she said. "Apparently one guy did it years ago, like fifty something years ago, but that's just a rumor and no one can prove it."

Chris stood up quickly, leaned across the table and grabbed the book from her, sliding it towards himself. He read over the page, taking the information in. This might not have been so crazy, after all.

"Alright, I think we're done for the day," he said.

He picked up the books that were in front of him and put them back on the shelves where he'd found them. Maddie did the same.

Chris then left the library, with Maddie not far behind.

"Something about that give you an idea?" she asked as she caught up to him, walking next to him under the streetlights as they headed back to Chris's residence.

"I know someone who can shadow-step," Chris said. The urgency in his pace made Maddie have to keep jogging a bit to keep catching up. "That might be our way out."

Once they were back in Chris's house, he grabbed a pen from the desk in the bedroom, then went back out into the kitchen, sitting down and opening the notebook.

"Another letter?" Maddie asked, standing near the front door and watching him.

"It's the only way I can contact anyone back home since Ash never responded to my last letter about the other way we could communicate. So yes, another letter," Chris said in a mildly defensive tone. "And if it helps us get out of here, I'm more than happy to write another letter."

CHAPTER TWENTY-FIVE

A Change of Plans

"Remington's here to see you, but they won't let him through the gates."

Craig got up from where he'd been sitting, the urgency evident. Ash quickly followed him out of the barracks, past quite a few people who'd already heard about what was going on down at the gates and who were also heading there.

"What's going on?" Craig called as they got close to the gates.

One of the gates was open but many recruits were standing in the way. Other residents of Banshee's End kept their distance but still wanted to know what was going on.

Everyone moved out of the way as Craig reached the gates, with Ash trailing behind.

"Commander," one of the recruits closest to the gate greeted him. The recruit indicated to the space outside the gates. "They won't come through until we let their friend in with them."

Craig frowned, moving past him to see what was happening. Sure enough, Remington was outside the gate. Alex was with him, and Cole too. Craig's expression fell, understanding now what was going on.

"You know we can't let him in," Craig said, indicating to Cole as Alex shifted awkwardly where he was standing on Remington's left. "We can let you and Alex in, but we can't let him in."

"Well, you're gonna have to," Remington said. "Because we're not coming in until you let Cole in with us."

Craig sighed. He looked back at the recruits crowding the gateway, seeing all the residents still watching.

"Move them all back inside, it's late and we'll deal with this."

The recruit he'd spoken to gave a nod of understanding, doing as he was told and trying to get everyone to move back. Craig looked back at the issue in front of him.

"Why should we let him in?" he asked Remington, indicating to Cole.

"Because I'm asking you nicely," Remington said through clenched teeth.

Craig stared at him for a few minutes as he tried to decide what to do.

"If he does anything against the rules, I am holding you personally accountable!" he ended up saying, pointing at Remington. He looked at Cole. "I swear to God, don't screw this up for yourself."

Cole didn't say anything, and Craig shook his head. He indicated for them to come inside, moving back inside the gates. Alex rushed inside first, glad to be back in the middle of nowhere where the vampires were friendly and wouldn't try to kill them.

"I'll let Jacob know you're here and we'll set up once Matt gets back with everyone," Craig said, once everyone was safely within the walls and the gates were shut again. He stopped halfway up the hill, looking back at his group. "Get him down to processing so we can get him in and out with no issues."

A couple of recruits asked Cole to go with them, to which he obliged.

Craig looked at Remington. "You'd better have a damn good reason for bringing him here."

Remington scowled at him but didn't say anything in response, so Craig continued on his way, far from pleased with how the day had turned out.

Ash stayed with Craig, Alex hot on their heels as they headed towards the church. Remington stayed where he was, not following them or going anywhere.

"You know he wouldn't bring him here unless there was a serious reason," Ash said.

Craig didn't even look at her as he walked and didn't say anything in return. Eventually they reached the church, Craig clearly expecting to find Jacob down there at this time of night.

"I'll meet you guys at the usual place," he said before going up the few steps and disappearing inside.

Ash sighed, Alex shifting where he was standing next to her.

"Well, isn't he just cheerful," she said, arms crossed. She looked Alex over. "Are you OK? You didn't run into any trouble?"

Alex shook his head, and Ash managed a smile, relieved that he was all right.

"It was super scary, though," he admitted. When Remington appeared next to Ash, Alex's expression suddenly changed, a thought having occurred to him. "Oh! Did Craig get the pictures I sent through to him? Did they come through?"

Ash frowned. "What pictures?"

Realizing Craig more than likely hadn't seen the crucial information he'd sent him, Alex rushed off, up the steps of the church.

Ash and Remington just watched without saying a word.

"I'm gonna go find Cole," Remington said, leaving Ash standing on her own in front of the church.

Ash watched him go, waiting until he was out of sight before she also went into the church, needing to know what was happening down below.

"I don't think it's a smart idea having him here," Jacob was saying as Ash made it down to the operations room. Alex was shifting from foot to foot, eagerly waiting to tell them what he knew. "I get that Remington's vouching for him, but Cole runs his own team. He's in charge of the team that pushed through into Wonderland. It's not safe to have him here."

Alex raised his hand, wanting to interrupt, and Jacob indicated for him to say something.

"I sent you some pictures," he said.

Craig frowned and got his phone out and switched it on to see what he was talking about.

"From when I was in the vampire lair," Alex continued. "I found their operations room, managed to take a few pictures, thought they'd be useful to you and everything you're doing here."

They all stayed quiet as Craig looked through what Alex had sent him, watching as his expression fell.

"This is bad," he commented. He shook his head slowly. "This isn't good."

"I, I don't know too much of what I sent you," Alex admitted. "I sent you what I think is their strategy, their current movements, some hierarchy rankings, but anything else, I don't know."

Craig looked at him, Alex giving him an encouraging smile.

"First off," Craig began, all of them listening. "Did Remington know he's an Eighteen?"

Jacob raised his eyebrows. "Eighteen? That's six ranks higher than what we thought he was. That means that he outranks Graith."

"He didn't, but it's the only reason he's alive right now," Alex said truthfully. "Well, not 'redeceased' as they say in the vampire lair."

Craig sighed, messing his hair up and shaking his head as he took the information in.

"I think we need to talk to him," he said seriously, putting his phone away. "Cole might also know something, things that Remington doesn't. I know we're on limited time. Hopefully, Matt can get back here soon, unless he's decided to try and protect the outpost operation." He looked at Jacob. "Do we need to wait for him to discuss this?"

"We should have everyone here," Jacob said. He hesitated before speaking again. "Do we need to ask a few others to join us from Upstairs?"

Craig was unsure. Since they'd been working on their operations over the last twelve months, after Marion and Chris had vanished into a different dimension, everyone else, as far as he was aware, who didn't belong down here, had gone home.

That was why he'd been so surprised to see Matt turn up out of nowhere. He hadn't just stopped in for a friendly chat. He'd, for sure, come to check on what was happening, and now he was still here for some reason.

No one else had come down with him, though, and that was a big indication that there was a high chance that they wanted nothing to do with the operation.

But it *was* going to be their problem when the Legion broke through Upstairs.

"We need to get that outpost finished," Craig said. "Someone contact Matt and tell him to do whatever he has to in order to keep it under construction. He'll figure something out."

Arley didn't like what Matt was doing, standing around and talking to someone on the phone. He'd been adamant about getting everyone out but, when she tried to get everyone to leave, she'd discovered that nearly everyone was opting to stay to try to complete more of the construction.

Danny and his team still weren't back, and it was a lot darker now, with snow falling a lot heavier than it had been earlier in the day.

"Leave it with me," Matt was saying to whoever was on the other end of the line. "I'll step in and see you once I'm done."

He hung up and put his phone back in his pocket. He wandered back over, stopping in front of Arley who just waited for him to say something.

"We've had a change of plans, Miss Beckett," he said, putting his hands into his jacket pockets. "Your lovely commander wants us to finish building this outpost and then get started on the next one."

Arley's expression fell. Was he serious? There was no way Craig would blatantly make them continue to work, not with a team of vampires headed their way. How long did they even have before the undead descended on them?

"So," Matt continued upon Arley's silence. "I have an idea on how we're making it through this, but you're going to have to keep a watch on things down here, and I have to step out real quick. Understood?"

Arley didn't really want him going anywhere. Everyone seemed to be abandoning their teams right now. Granted, Matt wasn't technically in charge of anyone's team, nor was he part of any, so he could come and go as he pleased.

"Where are you going?" she ended up asking. "How long are you going to go for? We don't even know how close the vampires are, how long it'll take them to get here. You're OK to leave us all undefended?"

Matt watched someone hurry past in the dull lantern light that they were all working by.

"Ten minutes, that's all I need. All you have to do is hold the fort until I get back, OK?" Matt could see Arley was very unsure about this proposal, but he wasn't giving her any choice. This wasn't a request, it was an order. "Look, Miss Beckett, if you're serious about being in a captain's position, you'll hold out until I get back, you'll take charge while I'm not here, and you'll get shit done. Craig's put you here for a reason, he has trust in you, and you need to trust yourself to make sure everyone here knows what's happening and what they need to do. So do your damn job, and I'll see you in ten minutes."

Not giving her the chance to say anything, Matt vanished into thin air.

Arley sighed and looked around as more people passed by. It was dark enough outside right now that Matt hadn't even had to find any shadows, he could just disappear as he liked from any location.

Arley really hoped he wasn't going to be any longer than ten minutes.

CHAPTER TWENTY-SIX

The First Line of Defense

Gates sighed and lit a new cigarette as Matt joined him and Zeke outside.

"The answer's no, Matt," Gates said without even waiting for him to speak. "I know where you've been, and I know why you're here."

Matt leant his chin on his hand, watching Gates take a drag on his cigarette, never meeting his gaze.

"I don't know why you're still bothering," Zeke commented, clicking his fingers and lighting his own cigarette without any lighter. "Blaine's not going with you, and neither am I."

As glad as Matt was that Zeke had somehow managed to restart his fire ability over the last six months, all he'd been using it for was smoking his life away. From all the reading he'd done when he was bored, he still hadn't figured out how Zeke's ability had restarted. But he wasn't going to question it, as he was going to come in handy if he agreed to help out downstairs.

"You can come straight back up," Matt said, holding his hands up in his defense. Zeke rolled his eyes, and Gates blatantly ignored the conversation. "I'll bring you here myself."

Gates sighed, looking at Matt who returned his gaze. "What's their issue this time?"

"Still the vampires," was the response, Gates shaking his head. "And it's going to be our problem very soon if we don't get onto this now."

"How?" Zeke asked. Skye stepped outside and Gates glanced over at her, getting a smile. Zeke lowered his voice, leaning in to keep the conversation between the three of them. "I don't know if you've noticed, Matt, but we're up here, and they're down there."

"And if we don't push them back *right now*, we'll be up here, and so will they," Matt said back harshly, also keeping his voice down. "So, I think it's in everyone's best interests to go on a *road trip* for a few days."

Zeke sat back in his chair. He exchanged looks with Gates who was clearly thinking about their best option. Gates watched Skye go back inside, before he sighed and responded.

"Alright, fine," he said, far from happy. He pointed at Matt. "This is on you."

Gates finished his cigarette, stubbing the remainder out in the ashtray. He pushed his chair back and left the table.

Zeke sighed and ran his hands through his hair, making it stick up everywhere.

"Has it gotten that bad?" he asked, watching Gates talk to Skye by the back door. "They're still a problem, even a year on?"

Matt nodded. "Yeah, I got bored so I went to have a look. It's not good."

He felt his phone buzz with a message. He got it out and unlocked it, seeing that Craig had sent him something.

Gates came back over but didn't retake his seat, just stood with his hands on the back of the chair he'd abandoned moments prior.

A frown crossed Matt's face as he read the message from Craig about something that had turned up for him at Banshee's End. He locked his phone. Craig would have to wait. He'd take deal with it once the immediate vampire threat was taken care of.

"We should head down. I told them I'd only be ten minutes."

Arley jumped as someone appeared next to her. She'd been nervously waiting for Matt to come back, and now he had, with two other people she didn't recognize.

Danny still wasn't back.

"Beckett, this is Gates and Zeke." Matt introduced his two companions, neither of whom looked thrilled to be here. "Boys, this is Arley Beckett, Craig's second in charge. I'd say we listen to her, but we don't." Arley shot him a look, Matt putting his hands in his jacket pockets. "Do we know how we're looking on the vampire front?"

Arley shook her head, moving a little as a few people bustled past. It was clear to her that at least one of the three in front of her right now had been smoking prior to turning up, and she wrinkled her nose at the smell. She was sure that it wasn't Matt, though. She'd have seen signs of it by now since she'd been hanging around him at the outpost construction.

"No one's seen anything yet," she said. "I have people stationed right around the site, but there's been no signs of any vampires yet."

Zeke looked around, not liking the snow. Obviously, Ash hadn't fixed the weather problem in the last twelve months.

"I need to go and check on Danny and his team." Matt looked at Gates and Zeke. "You boys know what to do." He looked directly at Zeke. "Keep it under control, man. It's taken all day to get this far with the structure, don't ruin it."

Zeke rolled his eyes and shoved his hands in his pockets as Matt disappeared.

Arley looked Gates and Zeke over, Zeke staring at her as she did so. Gates just looked bored.

"So, are you two our ... defense?" she asked. "No offence, but I don't see how two ordinary people can help in a vampire situation."

Gates looked at Zeke, something having occurred to him. Zeke returned his look, both of them ignoring Arley who wasn't happy about it.

Trust Matt to be friends with people like this.

"Do you think," Gates started to say. Zeke raised his eyebrows, interested to know what his friend was thinking. "That if they bite the barrier, it'll bite me?"

Zeke frowned. He hadn't thought of that. Arley had no idea what they were talking about, but she wasn't about to ask.

"Only certain vampires can turn people, right?" was Zeke's counter question, making Gates think this time. "So, like, unless it's a super strong vampire who can turn people, I think you'll be alright."

"I hope you're right."

Over in the next town, Danny looked at Matt who'd appeared directly next to him. Danny was still in the same place where Matt had seen him last, still with his arms crossed. It looked like he hadn't moved a muscle.

"Any progress?" Matt asked, watching some of Danny's recruits heading their way.

"Last one's being buried as we speak," Danny said. Matt nodded slowly to himself. "And so far, no undead in sight." He shifted, facing Matt more. "What's the plan? Are we going back to the outpost site, or are we going back to Banshee's End?"

"Craig's had a change of heart. We're defending the site," Matt said, Danny sighing, more in annoyance than anything else. "I can take you and your clique back if you want, we have our line of defense. We have to get this built, that's the priority."

"Whatever the commander wants, I guess." Danny whistled loudly and all his recruits looked at him. "Pack it up, everyone! Let's go!"

Having Matt with them meant they didn't have to go very far to get back to the outpost construction site. They were all back within literal seconds, Danny not liking the dizzy spell that came with the fast travel.

"Any progress on getting Chris back?" Gates asked, having made himself at home where Matt had been sitting earlier in the day. Zeke had set up camp next to him, although sitting on the ground. The two of them had been passing a lit cigarette between themselves. "Or has everyone given up on that now?"

Matt shrugged, while Danny indicated to his team to get back to work. His three thieves stayed with him, though, not about to let him out of their sight.

"That's Ashley's business," Matt said. Arley, again, listened in and had no idea what they were talking about. "Well, I was looking into it, but I keep coming up empty, I'm afraid."

Gates thought about it, taking his feet off the box. Zeke finished off the cigarette and leaned his head on his hand as he listened, watching someone moving essential pieces of outpost across the snow that had settled on the ground.

"Do you know if any areas cross over with the one he's in?" Gates asked. "I might be able to talk to him if we can find a crossover path, same way I contacted you when you stepped off the Yellow Brick Road."

"We'll figure it out once we get back to Banshee's End," Matt said, shaking his head. "Right now, we have more important things to worry about, namely, vampires."

Gates understood, pushing himself to his feet. "Tell me where you need me to set up."

"What's your coverage?" Matt asked, as Zeke hauled himself up off the ground. "More or less than when we were at the City?"

Gates let out a breath as he thought about it.

"Shit, probably more now?" he said. "I mess around with it when Skye's not home. I think I can get more than I was able to at the City." He looked around, calculating the area. "Yeah, this should be pretty easy, I can hold it up." He switched his gaze to Matt, very serious, now. "I'm not going to risk being turned into a vampire, though, Matt. Got it?"

Matt gave a single nod, Gates narrowing his eyes at him. They all heard someone shout from not too far away, signaling that something was happening.

Arley looked at Matt, worried, but trying very hard not to show it.

"This is what you signed up for, Miss Beckett," Matt said. He indicated to the group of them. "So, tell us what to do."

CHAPTER TWENTY-SEVEN

In Need of Backup

Chris stopped reading, exchanging looks with Maddie.

"Did you feel that?" he asked. She immediately nodded, the worry clear on her face. "That's not good."

Neither of them moved as the ground shook again. The few other people in the library also stopped and looked around, confused. Multiple books tumbled off the shelves, and everyone looked worried.

Chris had never been in an earthquake. He knew about the damage that they did, and he knew the signs, but something was telling him this was no normal earthquake.

He shut the book, leaving it on the table and getting up. Maddie followed him outside as the ground shook again. She almost lost her balance, grabbing onto Chris unintentionally to stop herself from falling over.

"How long do you think we have?" Chris asked, surveying the damage that had already been done.

Clouds had started to come over, signaling rain. Thankfully, no houses or buildings had been damaged yet, but there were a lot of cracks snaking across the ground. There were also shallow holes amongst the cracks, and a few trees had fallen over nearby.

"I don't know," Maddie said, answering Chris's question. "I've never been in this situation before. I don't know how long it takes between the earthquakes starting, and the dimension collapsing. It could be hours, it could be days. I really have no idea."

She didn't say anything else, neither of them speaking as the ground shook again.

All Chris could do was hope that Matt had received his S.O.S.

Gates pushed a vampire back off his barrier, the vampire falling to the ground from the force of it. Zeke quickly came over and set the vampire on fire, just as another came forward to try and break through Gates's barrier.

The burning vampire screamed and more of them joined up to try and push their way through Gates who was starting to lose his footing.

"We can't keep this up, Matt!" he shouted. He slid back a few steps as multiple vampires threw themselves against the clear barrier, using a lot more force than he'd expected. "They're gonna get through. The more they pile against me like this, the less space I'm gonna be able to cover!"

Arley watched, stunned, as Zeke lit up a whole row of vampires, all of them shrieking and unable to put the fires out. There were a lot more out here than they'd initially anticipated.

Danny had taken his crew further towards the back of the construction site to cover more ground there. Arley saw a few bright flashes of lightning overhead every so often, so at least he was doing his part.

"We're gonna need more people," Gates said, pushing hard against the vampires to keep them back. "I can't keep this up. I'm taking physical damage, Matt!"

Gates glanced at Matt just in time to see him disappear. He growled in annoyance, shoving the barrier forward again, and managing to push a group of the undead off and onto the ground. He was just going to trust that Matt knew what he was doing.

Alex jumped as Matt suddenly appeared next to him, and he moved out of the way out of pure instinct.

"We need more people," Matt said before Craig could get a word in. "Just enough to push them back. Blaine and Zeke can only cover for so long and there are more of them than we expected."

Ash raised an eyebrow. She should have known that he'd go and get his friends to help out. It was obviously a lot easier for him to convince them than it had been for her.

"How many do you need?" Craig asked. "We can't spare many, but we have enough that you can take some. Do you know how many you're dealing with?"

"Too many."

Craig understood without having to ask any further questions. He headed straight to the staircase that led out of the church. Ash and Alex followed, but Jacob stayed where he was in the operations room. The others down there with him also didn't move, knowing not to leave.

Matt was already waiting outside the front of the church by the time the three of them had opened the grand doors and stepped outside.

Not saying a word, Craig headed straight toward the barracks, barreling past people who just watched him as he kept up the fast pace.

Craig went into the barracks, the lights in the front room were already on, and none of them bothered to close the door. Craig headed further into the barracks, turning lights on as he went, not caring that there were some recruits asleep before their shift.

"Get up, let's go!" Craig called throughout the rooms as he passed through, drawing multiple groans of annoyance. "Five minutes and you're to be out the front, move!"

He did this for another three rooms before deciding that would be enough people. He stood at the back of the last room watching the recruits moving around.

"Commander!" Doug stopped in front of him. "If you need an extra hand, I'd like to volunteer."

Craig looked him over. "You sure?"

Doug nodded confidently to confirm it.

"Alright, if Jacob's OK with you coming with us, you can."

Doug nodded again to confirm that Jacob was OK with it. Even if he wasn't, Craig was just going to have to take his word for it. Matt was under the impression that Craig would be going with them, too.

Craig, Ash, Alex, and Matt followed the last recruit out to the dimly lit area at the front of the barracks, where the rest of them were waiting to be told what was happening.

"Here's what's going to happen," Craig began, addressing everyone. A few civilians walking by stopped to watch and listen, too. "We've got a siege happening over in Wonderland where we're trying to set up an outpost. It's crucial that we push the Legion back off this construction site, we need these outposts built, especially this one. They've requested more people, so that's where we're all heading.

What happens, happens, but as long as we can prevent them getting further through, we're doing our jobs. Is that clear?"

Everyone acknowledged they'd heard him, and Craig looked satisfied. He looked at Ash and Alex.

"Are you two staying here?" he asked.

Remington and Cole both stopped near him, and Craig switched his gaze to them, several of the recruits shifting uncomfortably. "Neither of you are leaving this outpost."

"We'll stay back with them," Ash spoke up, trying to take some of the pressure off Remington who just looked at her. Ash managed a smile. "We'll keep them out of trouble."

Craig didn't argue, having more important things to deal with right now than their informant and his pesky friend.

Matt took Craig not saying anything more as his cue and disappeared the group.

Once everyone had gone, Ash looked at Remington and Cole. Remington stared at her, while Cole purposely avoided her gaze, instead watching people walking past at a safe distance. As the local civilians left the area, they made sure to steer very clear away from the two vampires.

"Any ideas of what to do while we wait to hear any news?" she asked. "Since you can't go and help in the operations room."

"We were hoping we could have helped," Remington admitted. A sad look appeared on his face. "But I guess Craig doesn't want us to."

"I don't get why he's so mad at you," Ash said.

She got no immediate answer, as Remington put his hands in his pockets uncomfortably and just stood there.

"Honestly, Ash," was how he chose to start his response. "Craig's pissed off because he has no informant anymore and now, since I've come back with Cole, he's got his guard up." He glanced at Cole.

"I understand it, but he needs time to come around. He just has something a bit more important to deal with first."

Remington sighed and walked away, Cole taking the cue and following. He figured that was his best option, rather than standing around somewhere in a place that no one wanted him in.

Ash watched them go, Alex shifting uncomfortably next to her.

"I guess we just go and try to help the operations team," Ash said, turning and heading back to the church where she might be of some use to Jacob and his team.

Alex stood there, torn between following her and following his vampire friends.

CHAPTER TWENTY-EIGHT

A Means of Communication

Remington and Cole were sitting in the manor near the back of the outpost, minding their own business since they weren't allowed to help with anything. They were bored. If Banshee's End didn't have the operations room below the church, they wouldn't be in this situation.

Remington jumped as Matt appeared next to him.

"I thought you'd gone to help with the vampire problem," Remington said, leaning his head on his hand.

"I have more important things to work on," Matt said. He sat down on the chair closest to Remington. "Craig can take care of it, Blaine's there. I can only do so much."

Remington shrugged and Matt leaned back in his chair, putting his feet up on the table and crossing his arms. He looked at Cole with interest.

"Heard you might know a thing or two about Dimension Walkers," he stated. "Do you know how many we have left?"

Cole shrugged, also leaning back in his chair.

"Couldn't tell you," he said, which wasn't the answer Matt wanted to hear. "Most of us don't know who's who until we run into them. We're not connected to each other for a reason. Why?"

Matt took the information in. Without answering, he stood up and vanished. Cole raised his eyebrows, but Remington just shook his head, not bothering to say anything.

The barracks were quiet at this time of the night, mainly because Craig had taken the majority of the recruits to the Wonderland outpost as backup. There was not a sound as Matt went over to the desk in Craig's room, finding what he was after straight off. The letter addressed to him was sitting on the top of everything, just waiting for him to look at it.

He picked it up and turned it over, seeing that it was from Chris. Without hesitation, he opened the envelope, unfolded the letter and skimmed through it.

Normally Chris sent letters to Ash, but upon reading what was in this letter, he understood why it had been sent to him.

Seconds later, he was in the operations room. Ash was the first one to notice him.

"Did Chris send you details of an easier way to communicate with him?" Matt asked as everyone stared at him.

Ash nodded. "It was in one of the letters he sent me recently, but I haven't had the chance to read it properly. I don't have it with me, it's back at the castle in Wonderland."

Not needing any further clarification, Matt disappeared.

"What does he want to know that for?" Alex asked, confused.

"Your guess is as good as mine."

Back in Wonderland, Nixx looked up from whatever he was doing as Matt wandered over, looking at a piece of paper.

"Thought you'd be too preoccupied with the threat outside," Nixx commented, then went back to what he'd been studying before the interruption.

"Everyone else has a handle on it, they'll be fine. I'm sure they'll call if they need me," was Matt's nonchalant response. Matt stopped next to Nixx's desk and held the piece of paper out. Nixx stopped what he was doing again and looked at him. "Chris sent this over to Ash, recently I'd assume. Can you tell me if this is a safe method of communication?"

Nixx took the paper from him, and Matt waited patiently for him to read the information over, watching his mind ticking over as he did so.

"Hm," was Nixx's initial response. He stared at the words on the paper. "Mirror scrying is usually more to do with witches, but I guess it's not technically scrying, since you're not spying on people. It should be fine." He held the paper back out to Matt who took it. Nixx offered him a smile. "I doubt it'll drag you into the other dimension."

Matt chose not to bite at Nixx's jest and took his leave for the time being.

After having read the letter that Chris had sent, plus now knowing that he could talk to him through a mirror, and also getting no information of use from Cole, Matt knew that he needed to get a move on trying to get Chris back.

How exactly he was going to do that was the question, though. Sure, Chris had said there was a theory running around that shadow-steppers could possibly step between dimensions, but Matt had his doubts.

That would be too easy.

He went into one of the many empty rooms in the castle and found what he was after. He stood in front of the mirror and looked back to the piece of paper in his hand. At least the instructions Chris had provided were simple and easy to follow.

Matt was just hoping that this wasn't going to become a regular thing.

Chris looked away from his journal as he heard something. Maddie heard it too. He would have been surprised if she hadn't, considering her vampire hearing.

He stood up and walked through the small house trying to pinpoint the sound, Maddie rushing after him to see what was happening.

He found the right room—the one Marion had spent most of her time in—stopping in the doorway as he saw the light glow around the edge of the mirror on the wall. He and Maddie exchanged looks, Maddie indicating for Chris to go into the room first.

Knowing he couldn't stand there and wait it out, as he was sure that someone had finally decided to use the instructions he'd sent over to Ash, he hesitantly went into the room and stopped in front of the mirror. Maddie stayed back in the doorway, unsure.

She'd been the one who'd told him how this worked, so it didn't fill him with much confidence to see her reaction. Maybe she knew about it but had never actually done it before?

Chris cautiously reached out, being very careful as he touched the mirror. He drew his hand back again as the glow around the mirror intensified, connecting seconds later.

"God, you've no idea how happy I am to see you," Chris said when he saw Matt on the other side of the mirror.

"First time anyone has said that, but sure," Matt said with a smirk, crossing his arms. Chris mirrored his position. "How's the situation on your side?"

Chris shook his head and Maddie dared to come in and join the conversation. Matt glanced at Maddie but didn't comment on her presence.

"Not great," Chris said. "We're getting frequent earthquakes, with less time in between them each time, and they're getting stronger. It's really not good. I don't think we've got long left, to be honest, Matt."

"I got your letter," Matt said, and Chris was glad to hear it. Hopefully, this would finally be some good news. "Unfortunately, I think it's all just hearsay. I'm pretty sure I can't make it between dimensions, let alone back again. I'd know by now if I could, but I just don't think it's possible." Chris's expression fell. "Trust me, if I could, I'd come join you, but I don't think it's possible."

Chris sighed. That wasn't what he'd wanted to hear.

"So, what are we meant to do?" he asked as the ground started shaking again. Maddie quickly grabbed onto him to stop herself from falling over. "We probably only have a couple of days at the most. Hunter's already been and gone, so what are we meant to do?"

"I spoke to one of Remington's friends, Cole," Matt said. Maddie recognized the name straight away. "He said he doesn't know of anyone who can help. He was apparently one of the Dimension Walkers before the vampires got him."

"Yeah, we figured something like that had happened," Chris admitted. He sighed. "We're under the impression that Hunter's the last one. We have four people here that were Dimension Walkers, and with this Cole guy also being out, we have five out of six who are now vampires."

He waited as Matt thought about what to do.

"Hunter's not necessarily going to want to come back for you," he noted. Chris already knew that. "Unless we can convince him that he needs you. Do you have something he might want?"

"Like what?"

Matt thought again as the ground shook once more beneath Chris's feet. It wasn't going to get any better. It was only going to get worse.

"What did you do with your journal?" Matt asked, with sudden realization on his face. "The doctor's journal. Do you have it with you?"

Chris shook his head, and Matt's expression changed. There was that plan out the window.

"It was in my house Upstairs," Chris said.

Matt frowned upon hearing that, but maybe hope wasn't lost, just yet.

"I took it with me when we left," Chris continued. "If someone's been maintaining my house while I've been gone, it should still be there. Otherwise, I don't know what's happened to it. I don't know anything that's been going on since I've been stuck over here for the last year."

"OK, well, on the hypothetical, do you have something there that can masquerade as the doctor's journal?" Chris nodded. Now, that was what Matt wanted to hear. "OK, let me go and track down Hunter. Carmen will probably want that journal. If I can convince Hunter that you have something he wants, or at least that you know where it is, that might be your way out. Do you have anyone you need to bring with you when you come back?"

Chris immediately indicated to Maddie who raised her hand, Matt looking her over.

"Alright, leave it with me and I'll see what I can do," Matt said, the determination clear in his voice. "It shouldn't be too hard for me to track Hunter. I might already know where he's hiding out. Hold on for another twenty-four hours, just give me a day or so, and hopefully you can get out of there sooner rather than later. We have a real vampire problem here at the moment, so I'm going to have to go and check on Craig and his team before I get to work on Hunter. So, give me a little time and, with luck, you'll still be there when I can get back to you."

Before Chris could get another word in, Matt had vanished, and the mirror went dark. All Chris could see now was his and Maddie's reflections.

Chris sighed. "Let's hope he can find Hunter."

CHAPTER TWENTY-NINE

Desperate Measures

"We're gonna go down, Craig!" Gates called from his position not far from where Craig and a few of his recruits, Arley included, were stationed. "We can't keep this up!"

Craig looked over and saw Gates shove a small group of vampires back from his barrier. It was obvious he was getting tired.

There had been an overwhelming number of vampires continuously streaming into the construction site. Gates was right, there was no way they were going to be able to push them back, not with the amount of people they had compared to the Legion's numbers.

The Legion were adamant on making sure this outpost didn't get built. If they allowed that to happen, they knew that there was a lesser chance they'd be able to make it Upstairs.

Having looked at what Alex had sent him from the Legion's headquarters, it was obvious to Craig that getting Upstairs was what they were planning on doing and had been for a while.

Matt suddenly appeared and pushed a vampire away that was awfully close to where Craig was standing. Craig took a step back in alarm.

"Blaine's right, you guys can't hold out much longer," Matt said. He gestured at the amount of carnage around them. "You've lost too many people. They're pushing in from the back as well as the front here. Call everyone back, this isn't worth it."

Before Craig could say anything, Gates was knocked to the ground hard, his barrier vanishing instantly upon the impact.

The vampires, though, didn't initially continue their attack, standing over him instead. Now that the barrier was gone, they slowed right down.

Two of them grabbed Craig, forcing him onto his knees. Some of the others followed suit with Matt, Arley, and everyone else in the immediate vicinity.

Matt could have easily gotten free of the vampires' grip, as it was still rather dark outside where they were, but he was concerned that it would cause more problems. This wasn't how things were supposed to go.

Danny and his crew were brought from the back of the construction site by another group of vampires and forced to kneel with everyone else.

"I could kill you all right here, right now, if I wanted to," they all heard. They all knew that voice too well. Graith came to a stop in front of Craig, looking down at him. "And believe me when I say this, Taylor, I *really* want to."

"Then don't waste time with a monologue," Craig said. "Get on with it."

Graith smiled. He crouched down in front of him, getting himself level with Craig who did nothing but return his gaze.

"I would if I could," he said. He turned his attention to Matt. "I'm surprised you haven't abandoned the group yet. You're more than capable of it."

Matt gave him an unamused smile. "I have my own motives," he said, Graith amused again. "I like these guys, to a certain extent."

Graith looked back at Craig.

"Unfortunately, someone with much higher authority than I do wants you alive," he informed him. He smiled, showing his teeth this time. "For now." He stood up, looking around at everyone. "I know that you all respond to this man right here. I understand he's your immediate commander, which means that he makes all the decisions." He looked at Craig again. "Who's next in charge here if you're not?"

Craig didn't answer straight away. Matt could see that he was trying to work out what was the best thing to do in this situation.

He was going to need to throw someone under the bus, and he was trying to figure out who would handle it the best.

Matt knew who he'd be choosing. There was only one other person here who had any form of authority, and that was Danny.

"It would be within your best interests to answer me, Commander," Graith said, when he got no response from Craig. He was impatient. "Who's next in charge if something happened to you?"

"A captain's rank is below a commander's," was Craig's answer. He looked directly at Graith who was still standing over him. "As a commander yourself, you should know that."

Graith switched his gaze to Matt, deciding that he was the next biggest threat. "Is that your position, shadow-stepper?"

Matt smirked at him. "I don't report to anyone, so, no, you've got the wrong person."

Graith looked at who was next in line, next to Matt: Arley.

"What about the girl?" was his next question. Arley's expression became worried, but all it did was amuse Graith. "She looks like someone who'd be in charge if you weren't around."

"Danny's the only captain here," Craig finally said. "He's the next in charge if I'm not here."

Graith left his position, moving over to where Danny was on his knees and stopping in front of him. Danny met his gaze with hatred.

"I never thought you, of all people, Daniel, would be in this sort of position of power," Graith commented. He crouched down in front of him, Danny glaring at him the entire time. "But seeing as you're next in line if something unfortunate were to happen to Commander Taylor here, I want *you* to tell me what to do, what's right in this situation."

"He has no authority unless he's the only captain here, Graith," Craig spoke up, Graith looking back at him. Danny never looked away from the vampire in front of him. "I outrank him, outrank everyone here. You want something, you speak to me."

Graith thought about it for a few seconds before returning his gaze to Danny.

"We're going to pretend he's not here," he said. He indicated between himself and Danny. "You and I, we're going to have a conversation, Daniel. Ignore everyone else here, no matter what they say. You have your own division, which means that you have some form of higher authority. Correct?"

Danny didn't respond, so Graith continued.

"How many of your division are here right now?" he asked. He looked at the people closest to Danny: Shawn, Ted, and Jordan. "Your crew here, they're part of your division. They wouldn't be if you weren't in charge." He looked back at Danny. "How many of these people are under your instruction, including your bandit friends?"

Danny glanced over at Craig who was watching him. He shook his head slightly, Graith making Danny return his gaze to him.

"Don't look at him. Your commanding officer isn't here at the moment, remember?"

Danny hesitated but answered Graith's initial question.

"Twelve, including myself," he said. Graith's piercing red eyes never blinked as he stared him down. "Eleven of them are my team. You've already killed four of them. I had fifteen when I got here this morning."

"What a shame." There was no empathy in Graith's voice. He looked over at Craig again but didn't move from where he was crouched in front of Danny. "How many are directly under *your* division?"

"Why does it matter, Graith?" Craig snapped. "Everyone's under my division at the end of the day. They all answer to me, and they all do what I tell them to."

Graith indicated to Arley. "I know for a fact that she works directly under you, Taylor. I've seen a few of your recruits with your division badge on. Should I start with killing the girl before anyone else in your direct division?"

"You'll do no such thing," Craig shot back at him. He wasn't about to back down. "If you have any problems, you take them up with me. You leave my team alone, you leave Danny's team alone. They're all doing what they're told. The more of us that you kill, or turn, the more trouble for yourself you're causing. If you want to sort this out, it's with me, and it's with Jacob, no one else needs to get involved."

"Hm, well, we both know that Jacob's not about to show his face. I haven't seen him on the ground for a very long time, the entire time that Banshee's End has been running, in fact." Graith indicated to

Danny, not breaking his gaze from Craig. "I'm surprised he put a bandit in a captain's position. How much can you really trust thieves?"

Craig didn't answer, but Graith didn't need him to. He returned his gaze to Danny.

"I bet you're pretty mad about my people killing yours," he said. He was trying to elicit a reaction from Danny, who was somehow managing to keep himself from speaking, or trying anything. It wasn't because he had the vampires holding him, either. "You'd have to understand that as a captain, though, you're going to lose people when you're fighting for whatever cause you're resisting." He looked Danny over. "Tell me something, Daniel, you're not originally from down here, are you?"

"Not many of us are," Danny said. "A few people are, but majority aren't. What does it matter who is and who isn't?"

"Do you have a family Upstairs?" was Graith's next question.

"Yes."

"So, it'd be a shame if something happened to them?"

"Yes."

Graith nodded, pretending to think about what Danny had said. Danny wasn't about to offer up any further information about who he might have Upstairs, what family it was. Just because he'd been down here for so long, it didn't mean he didn't have anyone waiting for him to suddenly not be another missing person's case.

"I'm going to offer you a deal, Daniel," Graith said after a period of silence. He indicated to Craig. "We're going to continue to pretend that he's not here. This is a conversation between us. Commander Taylor has no authority right now, understood?"

Danny gave a single nod. He didn't know what Graith was playing at right now, but he didn't like it.

"As I mentioned earlier, I'd have killed everyone if I was allowed to," Graith continued. His voice was the only sound able to be heard at the present moment. "I have a higher authority back at our living arrangements who's told me not to kill anyone important. He's given me names and, lucky for you, you're on that list." He indicated to Craig. "He's also on the list, much to my disapproval."

He looked Danny over, pretending to think before he went back to staring straight into his eyes, Danny never looking away.

He wasn't about to let Graith push him around, no matter the situation.

"So, here's what's going to happen," Graith said. He again indicated to Craig, all the while staring at Danny. "*You're* going to make this decision, not him. You give me Commander Taylor, and we'll let the rest of you finish building your little outposts, and your defenses here in Wonderland."

Danny looked over at Craig.

"Think about what he's asking, Danny," Craig said. "You don't have to give him anything and you can't trust him."

Danny returned his gaze to Graith who offered him a rather amused smile.

"I'd prefer it if you shut your mouth, Commander," Graith warned, Craig's expression becoming a glare. "This is between me and your captain, so if you don't want further consequences, I'd let the man decide for himself."

"Danny." Matt was the next one to speak, Danny looking at him this time. "Craig's right, think about what Graith's asking you to do. Someone wants Craig alive. That's not a good thing."

Graith spoke again. "Let me give you another scenario, Daniel. Either you let me have Commander Taylor with no fuss, and you get to finish your defenses and outposts here. Alternatively, I kill everyone here myself. That will take less than ten minutes, and I'm more than happy to turn a few of you in the process. You can ask Remington what it's like. It's less than pleasant and you'll wish I'd actually killed you." He looked directly at Danny again. "It would be justice to make you a vampire."

"You'd also be stuck with me for eternity," was Danny's counter. "So, is it really worth it?"

Graith smiled. "I'm sure I could get used to it."

He looked him over again. "So, what's your decision, Captain? Are you willing to sacrifice one person for the greater good? Prolong everyone's lives for the sake of giving me your commander? Or is it worth killing you all instead, and then I'll just take Commander Taylor anyway?"

Craig went to say something, but Graith immediately interrupted him.

"You've no say in this, so don't even think of trying to sway him into something that he doesn't want to do." He looked back at Danny. "Well? I don't have all day. Five seconds and I want an answer, or I start killing you all one by one until you make your choice."

Danny hesitated as Graith continued to smile at him.

"Fine," Danny said, not even waiting for Graith to start counting down. Danny indicated to Craig. "Take him. We don't need him to finish the outposts."

"Danny," Craig warned.

Danny had the nerve to meet his gaze, Craig not happy with the decision. Graith got up from where he'd been crouched, walking over to Craig this time.

"Looks like your captains *can* make decisions without you," he said. He looked at the vampires who had been holding him down. "Let him up, bring him, let's go."

CHAPTER THIRTY

Dimension Walking

"You did *what*?" Jacob was far from happy with the current outcome of the outpost siege.

"What else was I supposed to do?" Danny all but yelled back at Jacob. Danny indicated to everyone in the room with them. "I would've thought that this was more important to you than one fucking person!" He held his arms out to his sides. "Do what you have to. I made the decision that was best for everyone. This isn't some ill will against Craig, Jacob. This is to get your Goddamned outposts built. Craig can handle himself. You know he would've done the same thing if Graith had made *him* make the decision. So, what? You would've preferred that I let them kill everyone who was there?" He waved Jacob away. "Fuck off, you would've done the same thing, but you wouldn't have hesitated as long."

"Danny's right," Matt spoke up. "If he hadn't agreed to let them take Craig, every single one of us who was there would be dead. Craig would have done the same thing, because he values his team, regardless of who's on it."

Jacob sighed, standing with his hands on hips. He knew what they were saying was true, but it was frustrating. "Did Graith say what he was going to do with him?"

Matt shook his head, as Jacob purposely ignored Danny for the time being. He'd rather deal with Matt. He at least was reasonable. To a point.

"He said that someone of higher authority wanted him alive," Matt explained. "We don't know who, or why. That's all that he said. It was either he kills all of us there, or he gets Craig and lets us finish construction to defend against when they *really* want to start up their siege to get Upstairs. There weren't a lot of options and, I'm sorry, Jacob, but I have to side with Danny on this."

Jacob looked at Alex who immediately tensed up. "You know where they might be taking him? Where you found Remington and Cole?"

Alex nervously glanced at Matt who only crossed his arms and ignored him. Alex looked back to Jacob.

"As much as I like Craig," he said nervously. "I don't think it's a smart idea to go over there with a bunch of people to try and get him back. The place is literally swarming with the undead, it's their lair. It's not worth it, going there and causing more trouble."

Ash was the next to speak. "Do you think Remington or Cole could help?"

Alex shook his head. "No. I think, after what I witnessed, they're more than likely exiled. I don't think they're going to be allowed back without getting killed."

Jacob sighed, messing his hair up as he tried to think of the best thing to do.

"Right now, we'll focus on getting those outposts finished," he began. "Danny, take your team back over there and get that finished. I don't want you back until it's done." He looked at Alex. "Do you think you can go and see if they've taken Craig to the same place you picked up Remington? You can at least get in and out without being seen. Keep an eye on him if he's there, and report back if there's anything we should know."

Alex wasn't pleased with the order, but he nodded, knowing it was within his best interests to do as he was told.

Jacob looked at Matt. "Once Gates has been looked over by medical, take him and Zeke over to the construction site. They can help look everything over and do something about any threats." He glanced at Danny. "They can take care of it if there are any issues. Can you go with them?"

"No can do," Matt said with a shake of his head. "I have someone else I need to visit. I'm working on getting Chris back before his dimension collapses, so that's my number one priority, now. Time's ticking, and I don't have long to work things out. You can contact me if you need me, but for the next day or two, I'm busy. I'll check in once I've done what I need to."

Knowing that Matt would do whatever he wanted anyway, Jacob didn't fight him on it.

"Alright, everyone knows what they need to do, get moving," Jacob said, waving his arms in the air to dismiss them all.

He didn't say anything more, leaving them to go their separate ways.

Danny shook his head and pushed past Alex, leaving the room, making sure that the door slammed shut behind him. No one commented on it.

Matt was the next to leave, just not through the door.

Ash looked at Alex and touched his hand. "Please be careful. Don't get into any trouble."

Alex managed a small smile, but Ash saw right through it. She'd known Alex long enough to know that he was faking the smile to try and reassure her.

"I'll be fine, I was the first time," he said, Ash not believing him. "It'll be fine, I promise."

Chris shut the door once he and Maddie got back to his place. Maddie quickly tapped him on the arm as he was locking the door.

Frowning, he followed Maddie's indication, his expression falling upon seeing what had caught her attention.

Hunter was sitting there, arms crossed and feet up on the table directly in front of himself. He looked far from pleased as he stared at Chris, ignoring Maddie who'd moved to stand more off to Chris's side than directly next to him.

"This had better not be a waste of my time," Hunter growled. He looked Chris over. "I don't know how Shade managed to track me down, but I don't appreciate it." He looked back at Chris's face. "Where is it?"

"You have to get us out of here before I tell you anything," Chris said. Hunter wasn't happy to hear it, and the ground shook, a lot more violently than it had before. "If I go down with this dimension, you're never going to know. You have to take me and Maddie back before I'll tell you anything."

Hunter sighed in annoyance, not even bothered by the shaking ground. He took his feet off the table, pushing the chair back and getting to his feet. Chris moved back slightly, standing right in front of the door.

"Just so you know, I don't actually care about those journals," Hunter commented. "They've got nothing to do with me. Marion's the one who wanted them. Now Carmen's insistent on getting them. I'm just the one they've decided is the right person to get them from all of you." He glanced at Maddie before returning his gaze to Chris. "Who else has them?"

Chris shrugged. "Can't tell you unless you get us out of here before we all die."

The ground shook again, a few cracks appearing in the walls of the house this time. Maddie's expression was worried as she watched several books fall off the closest shelf.

"Fine," Hunter bitterly agreed. "Get what you need, five minutes. Any longer and I leave without either of you."

Chris didn't need to be told twice. He went into the bedroom he'd been using for the last year, grabbing his journal and one of the bags he'd acquired in the time that he'd been here.

He took what he could, shoving everything in the bag as the ground shook. He was under the impression that Maddie didn't need anything as she'd waited in the front room with Hunter.

He was done in record time and quickly went back out to where Hunter and Maddie were standing and staring at each other, but not speaking. Hunter walked to the closest wall and waved his hand past it. The wall opened like a doorway, onto what looked, to Chris, like open space with stars and planets beyond.

"Move," Hunter said harshly.

Chris and Maddie moved forward through the doorway. Hunter followed, the doorway vanishing once he was inside. He moved past both of them, and Chris looked around as he and Maddie followed Hunter into nothingness.

There was nothing below them but darkness, pitch black, no path, nothing. On either side of them, stars and planets stretched out as far as he could see. Every few feet or so were doors hanging in the middle of nowhere, all the same colour, but they were all numbered.

Chris guessed that the numbers indicated what dimension was beyond the doorway. There seemed to be no particular order to them, as they'd just come through the one that was labelled with a 4, while the next one closest to them was numbered 208, and the next one after that 15.

Hunter didn't say a word as he walked a few paces ahead of them. Maddie stayed close to Chris, neither of them saying anything either.

There was no sound, not even their footsteps as they walked between dimensions. It was eerie, and Chris couldn't wait to get back to normality once they found the door they were looking for.

He assumed Maddie was OK with this. She must have done it before, since she'd been a Dimension Walker herself. He didn't know how long it had been since she'd done this, but it must have been for however long she'd been in Dimension Four, since that was where she'd been turned.

"Where did you leave Marion?" Chris asked.

Hunter didn't even acknowledge that he'd heard him, and they'd been walking for a while before he bothered to answer. "Doesn't matter."

Despite the vast space, there wasn't even any echo as they spoke. Chris briefly wondered if Hunter had taken Marion back to her original dimension, the one they were headed back to, but he remembered that Maddie had been with him to make sure he didn't do that. So she could be anywhere, behind any of these doors.

They seemed to walk for ages before Chris finally saw the door he hoped was the correct one. A door on their left numbered with a single 1.

Hunter stopped in front of it, glancing at his two companions before opening the door and indicating for them to step through. Maddie went through first with no hesitation, Chris following seconds later. Hunter shut the door behind himself once he was also through, and the door vanished behind them.

They were in front of the Dimension Portal, a short hike away from the town of Waterwall Incline.

"A deal's a deal," Hunter said, arms crossed, looking directly at Chris. "Tell me what I want to know."

"I appreciate the help, Hunter," the three of them heard Matt say as he appeared next to Chris. "Now, if you'll excuse us, we have something important to deal with."

Without any warning, Matt grabbed both Chris and Maddie by the shoulder and they vanished. The last thing Chris saw was Hunter's glare.

The next thing Chris knew was that his head was spinning, and he noticed Maddie was also rather unsteady. Trying to shake the dizziness, Chris looked around. They were in Banshee's End, not too far from the church of operations.

"We have a lot to talk about," Matt said. Several people looked curiously at them as they passed by. Matt looked at Maddie, extending his hand in an unusually friendly manner. "Matt."

Maddie accepted his gesture, shaking his hand in response. "Maddie."

Chris looked at Matt. "Thank you, Matt. I think you got us back just in time."

"It's no trouble," was the response. "I would have done something sooner if I'd been told that things were going wrong. No one communicated with me, so I assumed things were fine and that they'd worked everything out." He narrowed his eyes. "Why do I have to keep checking on everyone all the time?" He shook his head. "Whatever, we have more important matters to deal with. Go put your stuff in the manor at the back, and I'll meet you back there in a few minutes. I have to duck over to Wonderland and make sure Danny hasn't burned anything down yet."

Matt vanished again, Maddie quite impressed with the magic trick.

"Maddie!"

Remington came to a fast stop in front of them, accompanied by some other guy that Chris didn't recognize.

Maddie's expression turned to disbelief. "Oh my God!" she exclaimed.

She threw her arms around Remington, hugging him tightly as he returned the embrace, ecstatic to see her.

"I didn't know where you disappeared to," Remington said. Cole exchanged looks with Chris who did nothing but shrug. Remington let Maddie go, keeping his hands on her shoulders as he looked her over. His expression saddened. "I'm so sorry, how long have you been like this?"

Maddie shrugged. She gave Remington a sad smile.

"Almost two years," she admitted, the look on Remington's face not changing. She gave him a friendly push. "Don't worry so much, Rem, it's fine."

Remington wasn't convinced, and he pulled Maddie back into a hug.

Feeling awkward and like this wasn't his business or place to intrude, Chris took his leave, heading past the three vampires and towards the manor to put what little he had with him down.

Once he'd done that, he'd just hang around and wait for Matt to come back.

CHAPTER THIRTY-ONE

Familiar Tracks

G ates surveyed the area in front of him. He was bored. He lit another cigarette and passed the packet to Zeke, who hadn't left his side.

"Have you boys done anything while you've been over here?"

Matt stopped next to Gates who lazily glanced at him before shrugging and going back to watching the recruits and townsfolk working away in front of them.

Danny was nowhere to be seen.

"We're supervising," Gates said, taking a drag on his cigarette. He glanced at Matt who had followed his gaze and was also watching the workers. "I know it hasn't been that long, but any word on Craig?"

Matt shook his head and put his hands in his pockets. It was still cold, but at least the snow had eased off since he'd dropped everyone off here earlier on before going to wait for Chris.

"Nothing," he sighed. "I took Alex as close as I could get to the vampire area without causing too much of an alert, too much trouble." He sighed again. "I don't like the way Graith was talking, about someone with higher authority wanting Craig alive." He shook his head, thinking. "Who would want him alive? And why?"

Gates shrugged and watched Arley heading over to the three of them. "Whoever it is, Graith has to listen to them."

Arley came to a stop in front of Matt, not too impressed with the two smoking so close to her.

"What's up?" asked Gates.

Arley looked him over before turning her gaze to Matt, crossing her arms as she looked at him. Matt didn't even flinch at the slight glare on her face.

"Danny's found something up the back of the construction site," she said. "Wants someone to go over there and see what's going on." She looked Matt over. "Preferably an adult."

"You mean he didn't ask for *your* help?" Matt asked back with amusement, but Arley clearly wasn't in the mood for it. "See, this is why you're single, Arls."

Arley shot him a look, and Matt took her arm and Gates's, who also quickly grabbed onto Zeke, knowing that Matt wanted them to go with him to see what Danny wanted.

Danny looked over as they appeared. He was crouching down, looking at something. Ted, Shawn, and Jordan were, as usual, within close vicinity. They were almost all connected at the hip.

"What's the issue, Captain?" Matt asked as he casually strolled over. He stopped briefly, flinching. "That's odd."

Danny got to his feet and indicated to something on the ground. "This look normal to you?"

A frown crossed Matt's face as he unintentionally flinched again. Something was definitely wrong. Gates and Zeke came over as well to see what was going on.

Arley hung back, hugging herself to try to keep the cold out as she looked around. She hated the head spin that came with Matt dragging people through the shadows with him.

There weren't many people on this side of the construction site, but there were a few recruits—mainly Danny's team—working on burying the remainder of the people they'd lost to the vampires mere hours ago.

"That's not good," Gates spoke up when he saw what had caught Danny's attention. He looked at Matt who had crouched down, making sure he was seeing everything correctly. "I don't think it can wait until morning, Matt."

Matt could do nothing but agree, sighing as he stood up straight and put his hands on his hips. First the vampires raided their site, then they took Craig to do God knew what to him, and now, Danny had stumbled upon banshee tracks.

"OK," Matt started, taking a breath. He looked at Danny. "You stay here and keep overseeing everything, and we'll take care of this." He looked at Gates and Zeke. "You're right to help track?"

They both nodded, Matt giving a satisfied nod back.

"What's the issue exactly?" Ted asked, confused at what was going on.

Matt switched his gaze to him.

"We're dealing with a banshee problem," he explained. "Best we get on top of it before they get back here. They're somewhere close by, if we're seeing tracks like this, and I can feel it. The dark energy they give off, if they're nearby, I'll know."

"Don't banshees like ... scream and shit?" Shawn asked, sounding a little skeptical about the situation. "Surely we would've heard them by now if they were near us."

"Depends on how they're hunting," Gates said. "Either way, they need to be taken care of." He looked at Matt. "I didn't think banshees were in Wonderland. We've never seen them anywhere near here before."

Matt shook his head. "I'm not sure why they've migrated this far up," he admitted. "For all we know, it could have some connection to the Legion, but we don't know. The vampire presence in Oz might have caused the banshees to leave, try and move to a different area, who knows?"

That was a good enough explanation for Gates. He looked over at Arley, who was still standing a short distance away, just listening.

"Keep Danny and his boys in line while we step out!" he called to her, amused by the unimpressed look on Arley's face. "We'll be back. Hopefully."

Matt headed off in the direction of the banshee tracks. There was always something that he had to deal with, something always got in the way of their plans, and Matt was always the one who had to deal with the issues. Maybe he should have just stayed upstairs with Vivian and Riley.

The only problem was that if he'd done that, the vampires would be his problem a lot sooner than he wanted them to be.

That was the sad reality of it.

Ash was over excited to finally see Chris after what felt like forever. It had only been a year, so Chris didn't know why she was this happy to see him.

She almost knocked him off balance as she hugged him, Chris quickly grabbing onto her with a laugh.

"I can't believe Matt actually got you back," she said. She let him go and Chris gave her a smile. "Are you alright? Nothing bad happened while you were gone?"

Chris shook his head. "No, there were no real issues. Marion kept to herself, I kept to myself. I don't know where she is now. Carmen unbound us, that's the only reason I'm here and she's not, like, ten feet away from me. Hunter took her somewhere, I don't know where, though."

"Well, as long as she's out of our way, and can let us do what we need to, then that's what's important."

Chris agreed. Ash took a seat at the table, Chris following suit, sitting opposite her and resting his head on his hand.

"What's it been like down here the last year?" he asked, hearing someone coming their way.

It had to be one of the resident vampires, as there was no one else here as far as Chris was aware. He hadn't even seen Alex since he'd gotten back, and that was strange, since he was never far away from Ash.

Matt hadn't come back from his check-in with Danny yet, either.

"It's been rough," Ash admitted, as Remington wandered into the room. He couldn't be curious as to their conversation, since he'd have been able to hear it no matter where he was in the outpost. "More so over the last few weeks, or months, really. The Legion's started pushing forwards more and more. They're trying to get to the Room of Doors; they want to get Upstairs."

"And now with Craig gone, it's going to be a lot harder to keep order on the ground," Remington commented with a sigh as he collapsed onto the chair at the head of the table.

Chris frowned. "What do you mean, Craig's gone?"

Remington looked at Ash, and Ash shrugged awkwardly, not wanting to be the one to break the news to Chris. She was too close to Craig to want to talk about it.

Chris had only known Craig for the time they'd been at Banshee's End, so he knew him to a certain point, but he wouldn't have said he knew him very well. He did know that Craig was an integral part of the operation, though, especially the ground team.

"There was a siege a few hours ago," Remington explained since Ash wouldn't say anything. "They've been trying to build outposts over in Wonderland, to try and get reinforcements to at least slow down the inevitable assault." He hesitated before saying the next sentence. "Graith has Craig, they had to exchange him for everyone else's lives. Alex has gone to keep an eye on the situation, but we haven't heard anything yet. He's probably beaten them there, in all honesty. It'll take time for them to cover that distance from where they were in Wonderland."

"So, he's essentially going to be killed," Chris stated. This was not good. "Is there a plan on how to get him back before that happens?"

Remington gave an awkward shrug. "Cole and I have been exiled, so there's nothing we can do, hence why we're sitting around. Alex can at least tell us what's happening. From what Matt was saying earlier down in the operations room, someone wanted Craig alive, so that's one positive, I guess. Less chance they'll kill him straight away."

Chris wasn't convinced. Right now, though, there was nothing that he could do.

CHAPTER THIRTY-TWO

Banshees are a Girl's Best Friend

The forest was quiet, and Matt, Gates, and Zeke had walked in quite far.

Matt held his hand up, and the three of them stopped. He listened, flinching from the dark energy that was within the area. They were definitely close to their destination now.

"Alright," Matt said, keeping his voice down so as not to attract attention from any unwanted foes. "Be cautious. Try and find where they may be burrowed. I'm going to go back to Banshee's End and see if someone there has a silver blade so we can take some of these banshees out. Don't get killed while I'm gone."

Without waiting for a response, he vanished.

Gates sighed and put his hands in his jacket pockets as he and Zeke were left in the dark forest by themselves. "I hate banshees. Let's hope there's not many of them."

Chris jumped as Matt appeared in the room, even startling Remington. Ash wasn't impressed, but then, was she ever?

"Anyone here know where to get a silver blade?" Matt asked without letting any of them speak. "I'm on limited time, so talk to me."

Chris frowned. "I thought you were over in Wonderland?" he asked.

"And I have a bigger problem to deal with. Danny has the outpost under control. As much as I don't trust his judgement on occasion, he's the best ... man ... for the job." Matt crossed his arms. "So, anyone wanna lend me their silver utensils?"

Chris and Ash exchanged looks, Remington sitting up properly, no longer lounging like he had been.

"You're after a silver blade," Chris stated, Matt staring at him and saying nothing in response. "That's very specific." It took a few seconds before it clicked, his expression falling. "Banshees?"

Matt nodded solemnly. Even Remington's expression had fallen upon hearing what the threat near the construction site was.

"You be careful with banshees," he said, tone dead serious. "They're very dangerous."

"Oh, I'm well aware, trust me," Matt said back. "This isn't the first time we've taken on banshees. We know the threat level."

"I'm not surprised they're coming out more, now," Remington mused, resting his chin on his hand. "What with the vampire activity happening, there's more present. Banshees are a class of vampire, in a sense."

Matt's interest was piqued. "Explain."

Remington hesitated and sighed when he realized Matt didn't know about the offshoot of vampires.

"Banshees are dead," he indeed did explain. "They're usually created from malicious spirits, from souls of people who've been severely wronged, or have some form of devastating trauma. They're a breed of vampire, on the vampiric family tree. Their bite won't turn you, they don't have that power, but it's still very painful and not recommended."

Matt nodded to himself slowly as he took the information in.

"The banshees we came across a few years ago," he said, Remington listening intently. "One of them was apparently created by a necromancer."

Remington's expression dropped again. "A necromancer?"

Matt nodded.

Remington exhaled and leant back in his chair. "That's not good, if that's the case. Necromancers have the ability to create banshees, sure, but it makes them ten times more dangerous because they partially resurrect the person, which means that they still have some of their autonomy. They're more aware of what's going on. Hell, you could even talk to them and not even realize they're a banshee. They look like normal people, and respond to their name, if you know it. The giveaway, though, is their sharp teeth. They're only really dangerous when it gets dark and they're hunting, that's when that banshee animalistic side comes out."

Chris could see Matt's mind ticking over as he listened to Remington's words. He'd clearly picked up on something that he and Ash hadn't, but Matt was very attentive.

"Interesting," was all that Matt said before vanishing.

Matt's next destination was still at Banshees End, but outside. He watched everyone milling around, minding their own business, a few people glancing at him warily, hurrying past that bit faster.

He was looking for someone in particular, and he wasn't going to leave until he found them.

Moving from place to place at a fast pace, Matt found Colin talking to his son about something.

Colin looked at him as Matt stopped next to him, pretending to look at the food that was on display at the stall.

"Something tells me you might be able to help me," Matt said. He stopped pretending to look at the stall. "What did you do with the silver blade?"

Colin looked caught off-guard at the question.

"It's back at our old house," he stumbled. "I ... it wasn't really something I thought of taking with us. We left everything behind; we have absolutely nothing."

"I'll make good use of it, then."

Just as Colin went to speak again, Matt vanished, having the answers that he needed and not hanging around to make small talk.

"This is it."

Gates and Zeke stopped in front of a tree with a deep hole directly next to it. There was no doubt in Gates's mind that this was the banshee burrow.

"Well, at least we know where it is," Zeke commented. The small fire above his hand continued to illuminate the area around them. It wasn't quite so dark with the light around. "Are they're home, is the question."

"And how many might be home," Gates said. He sighed, messing his hair up in a frustrated gesture. "Why are we always the ones to deal with this sort of stuff?"

Zeke shrugged, a bored look on his face as he took in the forest. It was all trees, with some smaller green plants nearby in the undergrowth, but nothing even remotely exciting. Sometimes, Zeke missed their old domain.

"Hi there!"

Both men spun around, startled by the childish voice. Standing a few yards away, was a young girl. She couldn't be any older than six at the most.

Zeke and Gates exchanged looks. The little girl gave them both a nice smile, but Gates noticed straight away that she had very sharp teeth.

This wasn't good.

"What are you doing?" the girl asked, tilting her head to the side as she regarded the two men in front of her. She had her hands behind her back, and she shifted her weight back and forth, from one leg to the other, as she spoke. "It's dangerous to be out at night like this."

Gates and Zeke both stayed silent. The girl took a step forward, causing them both to step back. She tilted her head to the other side upon the movement.

"What's the matter?" she asked. She pouted. "I'm not scary, I promise!"

"You're Angel, aren't you?"

Matt appeared on the left side of Gates, looking unsteady for a second, due to the mass amount of dark energy in their immediate area.

The girl's face lit up with a cheerful smile. She nodded and indicated to herself.

"That's me!" she said. The smile never left her face. "Who're you?"

"I'm Matt," Matt introduced himself. He indicated to his two companions. "This is Blaine and Zeke."

"Hi!"

Gates and Zeke had no idea what Matt was doing. He obviously knew something that they didn't.

"Can I ask you something, Angel?" Matt asked. Angel nodded, still shifting her weight back and forth in a playful gesture. "How many of you are around here at the moment?"

Angel put a finger to her chin and tapped it, looking away from Matt and up at one of the tall trees close by.

"Mm, there's three of us," she said after some hard thinking.

"Is that three with you counted as well?" Angel nodded, Matt nodding back. "Well, Angel, I hope you know that nothing's personal, but we can't really let your friends stay here. This is an important place, and we need to make sure that the area is clear, OK?"

Angel pouted again, arms crossed. She was stubborn.

"But I like it here," she complained. She looked Matt over, a bitter look having replaced the pout on her face. "What makes this *your* forest?"

"It's not, but we've run into a vampire problem. I know that you and your friends are on that family tree, but, somehow, I don't think you're as big of a threat as they are."

Angel scrunched her face up. "I don't like the vampires. They're mean. They pushed us up this far, and now I don't get to see Daddy or Mommy, anymore."

"Well, we're working on trying to take care of the vampire problem. The only issue, Angel, is that we need this area cleared. Will your friends move for us?"

Angel didn't seem too pleased with the idea. Without warning, Gates moved, quickly putting his barrier up and something hit it incredibly hard, almost knocking him backwards. He was going to be sore in the morning.

This was an all too familiar situation.

Matt looked back at Angel, whose expression had fallen upon seeing the defensive maneuver by Gates. Gates kept the barrier up on all sides of the three of them, not about to take any chances.

"Oh, you're *them*," Angel said with disappointment. She stamped her foot. "That's not fair!"

"What's she talking about, Matt?" Gates asked.

"This is the little banshee girl we tried to kill when we first ran across their burrow in Oz," Matt explained.

Gates almost stumbled off balance as something slammed hard into the barrier again, a few scratches appearing on it. He felt the sting on his left arm at the contact. Banshees were definitely a problem for his physicality, and these ones felt more powerful than when they'd faced them a few years ago.

Angel put her hands on her hips in disapproval, and Matt never looked away from her.

"Remington said she'd be a lot more aware than the other banshees because she became one via necromancy, not by natural means," Matt said. "It's complicated and I can explain at another time, if you need to know."

Gates didn't have the chance to say anything, as the barrier was hit, yet again, this time from the side that Zeke was on, startling him.

Gates winced in pain. The pressure would get too much if this didn't get sorted out soon.

"You're mean," Angel said. "You killed one of my friends."

"Because they were trying to kill *your* family," Matt shot back. He wasn't about to lose to a six-year-old girl, banshee or not. "Can we make a deal, Angel?"

Angel crossed her arms in displeasure but nodded.

Matt spoke again. "You and us." He indicated between her and the three of them. One of the banshees was lurking next to a tree close by, waiting to be told that it could attack. Zeke could see it by the light from the flames. "We all hate the vampires."

"We do!" Angel said, nodding importantly, the cheer back in her tone from earlier.

"If you leave our team alone, the ones who're building in this area, plus anyone associated with us, we'll take care of the vampire problem, and you can go wherever you want to. You just have to give us some time, that's all I ask. What do you think?"

Angel tapped her chin in thought again, the second banshee moving closer to where she was standing.

"Mm, OK!" She smiled, unintentionally showing her sharp teeth. "You have a deal, Matt!"

Matt smiled back slightly, more amused than anything. "Well alright, that's a good decision."

He indicated for Gates to take the barrier down. Gates hesitantly did so, and Matt looked back at Angel.

"Now, what can you tell me about the Legion?"

CHAPTER THIRTY-THREE

Unfriendly Faces

A lex ran through the slowly closing door, making sure not to get caught in it.

The little blonde mouse had been hot on the trail of Craig and the vampires that currently had custody of him, and they were in the middle of shoving him down the stairs, heading lower and lower into the lair.

This was all too similar to where he'd found Remington.

"I'm surprised you haven't put up much of a fight, Taylor," Graith commented as they descended lower still, the levels getting darker and the metal stairs getting harder to see with each step. He gave Craig a rough shove from behind, but Craig managed to keep his footing as he luckily reached the landing on the next level. "Shame, I thought you'd be more ... fighty."

"There's no point when you're the one with the upper hand," Craig said. His two vampire escorts forced him to keep moving. "It'd be stupid to bother, a waste of energy."

Graith was amused, and the group continued to descend, unaware that the little mouse was close by on the handrail of the stairs.

The lower levels were very quiet, not a sound to be heard aside from the group's footsteps. Making it to the right level, the vampires pushed a door open.

Alex had been right. This was the very same place that Remington and Cole had been kept. The moment the door opened, the noise started.

"Looks like some of our traitors are hungry, Commander," Graith commented. "It's been a while since they've eaten fresh."

Craig didn't say a word as his vampire escort hauled him roughly past multiple cages and cells. The vampires in them all pressed right up against the bars, grabbing for Craig as he passed by.

Craig never let it get to him. He kept his head up as he was paraded through. Graith couldn't afford to let any of these vampires get him, no matter the reason, and Craig knew that.

If someone within this facility wanted him alive, there was no way Graith would risk his own head for something so stupid. He was smarter than that.

Craig was led to an unoccupied cell right near the back of the large room. One of the vampires opened the cell door, and Graith did the honors by shoving Craig hard between the shoulder blades and into the cell.

Craig fell painfully to his knees, hands flat on the floor from bracing his fall as best he could. The door was shut and locked before he could make any form of movement.

"Don't let the noise get to you too much, Commander," Graith said. He looked Craig over, satisfied as Craig made no movement to get back to his feet, staying in the same position on the floor of the cell. "We'll talk soon."

Graith turned and strode away, his vampire lackeys following without being told to.

Once they were completely out of sight, Craig sighed, defeated. He pushed himself to his feet. He didn't bother dusting himself down, placing his hands on his hips as he stood in the middle of the small cell. The dirt from the floor was the least of his concerns right now.

The person in the cell directly next to his lunged at the bars, Craig instinctively moving away quickly, and his shoulder slammed into the bars on the other side of his cell.

Just what he wanted, a neighboring vampire.

At least on his left, where he currently was, there was a walkway, so there was no cell or cage directly next to him on this side. His cell was only attached to one other one, which was a positive.

If he could call anything about this whole situation that.

Craig sighed again, giving up and sitting down in the back corner of the cell, the vampire next door still trying to reach him. Craig leaned his head back against the wall.

"Great," he said to himself.

A squeaking noise next to him on his left got his attention. A little blonde mouse was staring at him from the other side of the bars.

"Can I help you with something?" he asked, already knowing it was Alex. "You here to help, or are you just gonna sit there and squeak at me?"

Alex squeaked in response, and Craig rolled his eyes, turning his gaze back to the front. He really wished that the vampire bordering his cell would stop.

The noise in this dungeon was really annoying.

"Another human, huh," he heard on his left. "Haven't seen one of you down here in a while."

It was a feminine voice this time, not Alex and his squeaking. Craig looked to his left again, across the walkway to the cell directly on the other side.

A girl was sitting at the same level as Craig, pressed right up against the bars, with what looked to be a smirk on her face as she looked him over.

Her clothes were filthy and torn, and her blonde hair matted and all over the place. Her hands, gripping the bars in front of where she was sitting, were dirty as well, and she seemed to have multiple scratches on her hands and down her arms.

How long had she been down here?

"What did *you* do to piss off the hungry biters?" she asked, amused for some reason. She licked her lips as she looked him over again. "Must've been bad for them to lock you down here with the bad vampires."

Craig took in her appearance before looking back at her face. He got a grin from her and saw multiple missing teeth.

"I could ask you the same thing," he countered, the girl clearly thinking that everything was funny. "You're not a vampire, I can tell."

The girl laughed, pushing her face against the bars more.

"Dunno why," she said. Her expression suddenly fell as she spotted the small mouse. "You!"

She made a violent grab for the little mouse, Alex squeaking in surprise. He dashed into Craig's cell and vanished. The girl growled in annoyance.

"You come back here, you little rat!" she screamed. Craig watched her hitting the bars in frustration. "Give me the mouse!"

"How did you get down here?" Craig jumped as Alex —no longer the mouse—spoke, standing next to him, making sure to avoid the vampire in the cell next to them. "You were still in the Emerald City when it went down."

The girl glared at him, making a grabbing gesture again as she pushed herself against the bars, really wanting to get hold of Alex.

"You all left me!" she screeched, Alex and Craig both flinching at the volume. The girl pointed at Alex. "You, you have to get me out of here! You owe me!"

Alex shifted awkwardly, unsure what to do.

"Uh, well," he began. He cleared his throat. "Craig, this ... this is Alice."

Alice bared her teeth at him, Craig switching his gaze back to her. She wasn't that scary.

"Nice to meet you, I guess," he said. He looked at Alex who moved to sit in front of him in the small space. "So, what's your mission? Jacob put you up to this?"

Alex watched Alice as she, again, tried to reach as far as she could through the bars. She had a long way to go.

"I've been put on watch duty," Alex explained. "Report if anything happens. I'm here to observe, and nothing else."

Craig sighed, resting his head back against the wall again. "Great."

Alex's expression saddened as Craig shut his eyes, trying to block out the never-ending noise. Alex looked over to Alice as he saw that Craig was far from the mood for small talk, or any talk in general, really.

"How did you end up here?" he asked Alice, the rabid girl eyeing him off suspiciously.

She narrowed her eyes at him, looking him over. She looked back at his face and spoke.

"Where's Matt?" she asked. "Is he with you?" Alex shook his head. "Why not?"

"Matt's busy," Craig sighed. He crossed his arms, keeping his eyes closed. "He's not about to come down here and try to rescue us, we're on our own."

Alice growled and switched her dangerous gaze back to Alex. He shifted uncomfortably, not liking the look that she was giving him.

"I don't like *him*," she said, jabbing a finger at Craig. "Who's he think he is?"

"Commanding Officer Craig Taylor," Craig sighed. "Not that that means shit down here."

Alice frowned. "What's a 'commanding officer'?"

She didn't like big words. People she didn't know were so annoying. Then again, people that she did know were just as annoying.

Except for Matt. Matt was the exception.

"A commanding officer is someone you should listen to," a voice close by said. Graith stopped in front of Craig's cell, arms behind his back as he looked down at him. Alex had disappeared before he'd been seen. "Normally, I wouldn't come down here and bother my prisoners, but you're a special case."

"Is there something you want from me, Graith?" Craig asked, his tone rather bored. "I'm busy, right now."

Graith smiled in amusement.

"I want to talk to you about something," he said. "What's your plan, Commander? Surely, you're smart enough to understand that your group is outnumbered by us. Banshee's End doesn't have a lot of promise with their recruits, most of them are new and don't know half their job. What are you hoping to achieve?"

"Why do *you* want to get Upstairs?" Craig countered. "What's up there for you, Graith?

"If I told you that, Commander, then it wouldn't be as much of a surprise." His eyes scanned Craig and Craig stood up, moving to the front of the cell and stopping directly in front of Graith. "Do you have much of a family, Taylor?"

"Would I still be here if I did?"

Graith's expression became interested. Craig leaned against the front bars, arms crossed.

"You're from Upstairs, yes?" Graith asked. "You don't feel like you've been here for your whole life, not many people have. Most came down here at one point or another, some have been here longer than others."

"How long have *you* been down here?" Craig asked back with a slight smile. "Are you from Upstairs?"

Graith gave a very slight, almost non-existent, chuckle.

"I've been here for a very long time, Commander, and it's starting to look like you might be too."

CHAPTER THIRTY-FOUR

Dead Information

Nixx stood up so fast that his chair toppled over behind him.

"What are you doing?" he exclaimed. Nixx pointed directly to Matt's company, the little girl named Angel. "What're you doing, bringing her in here?"

Matt raised an eyebrow. Why was Nixx making such a big deal out of this? The madman was always so dramatic. He could obviously tell that Angel wasn't a normal little girl, but Matt would've expected nothing less.

"Where are we?" Angel asked curiously, moving back and forth as she looked around. She put her arms out and spun around. "This room is big!"

"It sure is, kiddo," Matt said. He switched his gaze back to Nixx who was standing very still near the table he'd been working at, chair abandoned on the floor. "This little girl knows a few things that I think you might find interesting."

"She's a banshee, Matt," Nixx said harshly. Angel paid no attention to him, instead still marveling at the size of the room. "What could she possibly know that's of importance to me?"

Matt directed Angel over to one of the close tables and made her sit down on the chair. Nixx didn't move, just followed their movements with his eyes. Angel swung her legs back and forth, not interested in Nixx in the slightest.

"Her friends are outside, and there's no need to be worrying about them coming in," Matt reassured Nixx. "Angel and I had a long chat before we came here, and she knows some—what I deem important—information regarding the Legion."

"So why is she here and not at Banshee's End talking to Jacob or Craig?" Nixx's tone was serious. He wasn't playing around.

"Craig's indisposed at the moment," Matt said, knowing Nixx wouldn't question it. "And I doubt Jacob would be very happy with me if I brought a banshee back to the primary outpost."

"Oh, and *I'm* happy with you bringing her here?"

"Never said you were." Matt looked at Angel who gave him a nice smile. Matt indicated to Nixx. "Wanna tell him what you told me?"

Angel shrugged. She looked unsure as she looked at Nixx. "He doesn't like me very much. Why should I tell him?"

Somehow managing not to roll his eyes, Matt looked at Nixx who now had his arms crossed, emanating displeasure.

"She was turned into a banshee by a necromancer," Matt explained. "She knows who that necromancer is."

Nixx's expression changed very fast upon hearing this new information. There weren't a lot of necromancers around and, if Nixx had done his calculations correctly, Dusk was the only one that was active and present at the moment.

The only thing he didn't know was exactly who Dusk was.

"She knows?" he asked after some hesitation.

Matt nodded. "She does, and she's agreed to help us out with the information in exchange for me not killing her, or her friends outside. We have a separate deal going on the side, but that's my issue, not yours."

Nixx bent down and picked his chair up off the ground, retaking his seat and resting his head on his hand. His gaze remained on Angel who stared right back at him.

"You're still connected to your necromancer?" he asked.

Angel nodded vigorously.

"And Daddy, too, since he helped bind me as a banshee!" she said. She sighed, mirroring Nixx's position. "But the vampires sent us away from Mommy and Daddy, so I don't get to see them anymore."

"That's a shame," said Nixx.

Angel nodded in agreement, a sad look on the little girl's face.

"So, your necromancer must be still alive, if you can still feel the bond," Nixx said.

"Yep! He's far away, though. He's been playing with those pesky vampires."

She stuck her tongue out in disapproval, the intrigue clear on Nixx's face.

Matt was happy with himself for setting up this impromptu meeting. It was paying off well.

"Is he with the vampires?" Nixx questioned, Angel back to looking around, some books close by getting her attention.

"Mmhm!" Angel jumped down off the chair and pulled a book off the shelf. "He lives with them, tells them what to do. He causes problems for them if they don't do what he says. They have a stupid council, but he's better than them, so he tells them what he wants and they do it."

"Do you know the name of this necromancer, by chance?"

Angel tapped her chin in thought, the book in her hands forgotten about for the moment.

"He says something about 'dark' or something like that I think." She shook her head. "I don't know. I don't like him much, so I don't listen."

Nixx's expression had fallen. He looked at Matt. "If she's talking about Dusk, then we have a very serious problem."

"Why? What's so special about this Dusk guy?" Matt asked.

He didn't understand what Nixx's issue was with this specific necromancer. If that was even who Angel was talking about. He didn't know much about necromancers, but by the look of Nixx's expression, plus the way that he was talking, didn't fill him with many good feelings.

"Dusk's a very powerful necromancer," Nixx explained. Angel was busy looking through the book, probably for pictures if Matt had to guess. "He's been around for a very long time. Some people think he's the one who originally created the vampires down here."

Matt frowned. "But everyone's been saying these Underground Worlds were created by Marion, so how could someone like this Dusk guy have been here for an eternity?"

"Well, we don't exactly know too much about Marion, how she got here, even how old she is," Nixx said. "But I think you're all wrong. From my research, Marion had nothing to do with the creation of these worlds. She was only tied to Wonderland because of magic and power. That way, if she went down, so would Wonderland and she'd take everyone and everything with her. The other counties would have stayed standing. It wouldn't matter, only Wonderland would've fallen. No one knows for sure how long these areas have been down here, it could be centuries, thousands of years, longer, even."

Matt wasn't convinced, but Nixx knew more than he did, or cared to learn for that matter.

"Vampires are undead," Nixx continued. "There has to be something that started their infection, yes? Necromancers deal with the dead, they bring them back, whether for good or for bad, so what's to stop one *making* the undead? He's more than likely spent time experimenting with…"

Nixx trailed off, his expression having changed upon his words. His stare was vacant. Matt waved a hand in front of his face, trying to get his attention back onto the conversation.

"Nixx?" He waved his hand in front of his face again.

"Oh no," Nixx said, continuing to stare at the wall across the room. It took a minute before he was able to tear his gaze away and look at Matt. His expression was concerned. "You said that Craig was indisposed?"

Matt nodded. What was he even asking for? What did it matter?

"We had a problem over at the outpost site earlier this evening," he explained.

Nixx was staring straight through him this time. Angel had retaken her seat and now lay with her head on the table as she watched the interaction, having forgotten all about the book.

"Danny had to trade him for everyone's lives," Matt continued. "Craig's with Graith and his crew, right now. We don't know exactly where they are, although Alex knows where their lair is. I dropped him off at a safe distance, so he should be inside at the moment keeping an eye on what's happening with Craig, if that's where they've taken him."

"You have to get them both out of there," Nixx said urgently.

Matt didn't quite understand. "It's a vampire lair. I can't get close enough to get in undetected. Dark energy fucks with me, even you know that. You saw it happen with the banshees a few years ago. I can't get anywhere near any form of dark energy, and there was some within the area where I dropped Alex off. That's why I had to leave him so far out. Even if I wanted to get in, I wouldn't be able to get back out. It's not possible."

"What about Remington, can he get them out?"

Matt shook his head. "He and Cole got exiled. They're at Banshee's End, right now. Remington's probably still moping around, knowing him. It'll be down to Alex to get Craig and get out of there. I don't know how, but there's nothing I can do."

Nixx was shaking his head slowly. He didn't like the way this was going.

"Why did Graith want Craig?" he asked. "You said he got traded for everyone else's lives?"

"Yeah, Graith said someone with higher authority than him wanted Craig alive. Why he couldn't kill him on the spot. What? You think this necromancer is the one who wants him? What could he possibly need Craig for? He's not dead, well, not yet I hope. It's only been a few hours since they took him."

"You need to figure out how you're going to get those two out of that area," Nixx said seriously. "I think I know who Dusk is."

CHAPTER THIRTY-FIVE

Preparations

Danny stared at Angel, who was busy minding her own business, sitting on the ground not far from where everyone was working.

The banshees so far hadn't done anything wrong, or even mildly threatening, but Danny didn't trust them. They'd have to go by sun-up, and he was hoping that was soon.

"Why are we babysitting a little kid?" Shawn asked. He stood on Danny's right with his arms crossed. "Aren't we meant to be focusing on building this outpost or something?"

Danny tore his gaze away from Angel who was now drawing in the dirt, bored.

"Well, apparently, they're going to make sure nothing attacks us overnight," he said, annoyance in his tone. He pointed at Angel who chose to ignore him for the moment. "They're banshees, Shawn!"

"I can hear you!" Angel called to him, Danny shooting a glare her way. She rolled her eyes, back to drawing in the dirt. "You're boring."

"We should be fine when the sun comes up," Shawn said, trying to lift Danny's spirits but it wasn't working. "The bloodsuckers haven't figured out how to day-walk yet, we'll get more built during the daylight hours."

Danny ran a frustrated hand through his hair. Right now, he didn't care about the outpost. Right now, he just wanted to sleep.

"What do you think they've done to Craig?" Ted asked, Danny switching his gaze to him.

Ted had relocated to sit in front of Angel on the ground, adding something to her dirt drawing. Angel's face lit up at the gesture.

"Dead if he's lucky," was Danny's comment. He indicated for Ted to get up off the ground. "Come on, get the fuck up and do something productive. She's a banshee, not a child. She'll eat your face off if you sit too close."

Angel pouted at him, and one of her banshee friends close by made some noise in disapproval, as well. Danny shot it a look, indicating that he was keeping a close watch on them.

"You're worrying too much, Danny," Ted said with a wave of his hand. "She's harmless. If she wanted to kill us, she'd have already wiped us all out!"

Danny rolled his eyes. His gaze was brought to someone who stopped next to him. It was his least favorite inseparable pair, Gates and Zeke.

"You boys wanna do something useful and stop harassing the banshees?" Gates asked.

"Yessir!" Ted got to his feet without any further coaxing. "We'll go do a check on everyone."

He and Shawn headed off. They didn't know where Jordan had disappeared to at this time of the night.

"Oh, so you'll listen to him, huh?" Danny called after the two of them.

He got no response, and Danny shook his head as he watched them walk over to the closest recruits to find out how things were going.

"Fucking idiots," he said, more directed at himself than the other two. He looked at Gates, the glare back on his face. "What do you want? Come to make sure I'm playing my part, or are you here to dismiss me?"

Gates held his hands up in his defense.

"We've got no authority here, Danny," he said. The glare on Danny's face only deepened. "You're the one in charge, we're just here on Matt's behalf. Do you want us to leave? You'll be completely defenseless by the morning once the banshees go back to their burrow until tomorrow night."

Danny chose not to say anything, instead going back to watching Angel who hadn't moved except to add more to her dirt drawings.

"Does anyone want to come back to Banshee's End?"

Danny jumped at the interruption, and Matt looked between the three of them. Gates and Zeke weren't bothered by his sudden appearance. They were used to it.

"I need to talk to Jacob," Matt said. "But it'll probably have to wait until the morning at this rate. It's too late now, everyone'll be asleep."

Danny sighed. He desperately wanted to go back and sleep, but he knew that wasn't going to be possible. He couldn't leave everyone here under anyone else's instructions. Who was going to be able to monitor the progress? Ted?

"Unfortunately, someone has to stay here and supervise," he said. Matt gave a solemn nod and Danny waved him away. "Get outta here, take these two with you. Someone'll be smart enough to wake me if anything happens."

"You're sure?" Matt asked, and Danny nodded, waving him away again. "Alright, we'll be back sometime tomorrow, depending on what Jacob wants to do about a few things. Call if you need help or if anything we need to know happens. I can bring people over if you need them."

Danny gave a single nod to show that he'd understood the instructions. Matt took Gates and Zeke, all three of them vanishing seconds later.

Danny wondered why he was always taking orders from Matt. He wasn't in charge, Danny was. But maybe Matt knew more than he did, maybe he was better at strategy?

It was better than taking orders from Craig, but only just. If he was just left to do his own thing, then there wouldn't be these issues.

It's not like Craig was going to be anywhere to order him around any time soon. The only problem was that Craig had proven to be incredibly good and useful when it came to strategies and overseeing everything that needed to happen.

As much as Danny didn't particularly like Craig, he had to give him credit for keeping everything and everyone in line and on track this entire time.

It would be just Danny's luck for everything to come crashing down now that he'd let Graith take Craig. He was unlucky enough on occasion that there was a high chance of it happening.

Danny didn't want to be around when the collapse happened.

"We'll talk to Jacob in the morning," Matt said. "Go get some sleep, it's late. I'll keep an eye on Danny over at the outpost, sleep a bit. Call if you need me for something and I'm not here."

Not waiting for any response, Matt vanished. Gates was the first to move, taking his leave to go to the room he'd used in the manor at Banshee's End last time he'd been here.

Zeke followed, not feeling like standing around and talking.

Remington watched them leave. He'd been in the dining room for hours, even after Chris and Ash had gone to their respective rooms to sleep.

It was late and Remington was bored. This was what he hated about not sleeping. He had nothing to do, and he couldn't sleep for hours to kill time.

Deciding to find something to do, he got up and wandered quietly through the manor.

He heard what sounded like a discussion happening in one of the rooms. He directed himself towards the right room, staying out of sight as the voices grew louder the closer he got.

Gates was in a bathroom and Ash stood in the doorway, leaning against the frame.

"You're doing OK?" Ash asked, Gates glancing over his shoulder at her.

"Nothing to not be OK about," Gates said, turning on the tap at the basin. He sighed. "It's been a long day."

Ash's expression saddened as Gates took his jacket off, dropping it onto the floor with no care. Ash could see multiple cuts on both of his arms, the blood having dried by now.

"Is that all from the vampires?" she asked, indicating to Gates's arms as he started cleaning himself up, wincing as the water hit his arm.

"The banshees, mostly," he sighed in response. "At least Matt was able to make a deal with them, so that should mean we're banshee-free for a while. How long that lasts, is the question. Any alliance right now, though, is a good alliance."

Ash could only agree. She didn't know what exactly had happened with the vampires or the banshees, but Gates had taken a lot of damage because of both scenarios.

"Do you know what Matt's plan is from here?" she asked. Gates did nothing but shrug, Ash taking the hint. "OK, sleep well, I guess. I'll be down the hall if you need something."

"I won't."

Ash took the hint and left, Remington having disappeared before she'd seen him. The last thing he wanted was to be caught eavesdropping on a private conversation.

Granted, it wouldn't have made much difference since Remington could hear almost everything no matter where he was in the manor. He'd have heard it even if he was outside the manor.

At least it had at least entertained him for a few minutes.

CHAPTER THIRTY-SIX

Deductions

Jacob sat down at the head of the table in the manor. From what he could see, not everyone was present yet.

It was only nine in the morning, but Matt had called this emergency meeting, and Jacob wasn't about to question it. Matt usually knew what he was talking about.

"Who're we waiting for?" Remington asked, looking around at who was already at the table.

"Matt's gone to get Danny and Arley," Jacob explained. "I want the two of them join the discussion because of their positions. Arley needs to be here since she works in Craig's division."

"Who's looking after the construction site?" Gates asked. "Because, honestly, without Danny or Arley, there's not exactly anyone else who can direct. Danny's not the best at directing a construction project to begin with, but everyone else is worse."

"And that's saying something," Zeke chimed in, Gates nodding to back up the statement.

"Danny's the one in charge, it's his decision," Jacob said.

Zeke and Gates weren't impressed but, at the end of the day, they knew it wasn't their problem, nor their business. Whoever Danny left in charge, wouldn't be for very long if this discussion went according to plan.

When did it ever though?

No one said anything else in the time between the short conversation and when Matt turned up with the two people he'd been sent to fetch.

Jacob gestured for the three of them to take an available seat at the table. Danny made sure to choose the seat furthest from the three vampires who were all seated together. The less vampires he had to deal with, the easier his life would be, even if the vampires in question had helped them out.

Matt sat next to Gates, and Arley hesitantly took a seat next to Ash who looked her over with strong judgement.

"Now that everyone's here, we can start," Jacob began. "First thing's first." He indicated to Chris. "This is Chris, since I know, Arley, you haven't met him before. He's been an integral part of the team and has just gotten back due to unforeseen circumstances. Chris, this is Arley Beckett, Craig's second-in-command in his division."

Chris offered Arley a smile from where he was on the opposite side of the table to Ash. Arley managed a very brief smile in return.

"Now, someone tell me what's going on," Jacob said, looking around at everyone. He didn't single anyone out in particular. "What's happening?"

Matt looked at Chris specifically. "You said that the journal you had is Upstairs in your house?"

"It should be," Chris responded. "Like I told you before, if my house is still untouched, it should still be there."

"OK, once this is done, we'll go for a step." Matt next looked at Jacob. "Nixx and I have had a long talk over this, and agreed it was best to bring the information over here and discuss it with the group. We ran into some banshees last night. The same ones we had the problem with when we first came into Oz."

"The ones with the girl?" Ash asked, Matt switching his gaze to her and nodding.

"We had a chat with the girl," he explained. Everyone who didn't already know the situation frowned. Remington wasn't in the least bit surprised by this news. "She's a lot more approachable than a normal banshee because she was turned into a banshee by a necromancer."

"You were able to talk to this girl?" Ash spoke up again.

"Someone else can explain it. Remington knows what I'm talking about." Matt went back to addressing Jacob. He had more pressing matters to attend to than explaining banshees to Ash. "This little girl explained that the necromancer who created her is still around, and he's working with the vampires."

It was Remington's turn to frown. Cole, though, was the one who spoke. "He's working with the vampires?" He exchanged looks with Remington. "Does that mean whoever this necromancer is, he's within the habitat?"

"She said he's the one in charge of the Legion," Matt explained. Remington and Cole exchanged looks again. This was news to them. "Apparently, he's the one that says jump, and they all jump."

Jacob looked at Cole and Remington. Maddie was in the conversation too, but she knew a lot less about what was going on since she'd been away for quite some time.

"You guys said you didn't know who was in charge of the Legion," he stated, Remington nodding. "Do you think it's possible that a necromancer—someone who's not a vampire—might be the one dictating everything they do?"

Danny slouched in his seat, arms crossed as he waited to hear what excuses the vampire would give.

Remington shrugged. "There's nothing saying that a vampire has to be in charge. It's not *not* plausible. It could really be anyone in charge at the end of the day, but, whoever it is, they have a *very* tight hold and a lot of power over the Legion."

"Nixx was concerned about it," Matt said. "We were talking about the possibilities, and he was more concerned because he thinks he knows who this necromancer might be."

That gained Jacob's interest a lot more than the start of this conversation. "He knows who it is for sure, or just speculation?"

"He mentioned a rather famous necromancer named Dusk."

Jacob's expression fell upon hearing the name. Remington and Cole's faces had also fallen.

"Dusk?" Jacob said. Matt nodded, causing Jacob to sigh. He wasn't happy to hear it. "If he's in charge of the Legion, instructing them, that makes more sense as to what they mean when talking about higher authority." He shook his head, thinking. "But why would Dusk want Craig specifically?"

Matt didn't know how to break the news to him. From his conversation and discussion with Nixx late last night, they'd come to a very disheartening conclusion on what Dusk wanted from Craig.

"Nixx thinks that Dusk might have been Marion's doctor," Matt made himself say. Chris and Ash exchanged looks at this news. "Apparently, he likes to masquerade different features depending on what he's doing. He more than likely won't look like the castle's doctor if we meet him again. That probably wasn't what he even really looks like."

"If he was the castle doctor," Chris said before Matt could say anything else. "He, ah, he was doing experiments on people, trying to figure out abilities and how they worked."

Matt nodded. Chris was on the right track.

"That's why we think he wants Craig. Craig has the fatal touch, that's his ability. I don't know about you guys, but if I were a necromancer, which I'm not, I'd want to try and find someone with any form of death ability and, if I could figure out how it works, try to replicate it?"

Jacob leant back in his chair, the serious look never leaving his face. This was a very bad situation if what Matt was speculating was right.

"Nixx wants the journals," Matt said when no one said a word. Everything was sinking in. "I have three of them, Chris has the fourth one, as long as everything's fine in his house and it's still there. Nixx wants to have a proper look through them, make sure he's right and not just assuming something that's not true."

"Are you sure it's a good idea to bring the journals back down here?" Ash asked, Matt's gaze flicking her way. "Because if they hold information on these experiments that the doctor was doing, and you think this necromancer is the same guy, wouldn't you want to keep the information as far out of his hands as possible?"

"It's a dangerous situation no matter which way we look at it." Matt's tone was dead serious. "I understand what you're saying, Ash, but I'd rather Nixx look through them and then we can decide what to do with them, whether we destroy them, or hide them somewhere so that no one can use them."

Danny pushed himself up into a proper sitting position, resting his head on his hand as he regarded Matt, a bored look on his face.

"Look, I'm just speculatin'," he began. Everyone let him speak which was an unusual circumstance when it came to Danny stating an opinion. "Ash has a point, you have a point, but you seem to be forgetting that it doesn't exactly matter where these journals are, does it? The Legion is pushing Upstairs, even if those books aren't down here now, they're up there, so there's a chance that they'll get them either way. Ever think that's why they wanna get Upstairs?" He moved, holding his hands up in a defensive maneuver. "Just thinkin'."

"Danny's got a point," Chris said. He crossed his arms and leaned back in his seat, exhaling and shaking his head. "We don't know the actual reason the Legion wants to get Upstairs, it could be for anything, including the journals."

"How would they even know where they are?" Arley finally had the courage to speak up.

She'd never been allowed to sit in on these sorts of meetings before, so she was feeling very out of place. This was Craig's environment, his thing, not hers, but right now, she was sitting in as his representative. She wasn't going to let him down by not trying to contribute.

"We don't know if they have any idea of where they are, or even if that's what they're looking for," Chris stated. Arley wasn't keeping up with why they were adamant on this, if they weren't even sure. "It's purely speculation until we can prove something." He indicated to Matt across the table from him. "Matt's right, I think we need to have Nixx look everything over. He can decide how we proceed. If he's right, and this necromancer is Dusk, and Dusk was masquerading as the Wonderland castle's doctor, Craig's in a lot of shit, and Alex will be too."

Arley was concerned to say the least. Maybe she'd been wrong, and she wasn't up for the responsibility of being a captain or anything more. Danny made being a captain look easy, and Craig made being a commander look simple.

Sitting in on this meeting was proving to be the complete opposite to what she'd thought. She didn't realize just how deep this operation was going and had been. No wonder they left Craig to do the strategy for the entirety of Banshee's End.

"Alright, here's what we'll do," Jacob said. Everyone looked at him. Jacob's word was law around here, so they would be doing whatever he said no matter what. "Matt, you and Chris go back Upstairs and get what you need, deliver them to Nixx. Danny, you take Arley, Gates, and Zeke, get that outpost finished as soon as possible and move onto the next one, fast. If you need to split the groups and get half started on the next one now, do it."

Danny gave a single nod.

"Arley, if Danny splits the team, you're in charge of the second construction site," Jacob continued. Arley understood, even if she was nervous about the responsibility. "Remington, I know that you and Cole have been exiled, but I need you two and Maddie to start trying to find out what you can about how fast the Legion are moving, and if anyone in the surrounding areas knows what might be going on inside the habitat. Ash, it's up to you whether you go with Matt and Chris and help them Upstairs, or if you want to go and help with the outposts. Just let me know where you're going."

"I'll go back with Danny, and try to help there," Ash said.

Jacob was satisfied with the conclusion.

"Alright, everyone keep in contact and report in at regular intervals. Once we know what's actually going on, we can devise a plan to get Craig and Alex out of the habitat as soon as we can. Craig can hold his own for now, but we can't leave him down there for too long. Let's get to it."

CHAPTER THIRTY-SEVEN

Building Outposts

"Everyone get your asses over here, right the fuck now!"

All the recruits and civilians who had been working to get the outpost built heard Danny's call for attention and rushed over.

The recruits knew not to keep Danny waiting, as his patience quite often wore thin.

Danny gave it a minute to ensure everyone was present. He did a quick silent count to himself, seeing the main people he needed here, including Gates and Zeke, Arley and Ash.

Shawn, Ted, and Jordan were, as usual, standing up the front with him. They hardly ever left his side.

Danny readjusted his sunglasses, the sunlight harshly reflecting off the snow that had settled from the previous night. It was snowing lightly at the moment, and he was really wishing it would just stop completely. He never wanted to see snow again in his life after this crusade.

"Alright, listen up," he started once satisfied that everyone was here, recruits and civilians alike. "We're on a serious time crunch right now, so you'd all better listen and not make me repeat myself, clear?"

He narrowed his eyes behind his sunglasses as everyone nodded in intimidated acknowledgement.

"Here's what's going to happen, starting immediately," he continued. He indicated to Arley in the front row. "Beckett here is gonna take half of you and you're going to get started on the next site. We're running on a strict timeframe, and we don't have much time left to get this shit built. I've been instructed to split you idiots up and get more work done.

"So, anyone in my team, you stay here and you're going to continue with this contribution. Anyone on Craig's team, you go with Arley. People who don't belong to either team, or Banshee's End, talk amongst yourselves, and split as evenly as possible between here and there. You have five minutes to decide before Beckett takes everyone to the new site. Am I being clear right now?"

More acknowledgement from the group. There weren't as many as there had been initially, as the vampires had killed quite a few recruits and civilians in the siege.

"I don't wanna hear any excuses," Danny said, tone serious and voice loud enough that even the people at the back could hear him. "Remember, you're currently reporting to me, regardless of Beckett being over at the other site. Anything and everything goes through me before it gets done. I'll come and check in a few hours how it's going. Don't make me report back to Banshee's End and tell them you're all too fucking slack to get shit done."

He looked at Gates, Zeke, and Ash who were all standing off to the side.

"You guys do whatever the fuck you think is best, I don't care where you go," he said. "I'd prefer Gates, if you would go with Beckett to keep order in case she's too intimidated to take her role seriously and make the right choices." Arley shot him a look, but Danny ignored it. She wasn't worth the effort. Danny looked back at everyone in front of him, loudly clapping his hands and making a few people jump, startled. "Get moving!"

Everyone rushed to their assignments. Danny's team split themselves off to the side, Craig's division went over to stand near Arley, and they all waited for the civilians' final decisions.

Danny waited with his arms crossed. After what seemed to him to be about five minutes, he spoke again. "Move! Split yourselves and get to work! We're on a tight schedule, get going!"

The civilians split as best as they could, a few joining Danny and his crew whilst the others went to Arley. Danny waved her away, and Arley took the hint, leaving for the new construction site. Gates and Ash went with them.

Zeke had voted to stay back here for the moment. He'd go over to the other one in a while and switch with Gates halfway through the day. Granted, it was already nearly eleven in the morning, but that didn't matter.

Danny turned to face his small team as Zeke wandered over, already in the process of lighting a cigarette to kill some time.

"OK, here's what we're gonna do," Danny began explaining. His crew were used to the way he spoke and ordered everyone around. They always listened, and Danny knew he could count on them should push come to shove. They'd sacrifice themselves for anyone else in the team. Well, he wasn't so sure about Daniel. "Ted and I are gonna go and have a look at some of the close by towns, see if we can recruit more help. Zeke's gonna be in charge while we're gone. We shouldn't be more than an hour, maybe two at the most. You listen to him until I get back, got it?"

They all nodded, Danny nodding back.

"You build, and you fuckin' build quick, but you build safe. I want to see progress by the time I get back. Once I get back, I'll have to go and check on the other site, so Jordan will be in charge when that happens. You can all contact me if something happens, make sure you do, and fill me in when I get back. If something drastic happens, you hold your ground, you don't do anything that'll sabotage this outpost. We've got one job, and we're damn well gonna do it, and we're gonna do it right.

"I don't want to come back and hear excuses, you're all better than that. You get this damn outpost built, and you defend it with your life. The Legion shouldn't come back today, not while it's light outside. I don't know how much time we have until we have another siege but, hopefully, Craig's sacrifice has bought us some time."

Daniel timidly raised his hand. Danny looked at him, tipping his head at him to tell him to talk.

"Do you think that vampire, the one in charge, will hold to his word and let us finish this outpost, Captain?" Daniel asked, lowering his hand.

Danny shifted his weight. How was he supposed to tell this kid that nothing was ever set in stone? As much as he disliked Daniel, he had no ill-intent against him. He was annoying, sure, but he'd still signed up to help their cause and try to counter the Legion's attacks.

Danny, also, didn't lie to his people.

"No," Danny said after the brief hesitation. He looked around at his team. "I'm not here to lie to everyone, to fool the lambs to slaughter, you know I don't do that. It's not fair on you lot to hear bullshit. I'm here to tell it to you straight. Graith is a fucking liar. He doesn't care about us, he doesn't care about his team, he doesn't care about anyone but himself. Graith is in it for Graith, no one else. He'd rather kill us all than turn us all. He's full of threats, mostly hollow, but he's dangerous. Vampires aren't trustworthy, I don't care what anyone says. Graith's not about to let us finish anything. I'm expecting they'll hit again before we get the wall up fully."

There were a few disheartened looks within the group, but Danny wasn't going to stand here and lie to them, tell them that it would all be OK. It achieved nothing.

"So, this is why we're on a strict timeframe," he continued. He put his hood up as the snow started to fall a bit harder, the sun having disappeared behind some clouds now. Readjusting his sunglasses, not about to remove them due to the glare, Danny sighed. "We need to get as much built as we can before whoever's telling Graith what to do decides to send reinforcements and try to take us down.

"Like I said before, if that happens, you stand your ground, you defend this area with your life. We can't afford for these bloodsuckers to get through to the Room of Doors and get Upstairs. It'll be a shitty time for everyone, not just us. I won't promise any of you will be getting out alive, so I just wanna say, in case I don't get another chance…"

He paused, looking around at them all, no one speaking.

"I appreciate the time and work you've all put into this doomed operation," he said. It was unlike Danny to show this sort of gratitude, but he needed to make sure he did one nice thing on occasion. "None of you had to sign up for this, but the amount that turned up, this group of you in particular, who've been serving under my division for the last year, thank you for your dedication. I'm glad it was all of you and not someone else." He narrowed his eyes. "Now get to work! Don't make me ask you again!"

Gates glanced at Ash as he leaned against a tree, standing in the shade even though it was starting to get colder and snow more. The sun had gone, and there was nothing to warm him up.

"I thought you'd have stayed back with Danny," he commented, taking a drag on his lit cigarette. This was also partially why he was standing out of the way. "He's way more fun."

Ash couldn't help herself, rolling her eyes. She leaned against the tree next to him.

"Truthfully, Blaine," she said, Gates not even bothering to correct her anymore. "Danny's an idiot, but he's good at ordering people around. I think I'd rather be locked down with the vampires than have to hear him yell at everyone."

Gates smiled, amused.

"I bet you'd have stayed over at the other outpost if I had," he noted, Ash's expression becoming a glare. Gates looked her over. "So, what've you been up to over the last year? Nothing fun, looking at the circumstances."

Ash scoffed. She crossed her arms, her gaze going to the recruits working close by. Gates saw her watching Arley, specifically.

"There's not exactly lots to do down here, no matter what county you're in," Ash said. "Up until recently, everything's been fine in Wonderland. With Marion gone, there've been no threats, even from Hunter. He was too busy trying to figure out what to do about Marion. As far as I'm aware, he was with Carmen." She sighed. "I'd been hoping the vampire problem would never reach this far, but they went right through one of the outposts that bordered us, so I had to contact Craig. He set up these operations to try and push them back. Now look where we are."

"Yep," Gates sighed. "Craig's missing, the vampires are roaming, and neither of us are working."

Ash gave him a look, Gates smiling. She shoved him rather roughly, crossing her arms as he managed to keep his balance. He finished his cigarette and threw away the remainder.

"Does your girlfriend know about everything that happened?" Ash asked, back to staring at Arley. "Does she know you're here?"

Gates shook his head, putting his hands in his pockets, feeling the cold starting to seep in.

"No and no," was his answer. "I can't and haven't said anything. What would I even tell her? She'd think I'm crazy, and I don't really want that." He shook his head with a sigh, turning his gaze to watch Arley as well. "I won't say anything, she doesn't need to know this shit. As far as she's aware, Matt, Zeke, and I are on a road trip somewhere, and that's how it stays."

Ash understood. "Let's hope it stays that way and the Legion doesn't get Upstairs to change that."

CHAPTER THIRTY-EIGHT

Home

Matt and Chris stopped in front of the four different coloured doors.

The two men had gone through the Room of Doors, down the tunnel, and had finally made it to the doors that led to four different areas Upstairs.

They'd had to take the Room of Doors since Matt had never been to Chris's house, hence why he couldn't shadow-step them straight there. The doors were a lot quicker than being shadow-stepped into California and then having to travel to the other side of the country to get to Pennsylvania.

It had been a long time since Chris had come this way, and he was rather nervous about going back Upstairs. He didn't know what he should be expecting, what was waiting for him back home. There were endless possibilities, and the thought of that alone was really worrying him.

"Can we stop for a second?" Chris asked as Matt was reaching for the handle of the black door. "I have a question."

Matt let go of the door handle and indicated for Chris to ask.

Chris cleared his throat awkwardly. Sure, he knew that they were on a tight timeframe and, yes, he was stalling, but something had genuinely occurred to him.

"I have a favor to ask," he started. Matt raised an intrigued eyebrow. "Since we don't know if my house is still there, that it hasn't been sold or rented out, whatever, once we get there, can you ... I dunno, knock on the door first and see if anyone answers? If not, go inside and see if there's any evidence that it's still my house? I don't want trouble if someone else lives there now. We'll have to figure out what to do, if that's the case."

"Sure, I'll do anything, you know that," Matt said.

That was one of the good things about Matt. He was a lot more confident about these situations and would do pretty well anything he needed to. Chris couldn't think of much that Matt wouldn't do if he had to.

Matt opened the black door, forwarding through without waiting for Chris who rushed after him. He didn't want to be left behind.

As much as he was panicking about going back Upstairs, he wasn't going to stick around in Wonderland or Oz unless he needed to. He needed to know what the state of his normal life was like.

Once the two of them had made it Upstairs and into the right area, Matt let Chris lead the way. He knew his way around, no matter how long he'd been away for.

There was a lot of traffic and people around at this time of the day. It was a bit cold out today, but nowhere near as cold as Wonderland currently was.

"Have you been up here before?" Chris asked as they walked down the sidewalk. "Here in Pennsylvania, I mean."

"It's been quite a long time, but I've been in the state before," Matt confirmed. "Not since before I went to Wonderland, though. I haven't gone anywhere that exciting since I've been home. I might consider going on a holiday somewhere once everything settles down, but we'll have to wait and see what happens."

Chris understood. He hadn't been on vacation for quite some time, either, and it wasn't even because he'd been in a different dimension for the past year.

"Do you..." he started to say as they turned down a quieter street, no longer walking down the main road. They were in the proper suburbs now. "Do you ever wonder how some of the guys ended up down there?"

Matt shrugged. "Not really. I've got other shit to think about rather than what everyone's reasons for being Downstairs is. I've got better things to do." He glanced at Chris. "You do?"

"No one really talks about it," Chris said with a shrug of his own. "I've had a lot of time to think over the last year."

Matt said nothing, and they came to a stop outside one of the houses, presumably Chris's house, as they had no reason to stop at any other place.

"This is it," Chris sighed. He stared at the house. "It looks in decent condition, maybe someone else does live here now."

The front lawn and garden were all tended to, meaning that, even though Chris hadn't been around for over a year, someone was looking after the place.

"I was gone for eight years, Chris," Matt said, Chris looking to him.

Matt went over to the mailbox, opened it, and grabbed what was inside it, much to Chris's despair. It might not have even been Chris's mail.

"But I came home," Matt continued. "And my house was still in perfect condition. You've been gone for a year, big deal."

Chris crossed his arms, watching Matt sift through the mail.

"Your situation and mine are different," Chris commented. "Your family was looking after your place. My family might have taken a different approach."

"Well, unless someone else who lives here is also named Chris, we have a pretty good chance that you still own it."

He tossed the mail back in the mailbox and strode to the front door. Chris hesitantly followed as Matt knocked on the door, waiting to see if anyone would answer.

Chris felt his panic rise fast and they heard someone moving on the other side of the door. He exchanged looks with Matt, not having time to say anything, as the door unlocked from the other side and opened.

An older woman opened the door and looked between Chris and Matt. Realization appeared on her face as she looked back at Chris.

"Chris?" she exclaimed. Matt gave Chris a questioning look. "Oh my gosh!" She moved forwards, out the door, pulling Chris into a rather tight hug. "Where have you been?"

Chris returned the gesture. He wasn't about to forget his own mother.

"It's complicated," he said.

His mother let him go and stepped back, looking him over and getting a brief smile.

"We looked everywhere for you, you just dropped off out of nowhere," she said. She looked at Matt who gave her a nice smile. "I'm Paula, Chris's mother."

"Matt," he introduced himself, shaking the hand she held out to him. "A friend of Chris."

Paula smiled broadly and ushered the two of them inside, shutting the door behind herself.

"You've no idea the stress you've caused me, Chris," she said, going through to the living room. Matt looked around with interest as Chris followed his mother through the house. "I've spent a lot of time here in case you came back. Where have you been?"

"Like I said, it's complicated," Chris sighed.

Paula sat down on the couch, Chris staying where he was in the entranceway with Matt next to him.

Chris narrowed his eyes as he looked around. "You haven't gotten rid of anything, have you?"

Paula shook her head. "No, no. I haven't touched anything. Everything's still exactly where you left it."

At least that was one good thing to come out of this awkward situation. Chris would be able to find the journal and go back down to Wonderland to see Nixx.

Paula's expression saddened. "Harper's been so worried about you, too. She didn't know where you disappeared to, none of us did."

Matt gave Chris a questioning look which he ignored.

"I know, I'm sorry," he said. "Look, I can't stay long, I have something to take care of but, I promise, I'll be back as soon as I can."

"Chris..."

"I'm sorry, Mom, really." He looked at Matt. "I'll see if I can find it, then we can get back."

Chris left the room, and Paula sighed. Matt followed Chris through the house to his bedroom.

"You're sure it's definitely here?" Matt asked.

"Mom said she hasn't moved anything, so, unless the house has been raided while I've been gone, it'll be here."

Matt crossed his arms and leaned against the doorframe as Chris went to the bedside table, opening the top drawer. He knew where he'd left the journal.

"Who's Harper?" Matt asked.

He had an idea of who Paula had been talking about, but he wanted to get the confirmation from Chris himself.

"My girlfriend," Chris confirmed. Just as Matt had thought. "We started dating about a month after I got home after the first time." He sighed, taking the journal out of the top drawer. "Hope she can wait a bit longer."

"You never mentioned her before."

"No reason to." Chris held the journal out to Matt who took it. "This is it, where to next?"

Matt accepted the journal, opening it and checking that it was definitely what they'd been after. Chris could hear Paula moving around in the living room.

"We're going to California," Matt said. He snapped the book shut, making Chris jump. "Go see my beautiful wife and kid."

He walked out and back to the living room, Chris having no choice but to follow.

"Thank you for the hospitality, Paula," Matt was in the middle of saying as Chris caught up to him. "Chris and I have a few things to take care of, but he'll be home soon, unscathed, and ready to explain everything to you." Chris rolled his eyes. "I'll make sure he keeps in contact with you, so you're not worrying." He looked at Chris. "Let's go."

Chris gave his mother an apologetic look, before he and Matt left. She was obviously not happy about him leaving so soon after being missing for over a year.

Once the two of them were outside, Matt scoped the area out, finding an area down the street that was dark enough for him to shadow-step. He grabbed Chris and the two of them vanished, thankfully without anyone seeing them.

A second later, with Chris's head spinning, they were in the living room in a different house.

Vivian looked over, away from the TV, as Matt made Chris hold the journal.

"Chris, hi!" Vivian greeted him with a very nice smile. "It's been forever since I've seen you!"

Chris smiled back as his head stopped spinning and returned to normal. "It's been a very long year."

Vivian accepted Matt's quick kiss of greeting before he headed past her and out of the room.

"What are you doing up here?" Vivian called to Matt, turning the TV down so she could hear his response. "I thought you had business in Wonderland with the boys?"

"I do!" Matt called back as Chris awkwardly waited. "We're probably gonna run into a vampire problem up here soon. I'll be back before that happens, just make sure you're prepared."

"Mmhm." Vivian had gone back to watching the TV.

"Riley home?" Matt called.

Chris could hear him moving things around in one of the nearby rooms.

"He's at a friend's house tonight," Vivian said. When Matt reappeared in the living room, holding the other three journals, she looked at him and smiled. "Be safe, OK?"

"Always." Matt gave her a quick kiss again before looking at Chris. "Let's get going. We have to go and see Nixx, try work this out before it's too late." He looked at Vivian. "I'll be home soon, call me if you need something."

Vivian smiled, giving the two of them a wave. Matt put his hand on Chris's shoulder, stepped back, and the two of them vanished.

CHAPTER THIRTY-NINE

Necromancy

"Everything going OK over here?"

Danny switched his gaze to Matt who'd appeared beside him. The sun had started to go down, and everyone was now on edge since there was always a chance of vampires whenever it got dark.

"No issues yet," Danny sighed. "I have Gates and Zeke swapping outposts every few hours. At the moment, Zeke's back here, Gates is over at the one with Arley and her team. Everything's fine for now." He indicated to Zeke who was leaning against a part of the already built wall. "The banshees have decided he's the one they like, so they're hanging out with him tonight."

Matt and Chris both looked over to Zeke who was looking at something on his phone to pass the time. Angel and her two banshee friends were close, with Angel talking to Zeke about something. They were out early tonight. The sun hadn't even fully gone down yet.

"Well, as long as you're all safe for the moment," Matt said. "OK, Chris and I are going over to the castle to talk to Nixx. Take shifts to sleep, keep working, we'll come and check in as soon as we have answers."

Matt and Chris vanished again, leaving Danny to his business.

Nixx glanced up as Matt wandered over. He was at his usual table, in the middle of looking at something.

Matt placed all four leather-bound journals on the table next to the papers Nixx had been sorting through.

"You got them?" Nixx slid the journals towards himself. "Wonderful."

"Do you think you're going to find what you're after?" Chris asked. "What are you even looking for?"

"It's nice to see you too, Chris."

Chris chose not to bite, and Matt pulled out a chair, scraping the floor in the process. He sat down, leaned back, and crossed his arms as he waited for Nixx to get started on his task. Whatever that consisted of.

"To answer your question, Chris," Nixx began. He opened the first journal, the one that was on top of the pile. "I'd like to assume that Matthew's told you about my speculations. You were in the team meeting this morning?"

Chris nodded, indicating that he knew.

Nixx continued, his focus on the journal the entire time. "If what I think is true, and the necromancer that we're dealing with is Dusk, these books will tell me. I've only looked through one partially. If he was parading around as the castle's doctor, then he would want these notes. He's very dangerous and, if he has his hands on Craig, he'll want to know how his ability works. Fatal touch isn't that common. I've never heard of anyone else with that ability. It's incredibly rare, and Dusk will want to use that to further his research and power when it comes to necromancy."

"Do you think he's going to kill Craig in order to figure it out?" Chris asked.

He was worried that if Dusk couldn't find what he was after, he'd resort to killing Craig and possibly Alex if he knew he was there too.

"Not straight away," Nixx mused, turning each page with caution. "He'll keep experimenting until he gets what he wants, or unintentionally kills his victim. The doctor always tortured until his victims perished, or he killed them himself. Why do you think Alice is how she is? She was a prime experiment for the doctor, yet he got bored when she showed no signs of interest, left her down in the dungeons, and now here we are."

"Do you know how abilities work?" Chris asked curiously.

Nixx shook his head.

"Haven't have the foggiest. Besides the few common abilities, such as Zeke's, every ability is unique to everyone, for the most part. There are multiple theories on why that is, but there's no real answer, no real explanation for how someone's ability manifests, why people end up with the ones that they do." He shook his head again, moving the first journal out of the way and opening the next one. "Some, like the fatal touch, are a lot more rare than others. From everything that I've read, people only ever speculated that the fatal touch was a possible ability, no one was ever able to confirm it. But as a death ability, necromancers will want to utilize it to their advantage, hence, Craig's predicament."

"If this guy in charge of the Legion is actually this fabled necromancer?" Matt was skeptical. "What are we even meant to do if this turns out to be true? Not just speculation? What do we do, because we can't exactly waltz up to the vampire habitat and ask for Craig back."

"That's a discussion to be had as a group."

Matt wasn't impressed, but he didn't push the matter any further. Nixx wasn't going to have all the solutions, even though Matt would have liked someone to have an idea. They were just going to have to wait for the final conclusion.

It had been quite a while since there had been any sign of anyone, and Alex didn't know how long they'd been down here. He hadn't been game enough to return to his human form ever since Graith had come downstairs to the dungeons last time.

Alice had been staring into Craig's cell for what was more than likely literal days, not saying a word, but occasionally making a grab for the tiny mouse when he wandered away to check for anything that might have been happening further in the dungeons.

So far, nothing even mildly interesting had happened.

Alex squeaked as he heard the buzz from Craig's phone. Neither Graith nor any of the vampires had bothered to search him, figuring that even if he managed to get out, he wouldn't get very far.

Craig reluctantly reached into his pocket and took out his phone. He was too tired to deal with other people's problems.

He hadn't expected his phone to even work down here. Granted, like everyone else's phones, this one had been upgraded thanks to technical magic. He didn't question it and had no desire to.

The battery wouldn't last forever, though, and it was already down to five percent, when he hadn't even been using it. He'd figured there was no point and hadn't even realized he'd left it on.

Alex squeaked again, Craig ignoring him and going to his messages, seeing that he had a new one. The vampire in the cell directly next to him was still going at it, trying to grab for him any chance that it got.

Alice watched with interest as Craig kept his gaze on his phone.

"What's that?" she asked, pointing to the phone.

"Work," was Craig's answer. He sighed, seeing the new voice message from his bandmate Upstairs, Astin. "I don't know why he bothers."

This wasn't the first time this had happened, that Astin had tried contacting Craig. He got voice messages every so often, and had been for quite a long time, since he'd disappeared from Upstairs. For some reason, Astin hadn't given up hope.

Craig didn't even know if it was possible for him to go home anymore.

Hesitating, Craig stared at the unheard voice message. Alex was waiting to hear it and, making his decision, Craig gave in, playing the voice message to see what it said.

"Hey man, me again," was the sighed beginning of the message. The tone was sad, just like every other one Craig had received from him. "Look, I know you're getting these, or well, someone is anyway. It tells me you've seen them, or well, whoever's got your phone, I guess." Astin sighed sadly again. "I know it's already been four, no, five years now, but I just wanna know you're still alright, wherever you are. I know you're still out there somewhere, where, though, I've no idea, but just know, we're all still here when you can come home. We miss you, man. Please look after yourself, get in contact soon, OK? We love you, man."

The message ended and Craig sighed to himself, relocked his phone and put it back in his pocket. He crossed his arms and shut his eyes again. He was too tired for this.

"How did you end up down here?" Alex asked, no longer the mouse, sitting in front of Craig, out of the way of the grabbing, rabid vampire in the next cell.

Craig kept his eyes closed as he answered.

"No idea," he said. Alex frowned. "If I knew for sure, I'd tell you, Alex, but as things go, I don't remember. We played a show, and the next morning, I woke up down here. I'd given up heavy drinking by then, too, so I can't even use an excuse of having drunk too much." He opened his eyes and looked at Alex directly seated on the floor in front of him. "I don't know how much you know about Upstairs, the way some things work."

Alex shook his head. "Not well, even though I'm apparently from somewhere up there. I don't know anything at all, didn't even know until we got to Banshee's End that I wasn't from here."

"So, I was the frontman of this rock band," Craig explained. Even Alice was listening with interest, even if she didn't know what in the world he was talking about. There was a lot about the world she didn't know, since she'd come down here a very long time ago. "We were pretty successful, not gonna lie. Part of that 'rockstar lifestyle' heavily revolves around partying, drinking after shows, wouldn't be unusual to go out after the shows and stay out all night, and then do it all again the next night.

"Like I said, I'd stopped drinking by that point. I had no control over my intake when we were out. I managed to give it up completely for a few years, the stress of all this shit, though? Caused a minor relapse not that long ago, but whatever. My point is that it's no excuse for me not knowing how I got here. I'd love to say that, but it's not true. I genuinely have no idea how it happened."

Craig shut his eyes again.

Alex frowned. "Strange. How old were you when you came down here?"

"Shit, what am I now?" Craig had to think for a second. "I would've been about twenty-eight."

Alex was very interested, but he didn't have the chance to say anything else, as someone was approaching the cell. Within seconds he was a mouse again, falling back into the darkness of the cell so as not to be seen.

"Commander," Graith was back. Craig opened his eyes, not in the mood for whatever Graith wanted. "You're wanted downstairs, hope you're not in the middle of something."

"I was trying to sleep, but I guess I can spare some time, since you asked so nicely."

"I heard you talking," Graith said. He glanced at Alice, then back at Craig. "Talking in your sleep?"

Graith was amused by Craig's silence and one of the vampires with him unlocked the cell door. The vampire lackey hauled Craig roughly to his feet and shoved him out through the door.

"Where's he going?" Alice called as Craig was escorted away from his cell, heading back the way they'd come days ago.

"You'll be next, don't fret," Graith called back to her, the amusement in his tone the entire time. "No need to worry yourself with Commander Taylor's business downstairs."

Craig chose to stay quiet, seeing the little mouse dashing around to keep up with the small group. The last thing that Alex wanted was to lose track of Craig.

Graith pushed a door open, and Craig was escorted through the room and to another set of stairs that led even deeper into the habitat than the dungeons. It was dead silent as they descended, their footsteps, again, the only thing echoing off the walls.

At the end of the stairs was a long corridor. Once at the end, Craig was pulled to a halt. Graith knocked on the solid wooden door, waiting for some sort of cue to tell him that he could enter.

Craig glanced to his left, seeing the little mouse hiding close by.

The door creaked open slowly, and Graith signaled for the vampires to push Craig in and follow. They did just that, Craig having no choice but to go with them, the door swinging shut behind them.

The room they were in was rather large, and Craig felt a hint of unease for the first time since he'd been here. The room contained shelves and shelves of books, from floor to ceiling, a few metal surgical tables pushed out of the way, and multiple chairs with straps for wrists and ankles.

The most disturbing part—what had made Craig so uneasy—was the number of coffins lining the walls. Some were on the floor, while others stood up against the walls.

None were open, but Craig wasn't going to take that as a good sign.

"Craig Taylor," he heard as he was pulled to a stop. He didn't know who'd spoken. "It's a pleasure to finally meet you in person, I've heard a lot about you."

"Can't say the same about you," Craig said back, doing a quick scan of the room to see what would stop him from leaving or making any form of move.

There was a low laugh. The vampires pushed Craig harshly to his knees, holding him there. The floor was glass, and Craig saw the endless number of coffins below the flooring. A dark figure strode over from somewhere near one of the bookshelves, the dark clothing hiding most of their features.

The figure stopped directly in front of Craig who didn't move.

"Trust me, Commander, you've heard of me," the figure said. "And we're about to get to know each other a lot better."

CHAPTER FORTY

Sinking with the Ship

"What do we think?" Jacob asked.

Nixx was standing in front of the noticeboards lined with information, multiple years worth of notes and strategies alike.

"Well, we have a problem either way," Nixx said. He pursed his lips in thought. "I've gone through every inch of those journals, all four of them. There's a lot of information missing. There has to be more journals than just those four. Whether Dusk took them with him when he left the castle, or they're somewhere in the castle, I don't know."

"There might be some over in Carmen's area," Chris said, Nixx giving him a sidelong glance. "He was called in to torture Matt when he was in their dungeon. That was the last time we saw him."

"Hm," Nixx shook his head slowly. "It's a mystery."

"So, we're one-hundred percent sure that it's Dusk," Jacob stated.

Nixx nodded. He tore his gaze away from the information boards.

Everyone in the operations room listened. They all needed to know, and Doug took notes as they went.

"I have no doubt it's him," Nixx confirmed. "After going through every page, scouring over them over the last few days, there's no doubt in my mind that's who it is. Dusk is the necromancer, the one who's running the Legion's operations. It would be almost impossible for it to be someone else at this point. Necromancers are few and far between, and Dusk's been around for an incredibly long time. Someone with his amount of power is more likely to be running a legion of the undead than a novice."

Matt looked at Jacob. "So, what's the plan? Danny's team has almost finished the wall, a few buildings got completed overnight. Arley's team is about two thirds of the way done with their wall and one building is already done. We've heard nothing from Alex about the situation with the vampires, what's happening with Craig, nothing. We don't know when they're going to strike the outposts. So, what are we looking at doing?"

Jacob looked at Nixx who was facing him, hands behind his back as he regarded him, waiting for whatever he had on his mind.

"What do you know about Dusk?" Jacob asked. "Why would he be connected to the Legion?"

Nixx summed him up as he thought about the answer. Once he looked back to Jacob's face, he spoke, addressing him solely.

"Dusk's been around for a very long time, he's hailed as the original necromancer," he began to explain. Doug was scribbling madly, struggling to keep up with the notes. "He's had a long time to perfect his craft, but he doesn't know everything, clearly. He wouldn't be experimenting on people if he knew everything now, would he?" Nixx paused, turning back to face the information wall, walking slowly along it to look at all the information available. "There's rumor, theory, that he was the initial creator of the vampires, was responsible for the first one. Whether that vampire is still around, no idea, but if that rumor is true, or has truth behind it, that'll give you an idea of why the vampires are under his control."

Matt leaned against the closest table, arms crossed. He watched Nixx, trying to think, taking the information in.

"If Dusk's the creator of the vampires," he began, getting Nixx's attention. "You know how there's always the lore behind vampires, well, Upstairs there is, that if you kill the head vampire, you kill them all?"

Chris nodded. He understood. "You think if you take out the first vampire, it'll knock them all off? That would kill Remington, too. You're willing to sacrifice him?"

"Yes," Matt said with no hesitation. "He hates being a vampire, we'd be doing him a favor." He paused, looking up at the ceiling, Chris following his gaze. "I'm sure he's listening outside as we speak."

Chris rolled his eyes, as Matt smirked. He really never changed.

"As good of a theory as that might be, Matt, I don't think you're on the right track," Nixx said. "We don't really know enough about the vampires to put something like that to the test, it could cause catastrophic events, or it could do nothing. As I mentioned, there's also no evidence that the original vampire, possibly created by Dusk, is still around. He may be long gone for all we know, hence, rendering your theory useless."

"So, how do we take the Legion out?" Chris asked. "I don't know about you guys, but I don't think we're going to out fight them. They have hundreds, if not thousands, of reinforcements. We don't have anywhere near that amount. You already lost people in the siege when Craig got sacrificed. We don't stand a chance against them."

"Even Blaine had trouble when they started forcing their way through," Matt said. "Blaine can put up with a lot, but even that got too much when they started piling on. We're lucky he didn't get seriously hurt. He can only keep them back for so long. We need to figure out what to do, and fast, because they'll for sure be launching another siege soon. It's been days since they took Craig. Graith won't wait much longer and, when he hits again, we're going to lose everyone."

Jacob sighed. He was coming up empty on a plan. Matt couldn't help but think that Craig would have come up with a plan by now.

"I'll do my best and try to dig up more information on Dusk," Nixx said when no one spoke. "There are surely more journals around the castle that I can access, try and work out some information that he might have written down in between his experiments. You're all just going to have to do your best to hold the Legion off for as long as possible and, if they get Upstairs, then you deal with it. There's nothing else you can do right now. Matt and Chris are right, you don't have the reinforcements to stop them, but you can try to slow them down for as long as you can. Give us more time to get more information."

Jacob looked at Chris and Matt.

"You two stay with Nixx, check in with the outposts before you go to the castle, make sure nothing has happened," he said, Matt mock saluting him. "We'll try and work out a way to get into the vampire habitat to get Craig and Alex out."

Nixx went over to Matt, since he would shadow-step him and Chris over to the outposts before going to the castle.

⋅⋙✦⋘⋅

Gates looked over as he saw Matt.

"No news is good news," he sighed, Nixx surveying the area since he hadn't been to the construction site yet. He'd been too busy in the castle. "It's dark, I don't have a good feeling about tonight."

"Where's Danny?" Matt asked.

"He's on his way back from checking the other construction site," Gates said. "Zeke's over there with Ash at the moment, thank God. Man, she doesn't know when to stop talking, sometimes." He looked Matt over. "You're going over to the other outpost?"

"If Danny's already checked it, there's not much point in me disrupting your activities." Matt sighed. "Alright, hang in there, you know what to do if push comes to shove and tonight's the night. Just don't get yourself killed, Blaine, that's all I ask."

Gates rolled his eyes. "I'm not about to sacrifice myself like Danny's crew."

"Good. Call if you need anything. We'll be in the castle trying to work out a plan, so we won't be too far away."

Gates gave a single nod, and Matt put his hands on Nixx and Chris and they disappeared.

"Excuse me?" Gates heard someone off to his left. He looked to see who'd spoken and saw a recruit, no older than eighteen at the most. "Sorry, my name's Daniel, one of Danny's recruits."

"What's up?" Gates asked. He looked Daniel over. "Everything OK?"

Daniel shrugged, looking uncomfortable with the situation.

"You're in charge while Danny's not here," he stated, Gates nodding to confirm it. Daniel cleared his throat. "The ... ah ... some of the recruits up the front of the outpost thought they saw some movement about five minutes ago. They don't know what it was, if it even happened, but we thought we needed to report it in case it's actually something to worry about."

Gates indicated for Daniel to show him where, and Daniel led him through the half-constructed outpost. At least the wall was almost complete, that was a positive at least.

Reaching the front of the wall where the gates were going to stand, Daniel and Gates came to a stop. Daniel indicated out into the darkness, the recruits and civilians up here all very alert and on edge because of whatever they thought they'd seen.

"You think you saw something?" Gates asked, Daniel nodding.

No one spoke as Gates scanned the darkness in front of the wall, as far as he could see in this light anyway. There was no sound apart from the construction going on.

"There's not even any breeze anymore," Gates noted, hands on hips. "Strange." He looked up. "At least it's still snowing, that's a good sign I guess."

"Everything OK?" Danny stopped on Gates's right.

Danny indicated for Daniel to get back to work, the kid doing so immediately without question.

Ted looked over Danny's shoulder, trying to see whatever they were allegedly looking at. "What's the six, Captain?"

Shawn was now looking over Danny's left shoulder, the opposite side to Ted.

"The recruits thought they saw something," Gates informed them. He crossed his arms. "I can't see anything, but that doesn't mean there's nothing out there."

Jordan was the next to join the small group and try to see what was in the dark.

"OK," Danny said after some quiet and thinking. "OK." He turned around and looked at the people rushing around everywhere. "Everyone get over here, now!"

Hearing the call, everyone dropped what they were doing and came over. One went to get the rest of the recruits and civilians who were working up the back.

After a few minutes, everyone had gathered, and Gates kept a watch as Danny addressed the team.

"I'm gonna be straight up, things aren't looking good, right now," he said, seeing the worry on a few faces, Daniel one of them. "Be prepared for an attack tonight. Could be anytime. It could be in a few minutes, it could be in a few hours. First sign of commotion, move to your stations, and defend the outpost. Clear?" Everyone nodded. "Good, now get back to it until we get attacked."

Everyone scattered and Danny turned back to face the same way as Gates. Neither of them said anything, all they could hear were construction noises.

"Let's hope Arley can lead her team well enough to work through any possible problems," Danny commented. "She was a bit unsure when I was there just before, hopefully they listen to her or they're all dead."

Gates didn't have time to say anything, having heard something at the very last second. He put his hands out fast, the barrier appearing just in time as a vampire came running straight at him.

"Everyone fucking move!" Danny shouted, another vampire shoving hard into Gates's barrier. "Now!"

Everyone acted quickly, dropping and forgetting everything that they'd been doing. Many recruits took up the main front line position with Danny, Gates, and the other three bandits. Everyone else went to their designated positions, bracing themselves for the oncoming slaughter.

"I'm your first line of defense, but the moment I go down, you're all next," Gates said, shoving the barrier forwards hard, managing to knock over a group of three vampires. "Something tells me we're all going down with this ship."

By Daryl Walker

The Other Side of Andy

Motionless series
Motionless in Wonderland
Something Motionless This Way Comes
The Iron Army
Banshee's End
The Forsaken Dimension